The entire battle had lasted less than a minute.

Volo undid the black hood from the assassin nearest him to reveal its oriental elven facial features.

"Well," said Passepout, "that was easy enough!"

As if on cue, the assassins began to stand up, ready to resume their attack.

"It can't be!" Shurleen screamed.

"Undead elven ninja assassins," Blackthumb exclaimed.

Slower this time, the element of surprise gone, the assassins regrouped and prepared to resume their business, quickly and efficiently.

The smell of corruption, decay, and death pervaded the room, and the way to the door was clearly blocked by the assassins.

There was no escape and everyone knew it.

**FORGOTTEN REALMS**

FANTASY ADVENTURE

**Recommended Readings
for Realms Wanderers**

FORGOTTEN REALMS
FANTASY ADVENTURE

# Once Around the Realms

## A Picaresque Romp

## Brian M. Thomsen

# ONCE AROUND THE REALMS

Cover art by John and Laura Lakey.

First Printing: April 1995
Printed in the United States of America
Library of Congress Catalog Card Number: 94-68134

9 8 7 6 5 4 3 2 1

ISBN: 0-7869-0119-5

TSR, Inc.
201 Sheridan Springs Rd.
Lake Geneva, WI 53147
U.S.A.

TSR Ltd.
120 Church End, Cherry Hinton
Cambridge CB1 3LB
United Kingdom

# CONTENTS

**Dedicated to Donna
(and Sparky & Minx, too)**

## ACKNOWLEDGMENTS

Grateful acknowledgment is made to Jules Verne for his original masterwork, *Around the World in 80 Days,* and to Mike Todd for his cinematic multi-starred interpretation of it for the original inspiration for *Once Around the Realms.*

Grateful thanks to Realms Laureates Ed Greenwood and Jeff Grubb for research assistance.

And special thanks to Marty Greenberg, Mike Resnick, Bill Fawcett, Chris Stasheff, Ricia Mainhart, John Varley, Richard Gillam, and Ed Kramer, all editors who supported another editor who wanted to be a writer.

## REALMSLORE NOTE

Reader, be forewarned! This book was not written by the legendary Volothamp Geddarm, nor has it been authorized by him for publication. It is based entirely on rumor, unsubstantiated reports, and speculation. Though many real and famous characters of the Realms appear within these pages, they do so without their consent or authorization. The dark conspiracy described within is also unconfirmed, and dismissed as 'poppycock' by many esteemed leaders in high places, but then again, isn't this the fate of all such conspiracies?

# AT THE GATES OF SUZAIL

## OR

### How Volo and Passepout First Meet

"Great! A group of holy men is just what we need to liven up our day," said the guard known as Kirk, his teeth clenched in obvious perturbation.

"Just calm down," said Duke, his partner-in-arms for nigh unto forty years. "They're on some sort of pilgrimage, and Azoun has offered them the best of Cormyr's hospitality as they mosey on through his territory, and that includes the safety and security of Suzail's city walls as they pass a night's respite under the protective watch of his Purple Dragons. After all, there are thieves about, and . . . " lowering his voice in mid-drawl, ". . . who knows what else, given our orders for extra security."

"Bah! You're making a mountain out of a molehill. It's only one more thing for them to get on our backs about. Vangerdahast is probably just having a party or something."

"I wouldn't call a special meeting of the College of War Wizards a party. Sounds like serious business to me. Why else would he have ordered the city closed to all non-registered magic users? I'll bet it has something to do with some unseen menace that is lurking on the horizon, like that Horde invasion. Boy, we really kicked some butt back then."

"Don't get my hopes up," Kirk replied, drawing his chin betwixt his thumb and index finger till the two met at the distinctive cleftlike indentation that separated the right side of his jaw from the left. He nostalgically recalled the good old days. "Those were the times, weren't they? Fighting the barbarian menace. Overwhelming odds before us. Now all we're good for is night watch at the gate, and occasionally playing concierge to traveling holy men."

Duke looked down at his depressed buddy. Though separated by twelve inches in height and three years in age, the two veterans were cut from the same cloth, and were mirror images of what you would expect a great warrior to look like as he entered his golden years. They had fought side by side for years, saved each other's lives on numerous occasions, and together had more than their fair share of adventuring, carousing, and festing.

When Kirk had been assigned to permanent watch duty at the city gate, out of deference to his advancing years, Duke voluntarily put in for a transfer to this most boring of assignments just to keep his little buddy company. He never revealed to his friend that he, unlike Kirk, had chosen to join him on this assignment that was labeled by the youngbloods as the geriatric guard.

"Cheer up," Duke encouraged, punching Kirk in the shoulder plate. "I understand that there has been some trouble of late with battling brigands, and pickpockets masquerading as thespians. Maybe we'll get lucky and bag a few."

"Yeah," agreed Kirk, gaze now fixed on some invisible point on the horizon, then adding, "that's all we're good for, baby-sitting holy men and pinching pickpockets. Not what I'd call soldier's work. Purple Dragons, bah! Purple newts is more like it. Why don't we just retire?"

"Quit feeling sorry for yourself. Looks like we have company. Go give him the once-over."

Kirk took up his poleax, straightened his age-bent, five-two frame, and approached the oncoming traveler.

"Stop in the name of King Azoun," he bellowed, happy that at least his bass was in good form. "Who goes there?"

The lone traveler approached the gate, seemingly unthreatened by the harsh tones of the veteran of the watch.

"It is only I, Passepout the entertainer, star of stage, tavern, and festhall, and only son of the legendary thespians Catinflas and Idle. I've come to Suzail to share my talents with your most appreciative citizenry, and rumor has it that their generosity is legendary, if you know what I mean," rambled the traveler, jabbing Kirk in the ribs with his elbow with all of the self-assurance of Elminster at a magic show. The traveler's manner more than obscured his humble ensemble of threadbare pantaloons, homespun blouse thin and shiny to the point of silken, and a moth-eaten cloak that had as many worn spots as it had pockets (of which it had many).

"Passepout the entertainer," repeated Kirk. With a sneer, he added, "Never heard of him."

"I'm not surprised," responded the peripatetic Passepout. "A dedicated soldier such as yourself has too little time for the frivolity of theatrics and amusement. You are much too busy with the security and safety of all Faerûn, and for that, I might say, we are all truly grateful. Now, if you'll just let me be on my way into the city, I'll be sure to mention to His Royal Highness, King Azoun, what a splendid job you are doing."

Kirk lowered the blade of his poleax to block Passepout's way, and turned his head, calling, "Hey, Duke. Do you know of anyone we're supposed to be on the watch for who has an appointment with King Azoun?"

"Nope," replied Duke. "Not to my recollection."

Passepout interjected, "I didn't say that I had an appointment with King Azoun. I just naturally assumed that he would want to see me once he heard about my theatrical exploits, and, of course . . . "

"Nor mine," said Kirk, ignoring the pudgy traveler's explanation while still blocking Passepout's way as he continued his discourse with Duke. "Ever hear of an entertainer named Push-up . . . ?"

"That's Passepout," Passepout corrected.

". . . the son of Addled and Cant-floss . . . "

"That's Idle and Catinflas, the legendary thespians," insisted the son of Idle and Catinflas, beginning to think that he might better have chosen the south gate entrance to the city.

". . . the legendary thespians. Ring any bells?" Kirk completed.

"Nope," said Duke, approaching his comrade-in-arms. "Can't say it does."

"Sorry," said Kirk, handing his poleax to Duke. He turned back to the scapegoat of all of his geriatric frustrations. "We've never heard of any Passepout the entertainer, but you know what?"

"What?" whispered the now-meek traveler named Passepout, who was afraid that he would be spending the night in the dungeon for vagrancy, or some such other charge of which he was guilty.

"Duke here reminded me that rumor has it there are some pickpockets in the neighborhood who are trying to pass themselves off as entertainers . . . "

"Well, good sir," said Passepout, trying to regain some control, "if I should see any I will be sure to let you know, civic duty and all, and if you'll kindly allow me to be on my way, I'll . . . "

Closing in on the newcomer to the gate of Suzail, gently forcing him backward until his back was against the city wall with no place else to go, the cold surface of the stone chilling Passepout to the bone through his threadbare clothes, Kirk continued, saying, "Funny. Seems I do recall a pair of pickpockets named Idle and Catinflas from somewhere around Baldur's Gate. You any relation to them, punk?"

"You must be mistaken," insisted Passepout, not really answering the question, now sure that his night in the dungeon would be preceded by a beating, and dreading every minute of it. "I'm just a lowly street performer, and . . . "

"Do you know what we do to suspected pick-pockets in Suzail?" asked Kirk, balling his gauntlet-clad hand into the fist that he held dangerously close to the traveler's pudgy nose. "Do you know what we do?" he repeated. Duke stayed two paces behind, holding his poleax in his crossed arms, ready and waiting for the amusement that was sure to follow.

"Oh, good! A quaint local custom. Let me take notes," a new voice added to the city gate milieu.

Kirk turned from the cowering Passepout toward the source of the voice and confronted the latest traveler to attempt entrance at the gate.

"And who are you?" Kirk bellowed, disappointed that his fist's appointment with the pudgy little entertainer's face had been interrupted by this latest interloper.

"I am Volothamp Geddarm, but you can call me Volo," said the new arrival, a strange yet jaunty fellow dressed in exotic yet pragmatic finery, capped off by a well-traveled beret. He shrugged, adding, "Everybody does, after all."

Duke joined Kirk at the side of the new traveler, both still blocking any means of escape for the cowering Passepout, who still had his back to the cold city wall. He was thankful for the respite but dreaded the imminent resumption of his interrogation.

Duke scratched his head. "Seems I remember hearing something about you," he said. After a moment, he snapped his fingers and smiled, saying, "Sure, I know you. You're that book fellow, the guy with the guides, citizen of the world, home on the range, and all of that sort of stuff."

"Yes, I am Volo, traveler extraordinaire, and master gazetteer."

"Well, let me shake your hand," said Duke. He enthusiastically pumped Volo's extended hand and then turned to Kirk, saying, "This guy is the author of that book on Waterdeep, the one I used to find us that really good festhall last time we were on leave. You remember, that really expensive place where our old girlfriends worked."

"Yeah, I remember. Best leave I ever had, but you know I still can't figure it out," replied Kirk. "I thought that Katelyn had settled down with some rich merchant or something. She wasn't really the festhall type."

"Oh, you must be referring to the Hanging Lantern," Volo explained, ready to bring up that it had been run by a gang of doppelgangers. Then he thought better of it, simply saying, "Glad I could be of service."

"Darn tootin' you were of service. Best time I ever spent, outside of actual combat, that is," said Duke.

Just then the two guards and the two recent arrivals to Suzail heard a commotion, as if a mob were approaching the gate.

"That must be the holy men. I'd better go meet them and set things in order for their arrival," Duke said, heading toward the crowd. He turned back for just a moment to say, "It was a real pleasure meeting you, Mister Volo. Enjoy our fair city."

"Thank you, good sir. I'll be sure to add that the guards on watch are always courteous in my upcoming *Volo's Guide to Cormyr.*"

Kirk was in the process of turning back to resume his engagement with Passepout when Volo tapped him on the shoulder, asking, "So then I'm free to enter the city?"

"No skin off my nose," Kirk replied sarcastically.

"Then, I assume there is no problem with my bond servant accompanying me."

"Who?"

"My bond servant," Volo replied.

"I don't care what you do," Kirk responded curtly.

"Very well," said Volo, who motioned to Passepout, saying, "Come along, then."

"Wait a minute," Kirk interrupted. "He's your bond servant?"

"That's right."

"Well, he says he's an entertainer. Passepout the great and wonderful or some such, or so he claims. I think he's Passepout the pickpocket."

"No, he's just Passepout the bond servant. Come along, Passepout," Volo ordered. "I have much research to do, and none of it's getting done here."

"Yes, Master," said Passepout in what he hoped was a deferential enough tone.

"Now wait a second," ordered Kirk. "I don't care what research you have to do. If this here is Passepout the bond servant, then why did he claim to be Passepout the entertainer, son of Idle and Cantfloss?"

"That's Catinflas," corrected Passepout, wishing he hadn't after he had.

"Vanity, I guess," answered Volo. "After all, how would you feel if your parents were famous thespians and the best that you've managed to make of your life is as a lowly bond servant?"

"The reason doesn't matter; the fact is, he lied. And if I recall the Cormyr Civil Code, telling an intentional untruth to a guard on watch is an actionable offense."

"Well, I am very sorry," said Volo in his most conciliatory tone. "What is the fine? Will a gold piece do?" he asked, holding up a particularly shiny coin.

"Sure," said Kirk, knowing that it was against the Civil Code for him to accept such official fines outside a courtroom. He reached for the coin, only to have Volo snatch it away.

Volo propositioned. "How about this? You don't want to waste time in some courtroom turning in this fine, and I obviously don't really want to pay it. After all, a gold piece is a gold piece, and more than twice the value of a well-trained bond servant, let alone this one. How about I'll flip you for it, double or nothing? That way you have a chance to get another gold piece for your troubles, and I have a chance to be on my way. What do you say?"

Just then Duke called from the other side of the gate. "Hey, Kirk! I need a hand!"

Kirk called to his old friend, "Be right there," then turned to Volo, and said, "Okay, but be quick about it."

Volo agreed, and quickly tossed the coin in the air, calling, "Dragons, I win."

"Then, kings I win," said Kirk.

It came up dragons.

Kirk cursed and joined his comrade-in-arms at the gate dealing with the oncoming holy men, one of whom seemed to be quite obstreperous.

Volo and Passepout could still overhear the taller guard doing his duty, drawling, "Now see here, pilgrim, hold on and wait your turn, or you'll . . . " as they entered the city proper.

# ON THE PROMENADE

### OR

### Passepout Pledges Himself as Volo's Bond Servant

The Promenade was filled with the hustle and bustle of Suzail's citizenry returning home after a hard day of work, or venturing out in preparation for a long night's fun. Purple Dragons policed the streets as obvious omens of order, perhaps to impress the dignitaries that may or may not have converged on the city for the meeting of the College of War Wizards. Amidst all the melee of activity, the two travelers put greater distance between themselves and the gate.

"How can I thank you enough, O great and wonderful master?" implored the greatly relieved Passepout. "I was sure that I would be spending the next few days repairing my bruised and battered body in some cold, dark dungeon."

"Think nothing of it, good sir," insisted Volo. "I have lived the life of a vagabond for many years and have experienced more than my fair share of overzealous sentries and the like. I haven't always been of the stature to weekend at the beautiful estates of the Bernd family."

"You've stayed at Yonda?"

"You've heard of it?"

"Who hasn't heard of the most opulent family estate in all Cormyr?"

"I've just passed a few days there. Have you had the chance to visit?"

"Even famous thespians such as myself must wait for an invitation, and from what I understand they are few and far between."

"I'm sure your time will come. Bernd has an eye for talent and is a renowned patron of the arts. I'll see about putting the two of you together."

"Again I am in your debt."

"We men of the road must stick together. Now where is your great performance scheduled? As I will only be in town for a few days, I hope I will be able to catch it."

"Well, you see, O great and wonderful savior of the only son of Catinflas and Idle, my exact, uh . . . arrangements have yet to be solidified, and I had hopes of working out some sort of arrangement in town until several possible, uh . . . opportunities become more solidified."

"I see," said Volo, with just enough insight to make the down-on-his-luck thespian a bit uneasy.

"It's not like that," Passepout insisted. "I'm many things but not a thief, as those graying Purple Dragons at the gate accused. Times are hard, and an actor's life is not always an easy one. Even an accomplished thespian such as myself is entitled to a few dry spells. I had always heard that Suzail was ripe for dramatic harvesting, and if not here, well, then somewhere else."

"But more to the matter at hand," interrupted Volo, "what about tonight?"

"Tonight?"

"Yes, tonight. According to the post at the gate, a curfew is in effect. What will you do for tonight? There are several establishments I can recommend, if you would tell me your price range."

"Well, you know how an actor's life is. The journey here, roadside prices, and my appetite and all," offered Passepout, patting his ample belly, "have left me slightly deficient of means, if you know what I mean."

"You're broke."

"Exactly."

"Suzail is no place to be a penniless itinerant. There are laws against it and more than a few civil bodies ready to enforce them. As I saved you from the Purple Dragons' jaws at the gate, I feel I am obligated to continue in my role as your protector, at least for the time being."

Volo tossed the indigent entertainer one of his bags, the heaviest one, almost bowling over the unsuspecting fellow, who seemed to have lost a bit of his legendary acrobatic prowess through the acquisition of a few extra pounds of fleshly body cushioning. Passepout recovered, with a questioning look, but before he could voice his interrogative Volo cut him off.

"At the gate I identified you as my bond servant, and for the duration of my stay here in Suzail so shall you be. This will, of course, entitle you to share in my room and board, of course."

"Oh, thank you, O wonderful and good sir. I am in your debt," insisted the grateful, relieved Passepout.

"Think nothing of it. My accommodations are all comped."

"Comped?"

"Complimentary. Such is the advantage of being a world-famous author—and the most famous traveler in all of the Realms, if I do say so myself. My favors to you have cost me naught, and for them I now have an extra set of shoulders to carry my packs, and an eager ear to bend during my stay. For, you see, even more than traveling, I enjoy the sound of my own voice, and people sometimes look askance at you if you are talking to yourself, if you know what I mean. Think nothing of it."

"Your bond servant so shall I be for as long as you require. I owe you my freedom, and my board, and until such time as the debt is repaid, so shall it be."

"Only if you insist."

"And I do. Besides, maybe the accommodations won't cost you anything, but that doesn't change the fact that you were willing to risk two gold pieces in exchange for my release."

"No risk."

"But I saw you flip the coin with the guard."

"You did."

"So?"

Volo tossed the confused Passepout the coin, and said, "Flip it, and call it."

Passepout flipped, and called, "Kings."

The coin came up kings.

"Again," Volo insisted.

Again Passepout flipped the coin, this time calling "Dragons."

It came up dragons.

Volo snatched the coin from the befuddled Passepout's palm and then handed it back to him.

"Examine the faces of this lucky coin," he instructed.

Passepout looked down, and lo, the faces were blank, with neither a king nor a dragon evident on the golden surface.

Volo snatched back the coin again and put it in his pouch.

"See? Think nothing of it," he said, picking up the pace as they strolled along the Promenade.

"How did you do that?" asked the now-eager-to-please bond servant.

"I am also the author of *Volo's Guide to All Things Magical*."

"Wonderful."

"Not to mention the most famous traveler in all of the Realms."

"Of course."

"But we must hurry. The dark will soon be upon us, and the warmth of a good tavern beckons. Our destination lies just a few doors down."

# AT THE
# DRAGON'S JAWS INN

### OR

### As a Matter of Pride a Bet is Made

The Dragon's Jaws Inn, located on the Promenade was, as usual, bursting to the seams with patrons out for an evening frolic. Under the steady eye of bartender Milo Dudley, drinks were being served, rooms reserved, and schedules posted for the evening's activities of ax throwing and halfling tossing. Milo ran a tight ship and was at least fifty percent of the reason for the inn's success. No fight went longer than its repair bill outweighed its entertainment value, no paying customer was turned away for want of accommodation nor discouraged from returning by any lapse in satisfaction or quality. Before a mug was empty, Milo was at hand with a refill. Before a patron had passed out from overindulgence, Milo had already arranged a spot to sleep it off, and before an unwanted indiscretion had taken place, Milo was already there to discourage any unwanted advances. Innkeeper, bartender, referee, and bouncer, Milo always had his dwarfish hands full . . . and enjoyed every minute of it.

The other fifty percent of the tavern's success was undoubtedly the work of the actual proprietor, Gnorm the gnome. A former adventurer who had once left town with a bunch of drunken dwarves in search of a dragon's hoard to plunder, he returned four years later with enough booty to finance the inn for nigh unto a few hundred years, and support his own hobbies and habits as well. Gnorm never did any actual work; he left that up to Milo, the less than adventurous brother-who-stayed-behind of one of Gnorm's dwarven colleagues who never made it back from the dragon's den that was the source of Gnorm's prosperity. Instead Gnorm functioned as a sort of goodwill ambassador, glad-hander, and life of the party for the inn. It was entirely possible that casual patrons might be unaware that this jovial fellow for whom they had just bought a drink was actually the proprietor of the establishment, and the retired gnome liked to keep it that way.

To employees and patrons alike, he was just good old Gnorm.

Volo and Passepout had no sooner approached the threshold of the establishment when the door was thrown open for them by the ever-on-the-ball Milo, who bestowed upon them his enthusiastic greetings.

"Oh, Master Volo! You have returned to once again honor our establishment with your presence. Now, before you undo the drawstrings on your purse, I must warn you that your money will do you no good here. You are a guest of the house and entitled to any bounty it can provide," gushed the majordomo dwarf. "Mindy! Sara! Prepare a room upstairs for Master Volo and his, uh . . . "

"Companion?" Passepout offered.

"Bond servant," Volo instructed.

". . . and his bond servant, of course, and make sure the furniture's sturdy. There's nothing half-ling about this boy, no sirree," he continued with a slight chuckle, as if sharing some secret joke. "And Wolfgang, set up a new table over in Molly's area. I remember she was always your favorite waitress, and its location will give you a perfect view of the evening's competition without necessarily placing you in the line of fire. After all, no one enjoys the impact of a misfired halfling during their dinner."

"As always, you amaze me, Milo," Volo offered. He handed his packs to the waiting arms of one of the porters who would carry them to the bed chamber that had moments ago been reserved for them. "How do you do it?"

Milo shook his head as if to dismiss the implied compliment, answering, "Eo knows, someone has to," then quickly adding with a wink, ". . . and, Mister Volo, is there any truth to the rumor that your next publication will be a guide to Cormyr? Not that I would concern myself with such things."

"Right on top of things, as usual, Milo," Volo answered, "not that the Dragon's Jaws Inn has anything to worry about. Everyone knows it's the best-run establishment in all Cormyr, with no small thanks to you and its gregarious proprietor."

"From your lips to Eo's ears."

"Speaking of which, is the proprietor in?"

"Oh, no, Mister Volo," Milo answered, with just a hint of sarcastic disapproval. "It's way too early for Himself to arrive. Not that we couldn't use an extra set of hands with all the pilgrims coming through, and the War Wizards gathering. Of course, not that he would lend us those hands to begin with . . . but I am sure that he will be in soon and that he will be overjoyed that you have agreed to accept our hospitality. Now, enough of this blocking the doorway with chitchat and mutual admiration. I am sure that you and, uh . . . "

"His name is Passepout, son of Catinflas and Addled."

"That's Catinflas and Idle, the famous thespians," Passepout corrected, then, realizing his alleged station, added, "Master."

"Quite," conceded Volo, as if the distinction were unnecessary.

"Uh, yes," hastened Milo, not wishing to come between a master and his servant. "I am sure that you must be hungry from your long journey. Do you wish separate accommodations in the stable for your stout companion? I am sure that we can arrange a place for him in the stables, though judging from his build I fear the safety of the horses given the evidence of his appetite."

"No, no. Passepout stays with me," Volo answered.

"Wonderful," Passepout whispered under his breath, spying a roast that appeared to be being taken to the table that was to be their destination.

"As you wish, Master Volo," Milo conceded. "Tarry no longer. Molly awaits with two tankards of ale and a roast."

And with that the travelers were escorted to their place of honor, so that Milo could return to the other concerns of the house—however, not without instructing Molly to keep their tankards full and plates piled high.

The way to any critic's heart, the majordomo thought, was obviously through his stomach, or some other appetite that Molly could no doubt satisfy.

Passepout had just finished his third roast, and Molly was safely and cozily ensconced on Volo's lap, when the tavern's din was broken by a familiar herald.

"Hello, everybody."

"Gnorm!" the crowd roared.

"Time's a-wasting, and my throat is parched," declared the phantom proprietor.

Milo instantly appeared at his side, a full tankard in hand, which Gnorm proceeded to empty as the innkeeper whispered in his ear about their recently arrived honored guests.

Refilled tankard in hand, Gnorm hastened over to their table.

"Volo, you vagabond devil," he saluted, quickly adding, "no, don't get up. I see you have your lap filled. And you must be Passepout, son of Catinflas and Idle, the famous thespians."

"Oh! You've heard of them!" Passepout beamed from behind his grease-stained cheeks.

"Nope," Gnorm answered. Taking a chair and turning back to Volo, he continued, "So what do you think of what we've done to the place since last you've come this way?"

"What can I say?" Volo answered, gesturing Molly to forgo her throne for a few moments so that the circulation could return to his legs, and he and Gnorm could talk for awhile, all the while assuring her that her seat would be saved. "You've improved on perfection."

"Worthy of, let's say, four pipes and five tankards in that guide of yours?" the phantom proprietor queried.

"Oh, at least," the proud gazetteer replied.

"I owe it all to Milo," Gnorm offered. "I don't know what I would do without that dwarf. He's better than a wife, and that's no easy accomplishment, I'm telling you. Little did I realize when I promised his brother Thorn that I would make sure his kid brother was never wanting that I would be inheriting the best tavern keeper a sot such as myself could ever want."

Volo took his feet and raised his tankard high. "Then let us propose a toast. To Milo, the best tavern keeper, and the Dragon's Jaws, the best tavern in all of Cormyr."

"Hear! Hear!" Passepout concurred through cheeks bulging with mutton.

Once tankards had been guzzled and refilled, Gnorm replaced Volo in the toaster's stance.

"And I propose a toast to the master traveler of them all. Let us all drink to the master himself, Volo."

"Hear! Hear!" Passepout concurred, reveling in his good fortune at falling in with such wonderful company.

"Hear! Hear!" cheered the crowd, who downed their tankards, and quickly resumed their more private patters.

As the porters cleared the way for the halfling toss, the honored guests began to feel the pressure of the crowd closing in on them. A burly figure cloaked in black with staff in hand brusquely hastened past Passepout, rudely knocking the portly thespian into his plate of food, as he made his way to the shadows of a nearby table.

Passepout, who always considered himself an actor and not a fighter, scowled to himself but let the incident pass, so as to avoid a physical altercation.

Other tavern-goers also pressed in on the formerly private party of Gnorm, Volo, and his servant.

A young wench, who seemed to have her eye on the place of honor formerly held by Molly, approached the master traveler and gushed, "It's such a pleasure to meet the real Volo, the greatest traveler in all the Realms."

Volo's chest began to puff out, proud as a partridge.

"And I've always wanted to meet the real Marcus Wands," she added.

"Excuse me?" Volo replied, chest deflating, expression slightly perplexed.

"That's your name, isn't it?" she queried. "I know, you prefer to be called Marco."

"My dear, uh . . . " Volo answered with a momentary pause to scan her ample cleavage, ". . . lady, my name is Volothamp Geddarm. Volo to my friends and acquaintances, and I alone, and no other, am the master traveler of all Faerûn."

The buxom blonde, puzzled, continued her assertions, not realizing that in doing so she was not currying the favor of the guest of honor. "But I had heard that Marco Volo was the greatest traveler in all the Realms."

"An imposter, a braggart and a liar," Volo responded, losing patience.

Another patron joined in the discussion, perhaps wanting to curry the blonde's favor, asserting, "I too have heard of the travels of wondrous Marcus Wands. Perhaps there are two great travelers in the Realms?"

Partially due to the quantities of ale that had been quaffed, and partially due to the magnitude of ego that had evolved within Volo over the years, the master traveler lost his temper.

"I alone am the master traveler of the Realms," he boasted, "and anyone who says otherwise is wrong."

The cowled figure with the staff stood up and from the shadows interjected, "Can you prove it ?"

Volo turned to address this most recent assailant of his character, not able to make out any of the figure's features due to the spare lighting of the corner. "Of course, I can," he boasted.

"Would you be willing to submit to a test?" the cloaked one replied.

"Any test," Volo declared, "provided the tester is man enough to face me in the light, rather than hiding in the shadows.

"Then a test it shall be," agreed the figure, who emerged from the shadows and threw back the cloak that had been obscuring his famous bearded visage, black staff firmly in hand.

The cheering crowd, which had formerly been enthralled by the halfling-toss championships and had been managing to ignore Volo's arguments of ego, could not help but change the focus of its attention to the six-foot-tall, well-muscled figure that had emerged from the shadows, the torchlight flickering off the distinctive streak of gray that bisected his goatee.

Even Passepout interrupted his meal.

Milo quickly approached the figure.

"Khelben Arunsun," he addressed in the manner reserved for his special guests. "A thousand pardons. Had I known you were here, you would have received a much better table. I must be slipping in my old age," he offered, trying to defuse the situation as best he could.

The learned mage ignored him and continued to glare at Volo.

"You must be in town for the meeting of the Council of War Wizards," Milo continued to natter. "Imagine the Lord Mage of Waterdeep *here* . . ."

"Silence!" the imposing figure commanded, and nary a sound was heard in the inn. Approaching Volo with all the intensity of a jungle cat cornering its prey, he pressed, "Well, so-called master traveler, a test it shall be. Do you really believe yourself to be the greatest traveler in the Realms?"

"Yes, my lord," replied Volo, trying to maintain an uneasy balance between pride and deference for the archmage. "There is no question about it. I am the best, the most able, the greatest."

"A simple grand tour of Faerûn and beyond from west to east should be of no difficulty, then. Eh, master traveler?"

"None whatsoever, as I've done it many times before," Volo boasted, exaggerating ever so slightly.

"So you say, but what proof do you have?"

"My reputation and my word!"

"Perhaps you, and not Marcus Wands, is the liar . . . and what is the word of a liar?"

"Volothamp Geddarm is a man of his word," Passepout interjected, then quickly retreated into silence, stung by Khelben's baneful glare.

"So you say, but have you been a witness to these exploits?" Khelben interrogated.

"Well, no, you see, I'm new at this bond servant thing. I'm really Passepout, son of Catinflas and . . . "

"Silence!" Khelben ordered again. The thespian recoiled. "A liar I cannot abide, so you must prove yourself, Master Volo." The mage reached into his cloak and withdrew a bag of gems and a folded piece of parchment. "To prove your claims, you must, with this poor and portly excuse for a human being, thespian or otherwise, travel this globe, never setting foot on the same piece of land twice until you have circled all of Toril. Here!"

The archmage tossed the bag of gems to Passepout and the parchment to the traveler.

All eyes in the inn were now on Volo and he required a great deal of concentration to maintain the pompous and self-assured appearance that he believed the greatest traveler of the Realms had to project. *Appearance matters*, he thought, *damn it!*

"In that bag," the mage instructed, "are the legendary gems of the necromancer Kalen Verne. Together with that parchment, they will provide evidence of your travels. When each gem changes from green to red, it must be discarded in the place that the color change occurs. That spot will then appear on the map of Toril that will appear on the parchment, documenting your journey."

"A simple enough task," Volo offered, still maintaining the facade of self-assuredness, ". . . but I am a bit busy right now. You see, I have this book on Cormyr to write, and . . . "

"Silence!" Khelben demanded a third time. "Should you remain in one place for more than twelve hours, the magics that lie within the jewels shall consume you. Should you leave one of the jewels in a location before its color has changed, the magics that lie within shall consume you." Then, pausing to shift his eyes to Passepout, he added, "Should the map and the jewels part company, or leave the custody of those who now bear them . . . "

"I know," Passepout dolefully responded, cursing the luck that he had formerly claimed as good, "the magics within shall consume us."

"Correct," the archmage replied.

The crowd awaited Volo's response.

In his mind there was no alternative. His pride and ego could accept no less, and the preservation of his reputation demanded it.

"Molly, my dear," Volo called for all to hear. "Our packs and cloaks. I'm afraid that I will have to take a rain check on further festivities of the evening. If this is what it takes to prove my claim to fame once and for all, so be it. Passepout and I shall return here once our journey is completed, and we will bestow to the Dragon's Jaws Inn the map for all to see, as evidence of the exploits of Volothamp Geddarm, and his traveling companion, the distinguished entertainer Passepout, son of Catinflas and Addled."

"That's Idle," the companion corrected.

Turning back to the archmage, Volo extended his hand and said, "If this is what it takes, Master Arunsun, so be it. Let us part as gentlemen until we meet again with proof in hand."

"As gentlemen," Khelben agreed, "so be it."

The archmage accepted the hand of the world traveler and gave it one quick shake.

A chill went through Volo's entire being, which

he attributed to the feeling of power that effervesced from the archmage of Waterdeep. Quickly recovering his senses, he declared, "Come, Passepout, let us be on our way. Gnorm, Milo, lovely Molly, we shall return!"

Hoisting a pack upon his back, ready to meet the challenge, Volo jaunted out into the Suzail night, followed by the burdened Passepout, who dreaded the adventure that surely lay before them.

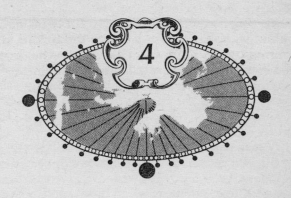

# ON THE ROAD

## OR

## The Trials and Tribulations of Always Being Hungry

"But, Master Volo, I'm just a lowly thespian, not a world traveler like yourself. I have never been out of Cormyr, let alone Faerûn . . . "

"Don't fret, brother of the road Passepout," assured Volo to his obviously discouraged companion. "Think of all the world as a stage, and you yourself merely a player with exits and entrances, and a bit more than the normal proscenium distance between stage left and stage right."

"That's easy for you to say, O great gazetteer. You are not already feeling the pangs of hunger of too many missed meals," bemoaned the portly Passepout.

Volo stopped in his tracks, and turned around to face his complaining bond servant, who had fallen several paces behind.

"Passepout, we are less than one day's trot from Suzail and less than an hour from the tavern we lunched at, and if I am not mistaken, you partook of more than your share of the venison stew they served."

"Maybe more than my share, but nowhere near my fill," he countered. "Besides, one must be careful to amply fill one's self with provisions when one doesn't know where or when one's next meal will be."

"Don't concern yourself with such mundane matters," Volo instructed. "Just look at me. A life on the road, yet I'm still as well fed as Lord of Waterdeep. I've never gone hungry when I could avoid it, and I avoid it at all costs. Now hop to. We're burning daylight, and the faster we get there, the faster we can get back to Cormyr."

"Get where?"

"A little place I know that is a bit north of here."

"But I thought that we had to go all around the world."

"We do . . . but I know a shortcut that will enable us to unload our gems over the vast globe of Toril, and still allow us to get back to Cormyr in enough time for me to finish my research, write the book, and hand it over to my publisher, before he wants his money back or my head on a pikestaff, both alternatives of which I assure you, I consider to be completely unacceptable."

With a sigh of resignation, the portly thespian joined the master traveler and continued on the road northward from Suzail.

After four days' journey northward, the two travelers' path intercepted that of a caravan bound for the grazing lands of the Storm Horn peaks with a herd of cows, sheep, and goats. The wagon master was a strong silent type fellow, reluctant to give his name (if he even had one), let alone engage anyone in conversation. The cook of the caravan, Stew Bone by name, more than made up the difference in gregariousness, and invited Volo and Passepout to join them for meals for as long as the drive and they shared the same road.

Needless to say, Passepout and Stew Bone became quick friends. Volo, on the other hand, made himself indispensable as a storyteller around the campfire, swapping stories with the herders well into the wee hours each night.

The journey proceeded quickly and almost painlessly for all parties concerned, until someone noticed when Passepout dropped the requisite gem at a certain spot along the road.

"Hey, Pudgy!" the rogue called. "If you have enough treasure of your own that you can throw it away, why don't you share it with your trail buddies?"

"That's Passepout, son of . . . "

Volo intercepted the conversation before Passepout could continue his correction. "My good sir, he is throwing only those gems away that have gone bad."

"What do you mean, gone bad?" demanded the rogue whom the others called Elam Jack. The others had already warned Volo of his dubious character and rumored stint for thievery in the dungeons of Suzail.

"Well," started Volo, "surely a man of such breeding as yourself knows quality in all things and obviously has no desire to partake of ale that has gone sour or an apple that has gone rancid or a jewel that has gone bad. Passepout is carrying home to his widowed mother up in Shadowdale . . . "

"Idle, the actress," Passepout interjected.

"That's right, Idle the actress," Volo conceded, "a sack of garden jewels. No real value for anyone except a farmer, really. You see, they only look like jewels. In reality, they are seeds for planting. That's why they are green. The red ones have turned and must be discarded before they spoil the rest in the sack. It's as simple as that."

Elam scratched his chin, and tried to consider the explanation for a moment, but then quickly dismissed it, saying, "I don't believe you, and even if you are telling the truth, I don't care. Why don't you just hand over to me the so-called rancid jewels?"

Passepout clutched the sack, fearing the inevitable.

Volo quickly jumped in once again. "He can't do that; you see, he is a . . . a druid. Yes, that's right, he is a druid, and is bound by his faith to return to the soil the remnants of its bounty even when it has already passed from green to red."

"What in the name of Bane is the reason for that? I ain't never heard of such a thing before. Religion or no religion, I want you to . . . "

Just then an unfamiliar voice lent itself to the discussion, saying, "I want you to drop it. A man's religion is sacred to him, no matter how crazy it might seem to everyone else."

A hush came over the traveling band. The silent caravan master with no name had spoken.

He continued to speak.

"Master Volo, you were told that we were only going as far as the Storm Horn peaks. Well, by my recollection, we should be there about right now. Now, I've enjoyed your stories, and all, but I'm afraid it's time for folks to go their separate ways, if you know what I mean."

"Yes," Volo assented, "we knew that there would be a limit on the amount of time that we would be able to bask in your hospitality."

"And a man must know his own limitations," the previously silent leader added.

"Indeed," Volo agreed. "Passepout, leave us be on our way."

Passepout gathered up his pack and hastened to Volo's side. The caravan master walked with them until they had reached the end of the camp.

"Tomorrow, me and my boys will set the herd up grazing. Where are you fellas heading?"

"North," Volo replied.

"Well, take care of yourselves and watch out for brigands. Elam isn't the only one of his kind around here. I know a lot like him. Grew up with many like him in the woods east of here. There but for the grace of Eo go I. Perhaps that's why I'm kinda close-mouthed. People jump to conclusions when they hear my accent, and expect some thug, sort of like him."

"I'd like to know the name of an honest man such as yourself, given the scarcity of your kind," asked Volo delicately.

"You can just call me Malpasso."

"Thank you, Malpasso."

"Now git. I don't want to leave my gang of wranglers for too long, especially Elam. He's a badun."

And with that, the caravan master rejoined his crew at the campfire.

"Nice guy, but kinda quiet," said Passepout.

"Men of few words are rarer than the words they speak."

"Now what?"

Volo put his arm around the thespian's shoulders and assured, "Worry not. We'll make our own camp over yonder, and tomorrow we head north."

Passepout fell in step with his master, paused for a moment, and inquired, "Still north? Where are we going?"

"Oh, didn't I tell you?" Volo replied. "To a great city I know."

"What great city? I thought we were going to take a shortcut."

"We are."

"So what city is this, that is also a shortcut?"

"It's called Myth Drannor."

Passepout was awakened from his sound sleep by the cold metal of a knife blade held against his neck, and a whiskey voice that demanded that he hand over all of his jewels . . . even the rancid ones.

During the night, Elam had tracked his way to their campsite and had already made plans to retire from trail riding on Passepout's pouch of jewels.

Passepout clutched the pouch closer to his bosom, as if his life depended on them . . . because it did.

Elam, now that he had abandoned the goat wranglers for good, was not about to take no for an answer, and reached across Passepout's rotund body, snatching the pouch from the thespian's hands, and in doing so, spilling its contents on the ground, forming a colorful pile of gems that reflected green in the campfire light, with a tiny glimmer of red on top.

"I should slit your throat just for the heck of it," the brigand snarled.

"I wouldn't do that," said Volo, who had awakened at the commotion.

"What are you going to do about it?" snarled Elam, the blade of his knife digging deeper into Passepout's double chin.

"This," Volo said, waving his hands in the air.

"Hah," said the brigand when nothing happened—only to slump to the ground, dropping the knife safely into Passepout's lap.

Malpasso emerged from the shadows behind Elam, a bloodstained club in hand.

"He shouldn't give you any more trouble. I'll tie him behind my horse and drag him back to the camp. That should teach him a lesson."

And with that, the trail boss hoisted the rogue over his shoulder, and returned to the shadows.

Passepout cried in gratitude, "Oh, thank you, Master Volo. You were wonderful, distracting that brigand while Malpasso gave him the whomp."

"Uh, yes," Volo replied with a touch of uncertainty in his voice. He quickly changed the subject. "Well, another gem has turned so it's time to move on. I suggest we leave by the dawn's early light and put more space between ourselves and Elam. I'm not too sure even a good two-mile draggin' will show him the error of his ways."

"On to Myth Drannor?" asked the bond servant, anxious to further separate himself from the disturber of his dreams.

"Yes," Volo replied. "To Myth Drannor, City of Gates and Shortcuts."

"Whatever you say, wonderful Master Volo."

The two lofted their packs and continued their journey on foot, as rosy-fingered dawn made her appearance on the horizon. Passepout continued his praise for Volo's help in saving his life, while Volo was noticeably silent, as if he were trying to solve a puzzle that he had only recently realized existed.

# MYTH DRANNOR

## OR

### When All Things Magical Don't Always Work

"Between Storm Horn peaks and Hillsfar lies a vast unbroken forest older than all mankind. There lie the legendary ruins of Myth Drannor. Also called the City of Crowns, Myth Drannor rises out of the Elvenwood like the forester's ax-head that its shape resembles: flaring blade to the west, narrow back running to the southeast. Its western edge is composed of lush, rolling meadows known rather obviously as the Westfields, the east is more forested and parklike, and to the north is a small glade that comprises the Burial Glen, a cemetery."

"A cemetery! Great!" said Passepout unenthusiastically. "Save me a plot. This place looks creepy."

Volo, undaunted, continued his travelogue. "The surrounding woods are filled with the usual dangers one would encounter in the wilds, with a particularly large contingent of orcs and bugbears prevalent. It is within the city, however, that the real danger lurks."

"Wait a minute! Master Volo, I know I agreed to be your bond servant in exchange for your saving me from a beating at the gates of Suzail," the discouraged Passepout interrupted, stopping both travelers in their tracks. "And I know that your good name demands that we follow through on this silly folly to go all around Toril, and that part of the agreement is that I accompany you, but enough is enough. I am tired, I am hungry, and I am scared. I've been attacked in the night, pressed beyond the endurance of a normal thespian, and starved for hours on end."

"We ate when we left camp, an hour ago."

"It's only been a hour? It feels like an eternity!"

"Cheer up, my good Passepout. Our problems will soon be solved."

"How?"

"At Myth Drannor."

"I didn't ask where. I asked how."

"And I was explaining it all to you when you interrupted."

"I don't need the introduction to the tourist's guide to Myth Drannor, though I know that is your specialty."

"Not really. Tourists are a rather fickle lot. In

my guides I always try to . . . "

"How is a ruined city going to help us distribute these accursed jewels?" cried the exasperated Passepout.

"Let me try to explain in a shorter, simpler way," Volo offered, once again taking to the road. The resigned thespian belatedly followed. "I believe it was Elminster who first pointed out that Myth Drannor is linked to many other places all over Faerûn, and beyond, by almost a thousand gates."

Passepout perked up. "You mean all we have to do is use these gates to teleport ourselves all over, delivering the gems until they run out, so that we can return home to the Dragon's Jaws Inn?"

"Sort of," Volo replied.

"So it's just a simple matter of garden-variety teleportation. We'll be done in no time!"

"Not quite," the master traveler responded. "You see, no normal teleportation or translocation magics work properly within the city, or into or out of its confines. You see, the magic is bent by the mythal, so that a traveler might find himself transported to some rather inhospitable destinations without a guaranteed way back."

"So how does this help us, then?" Passepout implored.

Volo continued, once again lapsing into his guidebook narrator's voice. "Aside from Elminster, masters of mythal are few. Learning to guide the mythal correctly requires much magical research, an aptitude for handling it, and at least a bit of on-site practice."

"So?"

"Well, I am the author of *Volo's Guide to All Things Magical*, a not too undistinguished conjurer, and I have passed this way before. Don't worry, son of Idle and Catinflas. We should do just fine."

Despite the ever-present threat of brigands and savage beasts, the two travelers' journey to the legendary city passed relatively quietly with the sole exception of the feral growls of hunger that emanated from Passepout's stomach. The woods soon gave way to a meadow. In the distance the skeletal shapes of stone structures that had once comprised the greatest city in the known world soon came into view.

"Isn't it grand!" exclaimed Volo.

"If you say so," Passepout begrudged, "but if you ask me, there's not much there, except some overgrown ruins, a few cellars without buildings, and . . . "

Volo interrupted, ". . . gates to more places than we have gems to distribute. I think we should be on our way home by nightfall if we play our cards right."

The expert traveler paused for a moment, put down his pack, and got his bearings.

"Now, if I remember correctly, the first gate that we can access is over by that staircase of stone. On the other side lies Halruaa. I sort of wish we weren't in such a hurry. You'd love it there, and they'd love you, too. A full appreciation of the arts is enjoyed by all there. You, the master thespian, would be in great demand."

"Perhaps we can tarry there just a little bit?"

"Maybe later. Right now we just want to cover as much ground as possible. Now, let me see." Volo paused another moment and then rushed closer to the staircase, Passepout in tow. "If I remember correctly, the gate is right here. Mmmm, I love the scent of mythal in the air."

"I don't smell anything."

"Of course you don't, but no worry."

Volo concentrated as if going into a trance, and muttered a few words under his breath.

"There! The way to Halruaa should be clear," he exclaimed, then, motioning to his bond servant to take the lead, he offered, "After you, master thespian. The people of Halruaa await."

"Thank you, good sir," Passepout responded, eager to see the glory of a living city after so many days on the road, and hear the roar of an appreciative crowd, even if only for a few minutes.

The son of Idle and Catinflas brushed off some of the dust of the journey from his less than regal robes, spit a spat into his hand, slicked back a lock of hair that was creeping down his forehead, and boldly took a step forward, feeling the power of the gate envelop him, until he felt himself once again on firm ground, where he stopped in his tracks.

Instead of a booming city of wonders, he was standing on a fiery cavern's floor, a ravenous beholder's eye-stalks turning their attention toward him as the gaping maw of its bulbous, levitating body floated in for the lunch that had just arrived.

As panic set in, the paralyzed Passepout heard a voice in the far-off distance from whence he came.

"You're blocking the gate," Volo called from the other side. "I can't get through with you in the doorway. Go on through!"

Passepout could maintain himself no longer and fainted dead out . . . falling backward, back through the gate, which promptly closed behind him, leaving the beholder lunchless.

"Get up!" Volo ordered, pouring a bucket of water from a nearby well over his traveling companion. "Wake up! We're burning daylight. This is no time to take a nap. I've seen people with a variety of reactions to teleporting, but passing out? Well, I guess there is a first time for everything."

Passepout groaned as he began to come around. Slowly he sat up, shaking his head to clear away the fuzziness, then quickly bolted upright and let loose with a scream of terror.

"*Mommy!*" he cried, his eyes darting back and forth looking for a place to escape to.

"What is the matter?" the master traveler asked. "You look as if you've seen a ghost."

Passepout cowered, eyes still searching for the monstrous disembodied eye that he had met on the other side of the gate.

"No, not a ghost," he said cautiously, slowly gaining his composure as the threat failed to materialize. "A beholder, and a hungry one at that!"

"That's odd," Volo responded. "I don't recall ever hearing of a beholder in Halruaa."

"Well, unless Halruaa is located in a fiery, sulphurous cavern, I don't think that was where we were headed."

"But I am sure that was the gate I used to get to Halruaa."

"Maybe something went wrong. Maybe that mythal stuff got in the way."

"I don't understand it," Volo said, a quiver in his voice. "Something like this has never happened to me before."

An idea popped into the master traveler's head.

"Relax," Volo ordered, "I need to scry your mind of the experience you just had in order to get a clearer idea of what is going on."

Volo placed his hand on his bond servant's forehead and concentrated with all of his might.

After a few seconds, the master traveler gave up.

"Nothing," he said. "I concentrate on your thoughts, and I find nothing."

"Thanks!" Passepout answered sarcastically.

"I didn't mean any slight; I just couldn't see anything. It's as if I am suddenly psionically blind."

"Maybe that's what happened at the gate. You mentioned that that mythal stuff can mess the magic up."

"No, it's not the mythal," Volo said with a certain amount of trepidation. "I fear it might be me. I should have sensed our visitor's approach last night, but I didn't. At the time I wrote it off to the fatigue of the road, but now I'm not quite sure."

"What do you think happened?"

"I don't know, but I fear that my magics have gone away."

"You don't suppose that grouchy old Khelben put some sort of whammy on you?"

"You mean when he bonded us to the jewels? I don't know. Maybe."

Passepout, now fully recovered from his terrifying adventure beyond the gate, stood up and once again brushed the dirt of the road from his robes.

"That's why I don't trust wizards. They're always out to play some joke on you. I hear that even Elminster likes to have his fun with the likes of us."

"Elminster!" Volo exclaimed. "He can help us. I'm sure that he can undo any dampening spell that Khelben cast on us. We must head to Shadowdale immediately!"

"Immediately?" asked a slightly apprehensive Passepout.

"Immediately!" Volo insisted. "The sooner I get my magics back under control, the sooner we can accelerate our distribution of the gems and thus clear the good name of Volothamp Geddarm, master traveler. There is no time to rest. Surely you must feel refreshed from your impromptu nap. I would have thought that you would like to see this whole thing over as soon as possible."

"Agreed, Master Volo," Passepout said cautiously, "but it wasn't my own feelings I was referring to."

"Then whose?" boomed Volo in a voice that echoed throughout the ruins.

"Theirs," answered Passepout. He pointed to a band of orcs who now blocked their only avenue of escape and were cagily closing in.

The orcs were an ugly bunch, obviously in search of treasure and fun. Unfortunately, one orc's fun is usually another person's torture, and neither Volo nor Passepout were adequately armed to fend off an attack.

"We're doomed," Passepout cried, once again ready to go weak-kneed.

"Now, hold on there, partner," said Volo. "Even without my magics we still have a chance. Lucky for us, orcs are stupid."

"Oh, you mean you can't read their thoughts, either," said the master thespian, temporarily relieved of his panic.

"Observe," Volo offered in a hushed tone. He approached the band and exclaimed, "Thank Eo you have arrived. I was beginning to worry that you might not come, and with such lovely weather it would be a shame to have to reschedule the show."

The orcs stopped their approach as Volo neared them.

"You there!" said Volo, approaching the leader. "You look like a stalwart fellow, an adventurer's adventurer if I might say. I bet the little woman is proud of you."

The lead orc scratched his head, feebly trying to figure out the curious human whom he formerly marked as their next victim.

"You know, you orcs lead such interesting lives. Right, Passepout?"

"Sure," said the thespian, hoping that his master would let him in on whatever he had planned.

"Don't dawdle, my good fellow. These orcs are in a hurry to get to Halruaa."

"Oh, yeah, right," replied Passepout, finally catching on.

"After all, we can't hog the gate all day."

"Of course not," the thespian agreed.

Volo put his arm around the head orc's shoulder and began to lead him over to the place of the gate.

"Now you have to hurry or someone will get the treasure before you."

"Treasure!" the band of orcs shouted.

"Well, yes, treasure. Halruaa is a land of treasure, and it's right through there," the master traveler instructed, motioning to the gate that still led to the domain of the beholder.

Immediately the orcs began to push and shove toward the gate.

"Halt!" grunted the head orc, still slightly skeptical of the two strange humans, yet eager to be the first through the gate if indeed treasure lay on the other side.

Passepout rushed to the other side of the leader in hopes of assisting his master in egging him on.

"You'd better hurry," he encouraged, then opening the bag of gems from Khelben he reached in and pulled out a handful. "See! There's lots more than this on the other side."

On the pile of green that rested in Passepout's

palm, a single gem of red glowed into prominence.

The head orc snatched the glowing red gem, and while Passepout quickly returned the rest to the sack, he proceeded to swallow it in a loud gulp.

"Not looking for treasure!" the orc replied, backing away from the gate. "Looking for lunch!"

With that the head orc approached the corpulent thespian, salivating at the meal that he was about to behold.

Passepout smelled the stink of orc's breath closing in on him, and felt himself going faint. He cried, "Oh, no! Not again!" as he looked to Master Volo for assurance.

Unfortunately, the look in the master traveler's eyes indicated that there wasn't any, and the brave gazetteer was preparing himself to meet his doom.

# RESCUED BY A CATLASH

## OR

### Good Company Is Always Appreciated, Especially When It Shows Up In the Nick of Time

*Snap!*
*Crack!*
Out of nowhere the lashes of a seven-strand whip sailed over the heads of the orcs, and slashed and cracked on the head of their leader, diverting his attention from his prey.
*Snap!*

*Crack!*

Again the whip came crashing down, its lashes striking two more orcs who quickly separated, diving left and right to clear a path between the holder of the whip and the orc leader and his prey.

Standing eight feet away was a tall, muscular yet thin woman with long brown hair, hard green eyes, and a seven-stranded whip whose twelve-foot range was deceptively disguised as two feet at rest. Behind her stood a band of no less than ten equally fearsome female warriors.

"We have been rescued by Amazons!" Passepout rejoiced.

Volo, knowing that Amazons were not indigenous to this area, nevertheless breathed a sigh of relief over the fortunate arrival of their rescuers and heard the orc leader mutter an orcish curse as he realized that his band was both outnumbered and outskilled.

One of the orc band, however, was neither as intelligent nor as perceptive as his leader, and with a loud war whoop, raised his blackened blade into the air and charged the newly arrived pack of humans.

An auburn-haired beauty, just slightly shorter than the company's leader, insinuated herself forward, and with lightning reflexes unleashed her rapier, skewering the oncoming orc before he had even realized that he was within striking range. With equal skill and facility, she withdraw her blade from the brute body, pausing only momentarily to wipe her blade on her victim's tunic to remove the remaining black flecks of orcish blood from its silver sheen.

Another equally foolish orc, dagger in hand, unaware that his comrade had already met his end, lunged forward at the bearer of the catlash who had dared to strike his father, the orc leader. His lunge, however, was quickly intercepted, blocked by the intervention of a quarterstaff whose bearer had vaulted herself forward to protect her leader. Thrown off-balance, the orc dropped his dagger and fell forward. He found himself pummeled across the side of his bovine visage by the oaken staff and spun around by its bearer, his orcish windpipe cut off from life-giving air by the staff that was now braced below his chin, his body coming to rest on the redhead's armored chest with his feet three inches off the ground. The former attacker's face was quickly turning white from asphyxiation.

Others in the orc band contemplated joining in when the orc leader barked an order; they all laid down their weapons.

The redhead looked to her leader, who responded with a sharp nod, and released her captive from her breathtaking grip. The asphyxiated orc fell to the ground, his air-starved lungs heaving, forcing the chest up and down, the only movement in his beaten body.

The orc leader focused on the catlash bearer, cruel stare meeting cruel stare.

The catlash bearer didn't bat an eye.

The orcs had met their match, and no further action was required.

The orc leader barked out another order, and two of his band came forward to assist their beaten comrade to his feet, chest still heaving in grateful inhalations. They bore him forward so that his father could face him. The leader's stern visage softened with relief as their comrade came around.

The leader tousled the bristles of his still-weak son's pate, and, turning back to the rest of his band, rapped out another order, at which point the rest of band started to retreat from whence they came. Father and son soon quickly joined them, following a lowly brute who dragged the corpse of their slain comrade.

Now alone with their rescuers, Passepout and Volo faced the band of female adventurers.

"O wonderful Amazons, thank you for your assistance," extolled Passepout, "but, of course, Master Volo and myself could have taken care of that loutish band on our own. In fact, I, myself, am well capable of handling twice as many orcs with one hand tied behind my back."

Volo whispered to his boisterous bond servant, "You know, brigands and rogues come in all sexes."

Passepout fell silent, fearful that they had just traded one set of predators for another.

The bearer of the catlash came forward and said, "Smile when you call my band brigands and rogues, or we are liable to take offense."

"None was intended, good lady," Volo replied. "I was merely stating a well-documented rule of the road."

The bearer of the whip scratched a white sword-scar on her cheek with the butt of the catlash before returning the weapon to its holster on her belt. "A rule of the road, you say," she continued, gesturing to Passepout, adding, "Porky here called you Master Volo."

"That is correct," the gazetteer assented.

"Marco, or the real thing?" she persisted.

"There is only one real Volo, my lady. Volothamp Geddarm, at your service," he declared, then quickly added, "and this is my, uh, traveling companion, Passepout."

Passepout bowed with a flourish, adding to Volo's introduction. "Yes, my lady. I am Passepout, son of Catinflas and Idle, and master thespian extraordinaire."

The bearer of the whip ignored the rotund actor's salutation, though several of the adventurers in her band found it very hard to stifle their laughter and amusement.

"Then you are Volo, the master traveler, and author of *Volo's Guide to Waterdeep*?" she persisted.

"Yes," Volo replied, "among many others. And whom do I bear the extreme pleasure of addressing?"

"I am Catlindra Serpentar, "she declared, offering her hand for Volo to shake.

Her grip was that of a warrior, reinforcing to Volo that even a beautiful woman such as this could be intimidating.

"And this," she continued, gesturing to her comrades, "is the Company of the Catlash."

"Wonderful," Passepout declared, eyeing the bevy of warrior beauties with ill-planned lust as he tried to make eye contact with the red-headed staff bearer. When he did, he gave a suggestive wink and a leer.

The redhead ignored his facial invitation, but the rotund thespian chose, in turn, to ignore her obvious lack of interest.

Two of her blond comrades giggled, amused at his obvious denseness.

"I have heard of you, and your company," Volo offered.

"I would expect no less from the master gazetteer," she replied. "You may call me Cat."

"It will be my pleasure, Cat, but if I recall correctly, you and your band are not usually this gregarious. Do you treat all of your rescuees like this?"

"Only those with whom I share a common goal."

"And what goal is that?" he inquired.

She tilted her head back as if to release a kink in her neck, and shook her luxurious mane of brown hair.

"There is enough time for questions later," she replied. "Our camp is on the other side of the city. Why don't you join us for dinner? Nightfall will be here soon, and you probably don't want to be wandering around these ruins then. No telling who or what you might run into during the day, let alone after dark."

"We would be honored," Volo replied.

"Wonderful," Passepout agreed, then quickly turned his attention back to the redhead with the staff. "Perhaps the walk over there can give us the time to get better acquainted?"

The redhead continued to ignore him and set off at a brisk pace toward the company camp. Soon the thespian fell behind, out of breath.

Volo adjusted his pace to stay in rank with his rotund, out-of-shape companion while keeping track of the company's progress far ahead of them so as not to lose their way amidst the confusion of ruins that had once been a great city.

"You know, Master Volo," Passepout sputtered between gasps, "I think that redhead really likes me."

"Indeed," said the gazetteer, glad that something had finally taken his companion's mind off food.

"I just hope she can cook," the thespian added.

Volo just smiled.

After a wondrous meal of hare and venison stew that no traveler on the road had any right to complain about—even Passepout confessed to being sated—Catlindra and her company gathered around the campfire, as was their custom, to wait out the digestion and passage of their meal with conversation, so that bodily functions would not interrupt their sleep later.

Volo listened to tales of the company's exploits, as related by some adventuresses who were probably hoping for a casual mention in one of his books. During a lull in the tale-telling, he turned to their hostess in hope of continuing the conversation from earlier in the day.

"You know, Cat," he started, "earlier I asked you about the common goal that you referred to. Do you care to elaborate now?"

Cat grew wistfully melancholy, and began her tale.

"More years ago than I care to admit, before I took to the road and adventuring life, I was just your typical small-town tomboy, getting into trouble, embarrassing my parents, the usual stuff. My parents didn't really mind. They knew I would outgrow it eventually. They were the best parents a girl could ever hope for."

"I know the kind of whom you speak," Volo offered, striving for a closer affinity with this bold adventurer.

"One day that all changed. I don't remember what it was I noticed first. All I knew was that there was something odd about my mother. I asked my father about it, but he laughed it off, figuring it was all just part of a girl's growing up. You know, a daughter feeling herself to be the rival of her mother for her father's affections."

"Sure," said Volo, not really understanding but willing to write it off as one of those tricky differences between men and women, and quickly noting that perhaps he should ask his mother about it at some later date.

"I persisted, and Father eventually lost his temper and locked me in the cellar. That's what he used to do whenever I used to throw a tantrum: lock me in the cellar and let me cool off. He was a loving father, and never struck me."

"I'm sure," said Volo, intrigued to see where this story was going.

"There in the basement, I found my mother's body."

Volo stifled a gasp.

Cat continued her tale in an emotionless monotone.

"You see, the thing that I had thought was my mother acting strangely, wasn't really my mother at all, but a doppelganger who had killed her and insinuated itself into our family."

"So what did you do?" Volo asked, still not aware what this had to do with the mysterious common goal that supposedly he and she shared.

"I escaped from the cellar and killed it before it could murder my father or me."

Cat paused for a moment to look in the flames of the campfire, then continued with the story, eyes still focused on the dancing flashes of red, yellow, and orange.

"Unfortunately, my father couldn't handle it. The death of his wife, his not recognizing her murderer's insinuation into their marriage bed. He went insane, cut himself off from the entire world, and retreated into his own little world. A friend of the family who was a cleric offered to take care of him. He's in a monastery now, still cut off in his own world, never making contact with anyone. I continue to send money to them, and they care for him as best they can."

"I'm sorry for your loss," Volo offered.

"Oh, others have had it worse. That which doesn't kill you usually makes you stronger," Cat said, trying to sound as matter-of-fact as possible. "Anyway, ever since then I've had this thing against doppelgangers."

"Well that's understandable," Volo agreed, still trying to figure out what all of this had to do with him.

"And when I heard about a certain travel author exposing an entire ring of murderous doppelgangers in Waterdeep, well, I knew I had to meet him."

"Who did that?" Passepout inquired.

"Why, Volo, of course," she replied.

"You did?" Passepout inquired of his shocked master.

"Well, I, uh . . . " Volo fumbled.

"Of course he did," insisted the company leader, who began to relate this tale of bravery previously unknown to Volo himself. "You see," she persisted, "there was a conspiracy in Waterdeep led by an evil doppelganger by the name of Hlaavin. His group called itself the Unseen. They were a consortium of shapechangers, thieves, illusionists, and assassins who had originally come from the Rat Hills to Waterdeep with a plan to gain control of the city by supplanting all of the most powerful people within Waterdeep society. At first their infiltration began slowly, taking more than ten years to maneuver impostors of a few minor functionaries in place, and then Hlaavin hatched an ingenious plan of setting up a high-class festhall to cater to just the types of society members that they wanted to supplant."

Volo finally saw where she was headed, and stated, "The Hanging Lantern."

"The Hanging Lantern?" Passepout questioned.

"Of course, the Hanging Lantern," Cat assured, "and you exposed it seven years ago."

"You did?" Passepout asked of his master incredulously.

"All I did was to say in my guide to Waterdeep that the Hanging Lantern was a festhall run by doppelgangers," Volo offered, trying to put his alleged heroic deed into the proper perspective.

Cat would not hear of it. "Oh, you are much too modest," she insisted. "That subtle little entry brought down the entire villainous plot without panicking the entire city. You were a genius."

"Well, I . . . "

"Unfortunately, they never caught Hlaavin," she continued, bringing the tale to an end, "but the Hanging Lantern was shut down, and you can't have everything, I guess . . . but anyway, any enemy of a doppelganger is a friend of mine."

Volo, glad that the story was over, changed the subject. "But that was seven years ago. We have new, more pressing matters at hand."

"Oh," said Cat with a gleam in her eye, "you're after the Bleth reward, too."

"The Bleth reward?" Passepout inquired, his eyes immediately seeing gold pieces.

Cat turned to Volo and, indicating the thespian at his side, stated, "I take it he's not too bright."

"I'm afraid that neither of us are," Volo replied. "This is the first I've ever heard of the Bleth reward."

"Oh, well, I guess I'm one up on you then," Cat conceded. "Lord Gruen Bleth of the Seven Suns Trading Company has offcred a huge reward for the safe return of his daughter, who was part of a caravan that was abducted while she was traveling through Thay. That's where we're bound, as a sort of general objective. Of course, if we don't find her, we'll find something to keep us busy. Still, the reward would be nice. Care to join us?"

Volo considered the offer carefully and graciously declined.

"Thank you, my fair lady, but I'm afraid we will have to decline due to prior commitments."

"Prior commitments can usually wait," Cat offered flirtatiously.

"If only they could," Volo countered, "but my word is my bond, and the matter is completely out of my control ."

Cat sighed. "A man of bravery, and a man of honor," she said wistfully. "I had hoped to share your company longer, but I respect your commitments. Perhaps we can travel together for a few days—say, until the road that leads to your destination diverges from the one that leads to ours. Which reminds me, if I might be so bold as to inquire, where are you and your roly-poly actor heading?"

"Shadowdale," Volo stated.

"Shadowdale?" Passepout questioned.

"Why Shadowdale?" the gracious hostess pressed.

"Because something has gone wrong with my magics, and I must have it corrected as soon as possible," he answered.

"Well, toward the Dalelands it shall be then," she stated, adding, "and then on to Thay. The hour is late, digestion complete, and time for sleep. Tomorrow, Shadowdale bound so shall we be."

A few hours later, still in the dead of night, Volo heard footsteps approaching, and mindful of their earlier midnight encounter, he quickly braced himself, dagger in hand beneath his blanket, and inquired, "Who goes there?"

A sheepish voice broke through the silence of the darkness.

"It is only I, Master Volo," said Passepout.

"Is everything all right?" Volo inquired.

"Sure," the thespian replied with all the enthusiasm of a slave bound for the block.

"All right, then," Volo answered, adding, "Get some sleep. The open road beckons us for an early departure."

"Great," said Passepout, with his usual lack of zeal.

Rosy-fingered dawn saw the Company of the Catlash, and their two new companions, ready for the road.

Volo noticed the auburn-haired staff bearer telling her comrades a story that invoked reams of laughter, which they quickly suppressed once they noticed his presence. His curiosity at the reason for their joviality and for Passepout's late-night stirrings was soon satisfied, when he saw the thespian at breakfast. Somehow during the night, his rotund bond servant had acquired a black eye, and a proclivity toward blushing whenever the redhead was around.

*Oh, well,* thought the traveler, *such are the risks of the inept Casanova.*

Vowing to himself never to mention what might have transpired, Volo helped his companion with his pack, keeping pace with him as they journeyed toward Shadowdale, subtly massaging the thespian's fragile, damaged ego.

By lunch, the embarrassment of less than twelve hours ago seemed to be forgotten, and the thespian's earlier braggadocio had returned, much to the chagrin of the rest of the company.

# SHADOWDALE

## OR

## A New Course of Action Is Required

"I will miss your company, master traveler," sighed Catlindra Serpentar.

"And I yours," replied Volothamp Geddarm.

"I hope you solve your problem," she added.

"In matters of magic, Elminster knows all," replied the departing traveler.

*"You mean we're going to see Elminster?"* interrupted Passepout, destroying the poignancy of the friends' farewell.

Cat kissed Volo on the forehead and with a sly wink rejoined her company along the road that would bypass Shadowdale.

Volo sighed for a moment and started down the road to Shadowdale proper.

"But, Master Volo," Passepout persisted, "I've always heard that Elminster is a bit of a curmudgeon and not really fond of unexpected visitors. And given the way we didn't exactly hit it off with Khelben, I don't think we can afford to get on the wrong side of another archmage."

Volo just shook his head.

"You can't believe everything you hear," he replied. "I'm sure he'll be glad to see us."

The sign read, *Trespassers May Be Polymorphed*.

"We're not trespassers . . . I mean . . . you've been here before," said the very concerned Passepout, who had no desire to pursue his acting career as a trained seal or some such other animal.

"Afraid not," Volo replied.

"But you have met Elminster before, haven't you?" the thespian persisted.

"Sort of."

"What do you mean, sort of?"

"He wrote introductions to some of my guides."

"Like *Volo's Guide to All Things Magical*?"

"Well, no," Volo hedged. "Now that you mention it, he was slightly miffed at me for that one."

"But that was a long time ago," the thespian demanded. "Right?"

"Sure was," Volo agreed, paused for a moment, and continued, "Now that you mention it, that was probably the last time we had business together. I hope he doesn't hold a grudge."

"Eo save us!" Passepout prayed.

At last they arrived at the most famous residence in the Dales, Elminster's tower.

The sign read *Enter At Your Own Risk — Have You Notified Your Next of Kin?*

Passepout did a one-eighty and took off back the way they had come, saying, "Darn it! I knew I forgot something. And it has been a while since I dropped a line to my dear parents. After all, what will Idle and Catinflas do without me?"

Volo reached back, grabbed his bond servant by the collar, and turned him around.

"Do you want to risk separating, given Khelben's spell?" Volo calmly asked.

"I guess not," Passepout reluctantly agreed.

"And don't you want me to get my magics back, so that we can divest ourselves of these accursed gems, complete our world tour, and get back to the city comforts of the Dragon's Jaws Inn?"

"Most assuredly, Master Volo."

"Well then," Volo pressed, "ring the bell."

Gently the thespian pulled the bell cord. Its tintinnabulation carried throughout the dale. If anyone were home, they would have undoubtedly have heard it—as would anyone else within a mile radius.

No one came to the door.

"Again," Volo ordered.

Again the chimes sounded, but still no one came to the door.

"That's odd," said the master traveler. "It's not unusual for Elminster to be away, but I would have expected Lhaeo to be around. Perhaps we should force the door, maybe look around some."

"But, Master, shouldn't we find a place to spend the night?" Passepout implored, trying to distract the traveler.

"We're not too far from the Old Skull Inn," Volo answered.

"Well, why don't we check in for the night and perhaps ask around for news about their whereabouts? It is getting late, after all, and you did promise me a night under a roof."

"So I did," Volo replied absently. "I guess we can check back tomorrow."

"Sure," agreed Passepout, discreetly dropping a red gem on the doorstep. "Sure," he repeated.

To himself he thought, *I'll wait until after dinner to remind Master Volo about not retracing our steps. We'll have to find a solution at someplace more friendly with fewer warnings.*

Jhaele Silvermane, proprietor of the Old Skull Inn, was a fine judge of human nature and a shrewd observer of new faces to Shadowdale who just happened to stop by her taproom. Given the Zhent troubles of the past few years, she was always on her guard and prone to "accidentally" overhearing conversations among new patrons. It was no surprise that she listened in on the two new arrivals, and even less of a surprise that she sent a messenger to Storm Silverhand when she recognized the mentions of Khelben and Elminster.

"But, Master Volo," Passepout implored, "we can't go back to Elminster's tower. You remember what Khelben said about retracing our steps."

"Why didn't you remind me of that when we were at the tower?" Volo blustered, having lost his temper with the rotund thespian for the first time.

"I forgot . . . and I was hungry . . . and think the raven-haired barmaid likes me . . . and I didn't think Elminster would appreciate us waiting inside, given all the warnings, and such."

The master traveler sighed, and conceded, "You're probably right. Normally I would have relied on my magics to alert me to any booby traps or such."

"What will we do now?"

"I don't know," Volo replied. "Since my magic has gone away, I feel helpless. If only Elminster had been home. He would have been able to crack this magic-dampening cloud that seems to be following me around."

Passepout eyed the crowd at the taproom, trying to find the barmaid whom he was sure that he had impressed with his tales of the theater and of his exploits on the road as Volo's right-hand man. Though he obviously felt sympathy for his master's plight, he couldn't help but wish that more magic users could experience how an average guy has to get by. It would serve them all right.

The raven-haired bartender was nowhere to be seen, and had he not known better he might have thought that she was avoiding him.

"Excuse me," offered a recently arrived patron, "did your friend mention Elminster?"

The speaker was a tall, good-looking young lady with silvery, long hair held back from her face by a tiara of silver, and the brightest blue-gray eyes Passepout had ever seen.

"Yes he did, milady," Passepout replied, acknowledging that the speaker was a much better catch for the evening than the barmaid would be any day. "We have an appointment with him . . . but he's not home."

"What sort of an appointment?" she pressed.

"Very important business," he replied, "but nothing to worry your pretty little head about. It will have to wait. So, in the meantime, why don't we get to know each other a little better?"

"I don't think so."

Passepout continued undaunted. "I am Passepout the legendary thespian, and this is the honorable Volothamp Geddarm, best-selling author of guides to Waterdeep, the North, and All Things Magical."

"I recollect El telling me about that one," she interrupted.

Passepout pulled himself up short, remembering his master's comment about the old mage's reaction to the aforementioned book of magic.

"You know Elminster?" he asked sheepishly.

"Yes, I do," she replied, "and I don't remember him telling me that he was expecting anyone, and I know he wouldn't appreciate strangers calling at the tower—probably as much as I enjoy the company of braggarts in my local tavern."

"I meant no offense," the thespian replied, trying to backpedal as fast as possible.

"I'm Storm Silverhand," she boomed, "and what business do you have with Elminster?"

"Storm Silverhand!" Volo exclaimed, breaking out of his stupor of self-pity. "I am Volothamp Geddarm, master traveler of the Realms."

"So he claims," Storm replied, "but I've heard of more than one fellow falsely claiming the Volo moniker."

Volo rolled his eyes. Again he was confronted with doubt and confusion due to that imposter Marcus Wands. *Reputation matters*, he thought, *damn it!*

"I am the real Volo," he replied, keeping his tones as measured as possible, "the one and only. I have come to Shadowdale in hopes that Elminster would be able to help me with a problem, but now that I think about it, it was all just foolishness on my part. He's probably back in Suzail at the War Wizards' meeting."

"You know about the meeting?"

"Sure. Vangerdahast has convened the college for some reason or other."

Storm considered the two strangers for a moment. There was always the possibility that they were not who they claimed to be, particularly the fat one . . . but Elminster would not want her to turn away someone who was really in need, nor would the merchants of Shadowdale want to risk alienating a famous gazetteer like Volo from writing kindly of their area. Either way, they looked harmless enough and posed little threat to a hardened warrior such as herself.

"For the time being, I will accept whom you say you are. If you have a problem, perhaps I can help. Let's go back to my farm, away from the crowds of Shadowdale's only tap house, so that we can talk."

"Sure," Volo agreed, picking up his pack. "Lead on."

Passepout scrambled to set his own pack in place and quickly fell in beside his master.

"Did you hear that, Master Volo?" he whispered. "Away from the crowd, she said. I think she likes me."

Yet again, Volo just rolled his eyes.

The chill from Storm's initial manner soon wore off in the confines of her farmhouse, where she fed the two worn and discouraged travelers ample portions of typical Shadowdale fare, washed down with freshly brewed Shadowdale ale. Between munches, draughts, and numerous expressions of gratitude, the gazetteer and the thespian told their tale.

"That doesn't really sound like Khelben," she observed, throwing another log on the fire, as the chill of the evening made its presence known.

"It was Blackstaff, all right," Passepout interjected. "I would have known him anywhere."

"Quite," Storm replied in a tone usually reserved for parents of opinionated and obstreperous children, then turned her attention back to Volo. "Well, it's obvious that your magics have been dampened by something. Maybe something happened when you tried to scry the gate at Myth Drannor. Sometimes the areas of wild magic cause an overload, a sort of mage hangover, you might say."

"My magics had left prior to Myth Drannor. I should have been aware of our camp's intruder the night before," he replied. "No, I'm sure it is something that must have happened to me back in Suzail, something linked to the gems, the bond, and the wager."

"If you ask me," Passepout interrupted, "it's just another case of a mage throwing around his powers, to have some fun with the less enchanted ones."

Volo ignored his servant's comments and continued with his train of thought.

"Now that I think back, I distinctly remember a chill passing through me as I shook his hand. I didn't think much of it at the time, but now . . . "

"No offense meant," Storm apologized in advance, "but it still doesn't sound like the Khelben Arunsun I know. He's more tolerant of braggarts than I am."

"What do you mean by that?" Volo asked.

"Well, you do seem to stake a lot on your reputation."

"It's well earned, and nobody ever questioned it

before that rogue Marcus Wands started calling himself Marco Volo."

"I know, but it's not as if anyone actually called you a liar."

"Well, no."

"And it's not like you were forced to accept the challenge."

"I had to. There is only one master traveler of the Realms!"

"And you weren't tricked into accepting the challenge?"

Volo hedged for a moment. "Well, actually, I do recall accepting it before hearing what it was to be."

"So even if the challenge had been that you must travel with a servant, dropping markers along the way, never retracing your steps, and never using your magical arts, you would have still theoretically agreed to it."

"Well, yes, I reckon so," Volo agreed, and then chuckled. "I guess I should keep my big mouth closed until I've heard all the details of a deal."

"This doesn't change the fact that Volo has been tricked," the thespian demanded. "How can Khelben expect us to pass this test without the help of Volo's magical arts?"

"Is that true, Volo?" Storm asked gently. "Is that the real reason for your reputation as a master traveler? Is it all just another magic trick?"

"No," he replied, a grin spreading on his lips. "Of course not. It just makes this harder."

"But not impossible," Storm added.

"No, not impossible," Volo conceded.

As the night grew long, Passepout once again became cranky and was about to suggest that they return to the Old Skull Inn when he realized that the ploy that he had used to prevent Volo from returning to Elminster's tower now prevented them from returning to the inn—and the arms of an appreciative serving wench who would probably like nothing better than to partake in an assignation with a famous thespian. Eyeing his hostess, he realized that maybe another alternative existed.

"You know, Storm," he declared in his most man-of-the-world voice, "life gets lonely on the road."

"I know," she replied in a respectful monotone.

"Particularly for a thespian such as myself who is used to the presence of many adoring fans."

"Of course," she replied in the same tone.

"And Master Volo is wonderful company . . . don't get me wrong . . . but I was wondering if . . . "

"You could spend the night snuggling up close to a more feminine warm body."

"You read my mind," he replied, leaning in close.

"No problem; it was easy," she answered, getting to her feet and helping him to his. "I was going to offer you one of the guest rooms, but I realize now that that simply won't do."

"Great minds do think alike."

"Uh, yes," she replied, leading him to the door.

Puzzled, Passepout asked, "Where are we going? Some little hideaway cottage?"

"*We* are going nowhere," she succinctly replied. "*You* are going to the barn. Mystia and Mandy are waiting for you."

"Mystia and Mandy?" he queried. He knew Storm had six sisters but couldn't recall the names Mandy and Mystia being among them.

Storm elaborated, removing any doubt of the females' identities, "My horse Mystia and my donkey Mandy will more than keep you warm."

"But the barn?"

"Yes!"

"What about the smell?" he insisted as she ushered him out the door.

"Don't worry," she replied, "they'll get used to it."

With that she closed the door and turned her attentions back to the master traveler, who had been conspicuously silent during this exchange.

Volo had fallen asleep, at the fireside, his head on his pack, his cloak as his blanket, and a smile on his lips.

*He's probably already solved his immediate problem. The loss of his magics won't stop the master traveler.*

Storm carried herself off to bed, vowing that she would be up in plenty of time to fix them a true innkeeper's breakfast.

After all, tomorrow they would be back on the road.

# NORTH ON LIGHTNING-HOOFED STEEDS

## OR

## Horse, Harbor, and Boat

In addition to Mystia and Mandy, the barn was also the home of other creatures, many noisy and nocturnal. Specifically, Storm never mentioned to Passepout about Roget the rooster, who decided to introduce himself to the ill-slept thespian with the dawn's early light.

Less than thrilled to be awakened by fowl crowing, Passepout stretched, brushed himself off, and headed back to the house. *Well, at least there's breakfast,* he thought as he tried to remove the kinks that had set into his joints during the chill of the past night.

The door had been unbolted from the night before, and a fresh fire raged in the hearth. Volo seemed to have been up for hours, despite his rested condition; his disposition was bright and sunny. In front of him were various charts and maps, plus the parchment that had been given to him when the thespian received the bag of jewels.

"Oh, you're already up, good Passepout," he said sunnily. "I was just about to call you. Storm had mentioned that you desired accommodations other than her guest room."

"Something like that," the thespian grumbled, wondering if his master had slumbered in the bower that Passepout had assumed was to be for himself.

"I don't even remember you leaving. I must have fallen asleep in midconversation, or something. But the hearth kept me warm, and the crackling of the flames serenaded me the way my mother used to, and now I feel well-rested and ready to go."

"Great," the thespian replied, less than enthusiastically.

"I've been studying the parchment that Khelben gave me."

"Where's breakfast?"

"Storm's fixing it. It should be ready momentarily. Now look at the parchment," Volo ordered. "Notice how the vague outlines of the lands that we've passed through have become clearer as the red dots that represent the discarded gems become more numerous."

"Great," Passepout replied. "A map whose detail

of a place is only usable once we've left there."

Volo ignored the remark. "Notice the zigzag route we followed from Suzail to here. Up to Myth Drannor, over to Shadowdale. . . ."

"I was there. Remember?" the thespian interrupted, loud enough to be heard over the rumblings of his stomach.

"Quite. Now if I remember correctly, we weren't told not to double back . . . "

"But . . . "

"Shush!" Volo continued as before. "We were told never to 'set foot' on the same land more than once. See, here is the dot for Elminster's tower, and when we leave here another dot should appear right around here."

"So you mean we could have returned to the Old Skull Inn last night," said Passepout growing more and more impatient.

"So the trick is to never set foot on the same general area once we've left there. This does not rule out other methods of transportation."

"But you can't control the gates . . . "

"I was referring to conventional methods of transportation."

"I don't understand."

"Until now I had only considered land-bound routes, but examining my other maps, other options seem to be open to us."

"Like?"

"Sea. Air."

"But . . . " Passepout sputtered, even more afraid of the implications that were being made.

Storm set down a large tray of buns, jams, and meats, at the hearthside. "I see what you mean," she interjected. "So what you really want to do is get to the open sea as soon as possible so as to minimize your risk of doubling back."

"Well, actually I was figuring on heading to the Moonsea, and from there down the River Lis, and farther south to the Sea of Fallen Stars."

"Not a bad plan," Storm replied, "but you have to watch out for the Zhents. If you venture too close to Zhentil Keep, your journey might stop there—for good."

"Zhents!" Passepout coughed, spitting out crumbs from his too-full cheeks.

"I am aware of the dangers, but such is the life of a traveler."

"But not of a thespian," the bond servant protested. "Why can't we . . ."

"There are things that can be done to minimize the risks," answered Storm before the question was even formed. "Through the Harper network I have contacts all over Faerûn, even in the Moonsea region. In fact, I have a delivery that must be made to a certain Harper in that region. Here's an opportunity to kill two birds with one stone."

"I wish you hadn't said 'kill,' " Passepout replied, as the conversation lulled to allow for a fuller enjoyment of the meal at hand.

After the morning meal, Storm escorted the two travelers back to the barn in which Passepout had passed the night. She indicated two horses.

"These are lightning steeds," she said. "They are the fastest mounts in all Faerûn. Marks lent them to two fellow agents who had escaped from Zhentil Keep, and they need to be returned to him. He'll be able to help you book passage on some trade ship heading in the right direction."

"Perfect," Volo replied.

"Great," said Passepout unenthusiastically.

"That's all I need, another sanctimonious Harper bending my ear."

"You won't have to worry about that with Marks. He's mute."

Storm outfitted both travelers with a full stock of provisions for the journey, and also a magical sack that could be used to render the pouch of necromancer's gems invisible to all eyes save Passepout's and Volo's. She then turned to Volo.

"I wish you well on your journey," she said honestly, "and should you ever pass this way again, be sure to stop by. There will always be a warm place for you to rest near my hearth."

"I assure you," Volo said with certitude, "I will pass this way again. As I am the master traveler of the Realms, I guarantee it."

For the most part, the trip north was uneventful. The steeds set an almost inconceivable pace, slowed down only by the needs of their riders to rest occasionally and, more infrequently, eat.

The ever-present rumblings of Passepout's stomach seemed to provide a chorus of thunder to accompany the steady drumming of the lightning steeds' hoofbeats. As they headed farther north, as if on cue, the sky darkened to an overcast blanket of storm clouds, reflecting the troubles and oppression of these non-Daleland residents living in the shadow of the Citadel of the Raven and other Zhent strongholds.

The steeds required neither urging nor directions to find the quickest and easiest paths home. They steered well clear of hostile outposts while still providing their riders with as easy a journey as possible.

Much to the saddle-sore thespian's relief, they

soon arrived at the home of the mute Harper Marks.

Nightfall had arrived, and Marks had apparently already turned in for the night.

Volo approached the entrance to his domicile, looking for a bell cord that could be rung to summon the master of the manor . . . but none existed. Instead, in its place, a bladder-horn was mounted by an open window nearest the door.

Volo squeezed the bulb.

The resultant blare trumpeted into the house with a cacophonous sound that hurt Passepout's ears.

The front door was quickly thrown open by a strange, wide-eyed man with blond curly hair, who rushed past the two travelers to embrace the necks of the two steeds who had returned home. His mouth moved at the rate of a mile a minute, apparently lavishing praise and affection on the noble beasts, though neither Volo nor Passepout could hear a word.

"Uh, Mister Marks . . . " Volo interrupted. "Storm Silverhand sent us, and said that you . . . "

In the blink of an eye, Marks turned his attention his two visitors, vigorously shaking hands and embracing them, lips still moving at the same silent yet frenetic pace.

Volo tried to continue his introduction. ". . . uh . . . Storm said that you might be able to help us get transport to the River Lis and southward."

Marks gestured to them with a jovial body motion that he would be glad to help them, but then held up a single finger to indicate that something else had to be done first. Turning his back on his guests, he took the reins of the horses and led them into their paddocks, one with the nameplate

Horsefeather, the other Coconut. He filled their troughs with a mix of barley and hay, with an oat mash sprinkled liberally on top.

Once his returned loved ones had been cared for, he once again assumed the role of the gracious host and ushered the two travelers into his house.

"Thank you, Mister Marks," Passepout shouted, "but we are very hungry, and . . ."

Marks slapped him across the face, just hard enough to get his attention, and covered his ears with his hands while shaking his head "no."

"I'm pretty sure he's telling us," Volo observed, "that even though he is mute, his hearing is fine, and there is no reason to shout."

Marks touched his finger to the tip of his nose and nodded. He then patted Passepout on the head, rubbed his stomach, and indicated the way toward a table where a meal had been laid out, awaiting the guests.

Passepout dove in, pausing only to observe, "It's as if he were expecting us."

The mute heard this, reached into the pocket of his robe, and extracted a small note that he handed to Volo to read.

"It's from Storm," Volo declared, "and she's outlined our needs to him. How did she get this to you before we arrived?"

Marks extended his arms out to the sides, and waved them up and down a few times. He then pulled them in, close to his body but bent, and began walking around like a chicken.

"By bird?"

Marks nodded.

"By carrier pigeon?"

Once again Marks signed that Volo was right on the nose.

Volo carried the exchange to its most meaning-ful question. "Can you help us?"

Marks paused for a moment as if for dramatic effect, then smiled and vigorously nodded. He then motioned to the traveler, rubbing first his own stomach and then that of Volo, then pointing to the set table as if to say, "C'mon, let's eat!"

Volo graciously complied.

The next morning, after the steeds had once again been cared for, Marks took out a map that he had annotated.

"It's a shortcut to Hillsfar," Volo observed out loud for the benefit of his bond servant, who was still stuffing himself at the table.

"Mmmmphlgh," Passepout replied with cheeks still bulging.

Marks pantomimed a spy skulking as if in shad-ows.

"It's a secret road."

Marks nodded.

Passepout joined the two, who had finished their breakfast at least an hour ago.

"What about once we get to Hillsfar?" he asked.

Marks extracted a packet from inside his robe and handed it to Volo.

"It's two tickets for a riverboat, sailing along the coast from Hillsfar to Harrowdale."

Again Marks nodded and then led them over to a slate that was hung on the wall. He wrote, *Alas, this is all I can do*.

"You've done more than enough." Volo replied, reaching to shake his hand.

Marks shook his head of blond locks, indicating that he wasn't finished. Using the sleeve of his robe he erased what he'd previously written and replaced it with *Remember: Dare & Beware*, and then offered his hand to Volo.

Volo shook it firmly, adding, " 'Tis the battle cry of the Moonsea Region."

Both nodded at each other, while Passepout simply shook his head in anticipation of the dangers to come.

The sign before the crowded community gate read *Welcome to Hillsfar* and then below it *Elves, Dwarves, and Halflings, Enter at Your Own Risk*, and then below that someone else had scrawled *We don't want you here!*

Passepout turned to Volo and said, "I take it you only visit really friendly places."

Volo was not amused. "I've traveled Toril over, and have enjoyed most elements of its diversity and variety, and for that reason I will never understand racism," he replied regretfully. "At least it doesn't apply to us and shouldn't interrupt our appointment with the riverboat *Greenwood Twain*.

Passepout stopped in his tracks, and pointed to a recently posted notice.It read, *Access to noncitizens only with governmental permission*, below which someone had written, *and you better have it or else*.

"Or else what?" asked the wary thespian.

"Not much," Volo replied, "probably just a trip to the arena as a gladiator-in-training."

The thespian shivered. "There are some lengths which even I won't go to for the sake of pleasing an audience. How do you plan on getting us past the guards at the gate?"

Volo watched the crowds at the gate. "Observe," he said. "Do there seem to be any exceptions to their spot-checks?"

Passepout studied the people. "Well, yes," he answered, "the guys in the funny helmets with the big red feathers."

"Correct."

"Who are they?"

"The Red Plumes of Hillsfar," Volo replied, slipping into his gazetteer voice. "They were mercenaries hired by Maalthier to defend the city. As mercenaries, they were free to wear their own insignia and uniforms, or lack thereof, so long as they wore their plumed helms—and who wouldn't want to, given the treatment those bearing the red plumes receive?"

"Too bad we don't have a pair of helms like that."

"Follow me," Volo ordered, venturing farther on, past the gate and behind a hedge that obscured easy viewing of the road from the gate guardhouse.

"What are you doing?" Passepout asked.

"You," he replied, not answering the question, "are going to tell a joke to those two gentlemen who are now leaving the city gate."

"A joke!"

"More than one if necessary," Volo replied, and with that scurried into a break in the hedge.

"A joke," Passepout repeated to himself, shrugged, marshalled his minute capacity of courage, and stepped out in front of the two oncoming Red Plumes.

"Hey!" called the thespian, doing a convincing job of not appearing scared. "How many halflings does it take to feed a wolf? Only one if he's fat enough."

The Red Plumes slowed, and then stopped to listen to the plump comedian.

"Uh . . . here's another," he sputtered, trying to think of a different one fast enough. "What is the difference between loading a cart with bricks, and loading a cart with dwarves?"

One of the Red Plumes raised his hand, and said, "Wait! I think I know this one!"

*Thud!*

With the sound of a makeshift bludgeon meeting the base of a skull, both Red Plumes went down, revealing Volo standing behind them, two stockings filled with coins swinging from each hand. A well-placed blow beneath their helms had succeeded in knocking the mercenaries out.

"Quickly!" Volo ordered. "Help me tie them up. I'm sure they won't mind if we borrow their helms. Where did you get such horrible jokes?"

"An entertainer must be prepared for any sort of audience," Passepout replied, and pitched in immediately with the divestiture of the mercenaries' headpieces. "And where did you ever learn that coins-in-the-sock maneuver?"

"At one time I was thinking of doing a book on self-defense for the common man called *Volo's Guide to Streetfighting*, but my publisher was afraid that it would become a how-to book for brigands. Oh, and one more thing," Volo added. "What is the difference between loading a cart with bricks, and loading a cart with dwarves?"

Passepout smiled.

"You can use a pitchfork when you're loading dwarves," he replied.

Volo just rolled his eyes. With the Red Plumes' helms upon their heads, they passed into Hillsfar without incident and immediately headed to the harbor, where the *Greenwood Twain* had just announced its final boarding call.

The trip eastward and south was uneventful but depressing. The riverboat that Marks had booked them passage on also trafficked in the slave trade, and once a day the poor unfortunates were brought on deck for their exercise. This jumping up and down would last for about twenty minutes, at which point they would be returned to the crowded, unsanitary hold.

Volo couldn't stand to watch, and would turn his back to look at the cold, clear, deep, almost purplish waters of the Moonsea.

"There but for the grace of Eo go I," he muttered, sickened by the inhumanity of it all.

Passepout was just sickened by the voyage itself. The cold north wind rocked the vessel on the unforgiving Moonsea. He wasn't able to keep down any solid foods until they reached the River Lis. He would only venture from their cabin to, at the proper time, throw a red gem overboard, or to heave the contents of his delicate stomach into the watery darkness below.

When the *Greenwood Twain* finally reached its destination of Harrowdale, Volo and Passepout quickly disembarked, leaving behind the depressing memory of the rolling waters and human chattel.

"Where to now, Master Volo?" Passepout asked. "It's good to be back on dry land."

"I'm afraid that I have bad news for you, son of Idle and Catinflas," Volo answered. "We will be booking passage on the first available ship heading south."

Passepout sighed with hapless resignation.

"But first," the master traveler added, "we will find a cleric who can cure you of your propensity for seasickness."

The thespian brightened a bit at hearing this, and responded, "Well, in that case, I guess another voyage won't be too bad. Thank you, Master Volo."

Volo braced at hearing the word "master," in

light of his shipboard observations.

"And another thing," he added, "consider the debt that you owed me to be filled."

"But, Master Volo . . . "

"No," Volo insisted, "you've more than repaid me for the incident at the gates of Suzail, so please don't address me as 'master' any longer. From this day forward, let the bond that exists between us be one based on the friendship of two companions on the road."

Passepout was almost speechless.

"What about the 'magical bond' that was imposed on us back in Suzail?"

"It is my hope," Volo answered, "that will be a temporary one, but the one we have forged out of friendship will last forever."

Passepout, sheepish in the gratitude he felt toward the master traveler, forced a slightly choked expression of gratitude.

"Thank you, Mast . . . , uh, Mister Volo."

"Thank you, Passepout, son of Idle and Catinflas," Volo replied, adding, "Now let's go find that cleric."

# SAILING THE
# SEA OF FALLEN STARS

## OR

## Pirates, Ho!

The cleric cured Passepout of his motion malady and assured him that he was now seaworthy. As the two travelers were leaving the healer's shop, Volo inquired if the cure would do for other forms of motion malady, such as air-sickness and the like.

*Air-sickness?* Passepout thought, *what's that?*

The healer assured them that it would, and the two left the shop, almost as quickly as Passepout's question left his mind.

The two travelers had pitched their red-plumed helms overboard before the riverboat passed through the River Lis, and felt confident in the safety of their true identities, or at least as safe as travelers could be in Faerûn.

Volo booked them passage on a merchant vessel called the *Amistad's Bounty* that was bound for Arrabar, down the Dragon Reach, and through the Sea of Fallen Stars, under the able command of Captain Bligh Queeg, a legendary ship captain and disciplinarian of the high seas. They were allowed first-class accommodations, which were private, provided they were willing to sleep in an above-deck storeroom rather than in crews' quarters or the hold.

The captain was at the gangplank when it was time for them to board. He was a short dumpling of a man who wore the uniform of a veteran of the Cormyrean Freesails and had a posture straighter than the main mast of the ship. In one hand he held a pair of metallic marbles, which clanked together while he extended the other hand to greet the new arrivals to his ship.

"*Mister* Volo, and *Mister* Passepout, welcome aboard," he declared with all of the formality of a Tethyrian noble negotiating a treaty. "We shall be setting sale shortly. Our cargo has been loaded, and we are merely awaiting the arrival of my first mate, *Mister* Nordhoff."

"What type of cargo are we carrying?" Volo inquired.

"Assorted metals, furs, and slaves for the coast of Zakhara."

"Oh," the master traveler replied, depressed that the cloud that had covered his early sea journey persisted in following him.

Queeg responded to what he considered to be a safety concern of his passenger.

"You need not worry about them," he explained. "They are all well chained in the hull, and, unlike other captains, I never allow them on deck until our final destination has been reached."

"Don't they need exercise?" Passepout asked, having witnessed a session on the riverboat during one of his bouts at the rail.

"Their condition is no concern of mine," Queeg answered. "I get paid no matter what shape they arrive in. Now, if you will excuse me, I have work to do. I am sure you will find your quarters suitable, and hope that you will be able to join me and *Mister* Nordhoff for dinner in quarters tonight. We will be serving strawberries for dessert."

Queeg did a perfect military about-face and headed for the quarterdeck.

The accommodations were all that the two travelers had been promised: a dry, but cramped storeroom above deck that rocked with the slightest movement of the ocean. If it hadn't been for the cleric's cure, both Passepout and Volo would have had an extremely unpleasant journey ahead of them. As it was, the two travelers slung up their hammocks in a corner and took a nap while the ship got underway.

Several hours later, Volo was awakened by the cries of someone being beaten on deck. Leaving Passepout snoring loudly, he ventured forth from the safety of their cabin to the front of the ship, where a half-elf was being flogged by a scar-faced dwarf with a whip.

Volo asked a well-dressed man who was standing by watching it with gritted teeth, "What's going on here? The captain said that the slaves would never be let out of the hold."

"The half-elf is not a slave," the man replied. "He's a member of the crew. Am I addressing Mister Volo or Mister Passepout?"

"I am Volo," the master traveler replied.

"I am Nordhoff, the first officer," the man replied. "My name comes from the orphanage in which I was raised."

"Nordhoff Hall in Westgate?"

"Exactly."

"Why is he being flogged?" Volo asked carefully, not wishing to seem presumptuous.

"Because the captain ordered it," Nordhoff replied. "He claims it instills discipline in the crew if one sets an example early in the voyage."

Even more carefully, Volo further pressed the first officer with a question. "Do you believe that?"

"Bloody no!" he replied with perhaps more vehemence visible than he had intended. "I also don't believe a ship's cargo should be kept secret from the first officer until after the ship has set sail."

"I take it you don't support the slave trade?" Volo pressed.

"Bloody no!" he answered, as if cursing under his breath. "But I follow orders as a first mate is expected to."

Volo returned to his cabin to arouse the still-slumbering Passepout, so that they might prepare for their dinner at the captain's table.

Queeg had already started his meal when Volo and Passepout joined him in his cabin.

"I hope you don't mind my starting without you gentlemen," said the captain. "You can never be too sure if land-lovers will be able to appreciate a good meal their first night at sea."

"It's quite all right, Captain," Volo replied.

"*Mmmpqgh*," Passepout agreed, his cheeks already bulging with fish chowder.

"I see that the sea has had a positive effect on his appetite, eh, *Mister* Volo?"

"No, Captain," Volo replied with just a touch too much formality, "he always eats like that."

"*Mmmpqgh*," the thespian agreed, nodding as he chewed.

Before the conversation could move on to the next level of courtesy, the cabin door opened and Nordhoff entered and took his proper place across from the captain.

"*Mister* Nordhoff, did you see that that crewman was flogged like I told you?" Queeg asked, not looking up from his bowl.

"Yes, Captain," the first mate replied.

"Good. I will always tell you what I expect of you, no more, no less."

"Begging the captain's pardon," Volo asked, "what was his offense? The half-elf, I mean."

"Nothing you should concern yourself with, *Mister* Volo," the captain answered patiently. "You can safely leave the running of this ship to *Mister* Nordhoff and myself." With that, he pushed back his dinner bowl and rang the bell for the cabin boy, saying, "Enough of this. It is time for dessert."

The cabin boy entered, looking as white as a ghost.

"Marlon," the captain bellowed, "where are my strawberries?"

"Sir," the boy whimpered, "they forgot to pack them."

The enraged captain leaped to his feet with enough force that Passepout could have sworn he felt the entire ship rock underneath him. "They forgot to pack them! They forgot to pack them! What are they, imbeciles?" the captain raged.

"No, Captain," Nordhoff answered, still sitting at his place, "they are men who made a mistake. Perhaps other concerns of getting the ship ready to sail took precedence. Or perhaps they were concerned with whom you would pick to flog, once we got underway, or maybe they just didn't think bringing your strawberries on board for your dessert was that important."

The captain's tone changed to one of controlled rage.

"*Mister* Nordhoff, your tone is mutinous," he said. "Earlier today you questioned my decency as a man for aiding and abetting the slave trade. Then you hesitated in following a direct order."

"The half-elf was innocent of any offense. He did not deserve to be whipped!"

The captain continued, not responding to the comments of his first mate.

"Now, you dare question my judgment in front of this ship's passengers. I shall not stand for this!" he bellowed. "Consider yourself relieved of duty and confined to quarters!"

Nordhoff stood up and turned as if to leave for his quarters, but turned back for a moment when he opened the cabin door and said, ". . . And you, Captain Queeg, can consider this a mutiny."

In through the opened door rushed three sailors, one of whom was the scourged half-elf. All carried cutlasses.

"Excuse me, gentlemen," said Nordhoff to the shocked travelers, "would you mind returning to your quarters temporarily? The captain and I have some business to attend to, and I assure you no harm will come your way."

Volo left his place at the table to head back to the storeroom, but Passepout hesitated a moment, raised his bowl, and asked, "May I?"

Nordhoff chuckled, and replied, "Sure."

The rotund thespian refilled his bowl and carefully followed the master traveler back to their storeroom, failing to spill a drop of the delicious fish chowder.

About an hour later, Nordhoff joined Volo and Passepout in their cabin.

"A thousand pardons, gentlemen," he offered. "You should not have been forced to witness what occurred. In reality I am a Harper agent who has been sent to disrupt the slave trade in these waters. As we speak, the captives below deck are being released from their chains. I had to wait until we were far enough from port to take control of the ship."

"What about the captain?" Volo inquired. Though Queeg was obviously a hateful fellow, Volo had no desire to see him killed.

"He has been set adrift in a lifeboat, a man against the sea," Nordhoff replied. "But don't worry. He's a sound seaman. He'll make it back to port. Besides, we also gave him a treat—a bounty, you might say."

"What?" Volo asked.

"His strawberries. We were lying when Marlon said they were left behind," Nordhoff answered.

"Are there any left?" Passepout queried. "The chowder was fine, but I could still really do with some dessert."

Nordhoff laughed.

"Well, it's back to the galley, I guess," he replied.

The demeanor of the crew for the following days was remarkably joyous. The former slaves joined in on the daily chores, and eventually a few joined the crew, while others were put ashore at safe locations along the coast. Even Volo and Passepout joined in on some of daily nautical labors, and in fact, both of them soon became quite expert seamen. Passepout also became an excellent fisherman, which was fortunate, since ship's stores had not taken into account his appetite when laying in provisions for the journey southward.

They were a few days out, off Telpir, when a pirate ship loomed into view.

" 'Tis flying the colors of Cyric," cried the half-elf, whose name was Starbuck, from the crow's nest. "She's a pirate vessel, and she's heading our way!"

"Dragon's teeth," Nordhoff swore, then turning to Volo and Passepout, he ordered, "You two better go back to your cabin and bolt the door."

Passepout was halfway across the deck when he heard Volo reply.

"If the ship is sunk, we're no better there than here," he answered. "We would be honored to fight at your side."

"Yeah, sure," said Passepout in his characteristic unenthusiastic manner, wondering which would be worse, drowning or being slain by pirates.

The pirate ship was commanded by the villainous Captain Ahib Fletcher, a lifelong member of the feared Brotherhood of the Red Tide, whose patron deity was Cyric. He ruled his crew with iron hook and whip, which had been magically forged to the ends of his arms to replaced his hands, lost due to earlier battle wounds. He was also missing a leg but managed to maneuver faster than any other seaman with the aid of an ivory and iron table leg that had also been forged into place on the leg's stump by one of the Brotherhood's clerics. Though rumored to be insane, he nonetheless kept control of his pirate crew. This despite many night's rages as he recalled the albino banshee who had stolen his son, and cursed "the infernal white wail" to the fear and wonderment of all present.

Nordhoff drew the crew close together. They would be helplessly outnumbered by the one-legged fiend and his cadre of sea marauders, but the mate had a plan.

"According to the rules of the Brotherhood of the Red Tide, the captaincy of a vessel is determined by trial by combat, and anyone can challenge the captain to a battle to the death for command of the ship. When we get within hailing distance, I will express our intentions. Then a plank will be thrown between the two vessels, and I will fight him for control of both of our vessels."

"What if you lose?" Passepout asked.

"Then it will be someone else's turn to defend the ship, and I wish them luck in advance."

The challenge was issued and accepted, and the two ships drew alongside of each other.

The horrible figure of the bloodthirsty pirate captain took his place on the opposite deck.

"Whosoever challenges me, come forward now and face me!" he crowed.

At that precise moment, the pirate ship *Raiding Queen* lurched, and Passepout was thrown forward, landing at the opposite end of the plank from Ahib.

"I see the challenger is almost as big as myself," Ahib crowed, "but he looks soft."

"I'm not the . . . " Passepout sputtered.

"Silence!" the pirate ordered. "Your challenge

has been accepted. Prepare to meet Cyric."

Volo and Nordhoff were powerless to intervene. They knew that Ahib would not listen to reason and that if they joined in, the ship's entire crew would be slaughtered by Ahib's men.

"But I'm not . . . ," the thespian continued in panic, "you want . . . "

"I said silence!" the bloodthirsty buccaneer crowed and, with a flick of his metal-studded whip, began his attack.

The lash flicked around Passepout in an effort to embrace him so that he could be pulled closer to the pirate on the plank. Luckily for the rotund thespian, it failed to gain a wrapping grip due to the length of the journey it had to make around his midsection. Ahib pull on the whip's butt, only succeeding in giving Passepout a nasty lash burn around his waist rather than dragging him onto the plank. Ahib, however, was thrown off balance by the absence of the expected pull of dragging his opponent's bulk closer to him; he was forced to fall back four steps before he could regain his balance.

"Jump onto the plank!" Nordhoff ordered. "Now!"

Without thinking, Passepout followed the order yelled by the first mate.

Ahib, who was about to lunge toward his prey, was once again thrown off balance, this time by the vibrating shock waves that passed along the plank from the resultant force of the landing of Passepout's bulk at one end. Once again, the pirate was delayed in his attack, and momentarily dazed.

Passepout was petrified with fear.

"How long does this have to go on?" Volo asked, his eyes riveted on the source of Passepout's terror.

"Until one of them can fight no longer," Nordhoff

replied, trying to strategize a new move for the panicked thespian.

"But Passepout isn't fighting now!" Volo implored.

"No, but he's still alive, and that at least is something to work with," the Harper replied, then shouted, "Passepout, jump!"

Again the thespian jumped, sending the waves of confusion along the plank that separated him from his doom. And the pirate was thrown off balance.

"Now run out into the center of the plank!" the Harper ordered.

Passepout stood stone-still, and Ahib had almost regained his bearings.

"Do it!" Volo cried. "He won't have enough room to swing the whip then."

"Oh," Passepout replied, rushing out to the center of the plank between the two ships. *Now he can't use the whip on me*, he thought with glee. Then he realized that Ahib still could use his hook to tear him limb from limb, and was immediately torn between retreat and allowing panic to paralyze him in place.

Panic won out.

"And now, me pretty seagoing butterball," said Ahib with glee as he approached his helpless victim, "I will finish you off with me hook."

Passepout could smell Ahib's fetid body odor, the result of many months at sea without a bath, and his eyes began to tear.

"Ah, the baby is blubbering," said the sadistic follower of Cyric, slowing down to play with his prey before slaughtering him. "Now you just stand there while I use my nice hooky-wooky to slit your throaty-woaty, and spill your guttsy-wuttsys."

The two men on the plank were now closer than an arm's reach, and within striking distance.

"Do something!" Volo implored of his panic-stricken companion, but Passepout could not hear him clearly with the crashing of the surf against the ships, and the crows and howls of the two crews.

Passepout knew he heard something, but didn't know what, so he assumed it was another order . . . so once again he jumped.

*Crack!*

The plank between the two ships could not take the combined weights of the two duelists, and the sudden extra force of gravity pushing down on it when Passepout landed. It obeyed the laws of gravity and responded.

The plank cracked, split, and broke, and the thespian and the pirate fell into the briny blue water between the two ships.

A millisecond of silence, followed by a *splash*, and a spout of displaced water came crashing down on the crews of the two ships.

Volo struggled to make out the two duelists fighting in the water.

Passepout was trying to tread water, and Ahib was slashing down with his hook, *splash*, then nothing.

Both men went under, with nary an air bubble.

Volo despaired at the loss of his friend.

Passepout bobbed to the surface, sputtering, and spit out seawater.

Volo cheered, "Passepout! You're alive!"

"But not for long! Help! I can't swim!" replied the chubby thespian, saved from drowning by his extreme natural buoyancy.

"Calm down!" ordered Nordhoff. "We'll throw

you a line!"

"Hurry!" Passepout screamed, taking in a full mouthful of seawater, which he spit out to add, ". . . and a pair of pants, too!"

The weight of the pirate's iron accoutrements had pulled him down into his watery grave from whence there was no return. His final lunge at the struggling Passepout had just missed its mark; it didn't hook the panicking thespian in the flesh but nonetheless snagged him at the belt line and that was enough to pull the pirate under. Even a belt that had managed to maintain order on the thespian's massive gut could not take the extra strain of the added weight of the equally corpulent pirate and eventually gave way, allowing the hook to lay claim and drag Passepout's pants along to the pirate's watery death, while allowing the thespian himself to bob safely up to the surface.

The Brotherhood of the Red Tide, formerly under the command of Ahib Fletcher, had no desire to serve under the captaincy of the rotund and soggy thespian who had apparently bested their captain, and a deal was cut where the two ships would agree to part and never mention the incident that had transpired.

As the pirate ship disappeared toward the horizon, Passepout, swathed in towels and blankets, had returned to his former self.

"Did you see that? Did you see that? No pirate is a match for the son of Idle and Catinflas," he crowed to his former master.

"None, indeed," Volo replied jovially, helping the thespian towel off. "Something should be left to mark the location of this august event."

Passepout nodded.

"I agree, Mister Volo," he replied, "and are you thinking what I'm thinking?"

"But of course," the master traveler answered.

Passepout nodded again, and opened the bag of now-wet gems, which he had managed to grab off his belt just before it gave way.

"Wet, but safe and sound," the thespian observed. Upon opening the bag, he noticed that indeed one of the gems had changed from green to red. He tossed it overboard in the general vicinity of the area in which the duel to the death had taken place.

The story of Passepout's brave and victorious battle with a fierce pirate captain spread from ship to ship along the coast, fueled by the lack of actual details of who was involved and how it occurred as in accordance with their agreement with the Brotherhood of the Red Tide. All along the Vilhon Reach stories true (Passepout won a hand-to-hand battle to the death, more or less) and false (a secret agent of King Azoun himself, using the disguise of an out-of-shape thespian, had infiltrated the dreaded Brotherhood of the Red Tide and crushed it from within) were being bantered about, giving the chubby thespian quite a reputation as a hero.

While traveling off the coast of Chondath, just a day out from their destination of Arrabar, Volo and Passepout were watching the shoreline as they passed by.

"Starbuck says that he heard that the people of Arrabar plan on offering you the command of their navy," Volo offered. "It's in a rebuilding phase after their recent war with the evil mage Yrkhetep."

"Sounds like a nice cushy job," Passepout answered. "Perfect for a soon-to-be-retired hero such as myself. Any idea how much the job pays? Just out of curiosity, I mean, after we've finished our trip, of course."

"Of course," Volo concurred, "but somehow I didn't think you would be interested in it at any price. All of the peoples of Chondath, particularly those in their port city of Arrabar, are highly lawful, and intolerant of pirates. I think that they see you as their savior, a warrior of the high seas willing to dedicate his life to wiping away the bloody scourge of piracy from their coastal ways."

Passepout chuckled.

"I think I'll pass," the thespian replied. "I don't think this legendary hero business is all it's cracked up to be. Besides, Idle and Catinflas would never forgive their only son if he forsook the stage for a life of bravery, heroism, and that sort of thing."

"Ah," replied Volo, "Arrabar's loss is the art's gain."

"Indeed!" the corpulent thespian responded, puffing up his chest almost enough to match his stomach. "It isn't easy being a man of many talents."

"Indeed!" Volo replied.

The *Amistad's Bounty* pulled into harbor at Arrabar without any fanfare whatsoever: no parades, no banners, no job offers for Passepout from the Lord of Arrabar who ruled the allied city-states of Chondath, nothing out of the ordinary at all. Apparently the rumors of the thespian's heroism were only outdone in their outrageousness by the rumors of the public's response to them.

"Well," said the slightly discouraged Passepout, who was putting his pack in order after the long ocean voyage, "I said I was going to turn it down anyway . . . but it would have been nice to be asked."

"Look at it this way, my friend," Volo offered. "I remember the story of a hero whose reputation had spread so far and wide that he was never able to go anywhere without being recognized. As a result he was never able to get any rest, as he was always besieged by petitioners wanting his help. Likewise, he was never able to rest, because there were an equal number of fellows who wanted him dead just so that they could claim his murder as another highlight of their infamous reputation. Rumor has it that eventually he had to sleep sitting up with his back to the wall of the farthest corner in any inn's accommodation so that he always would be prepared for whatever the fates threw at him."

"Whatever happened to him?" the thespian inquired.

"He joined up with six other heroes to save a small town that was being besieged by bandits."

"So what happened?"

"The bandits were routed, but he was killed. They buried him in the town cemetery. A last he had a place to rest. The local children still put flowers on his grave."

Passepout shivered.

"I guess being a hero isn't all it's cracked up to be," the thespian observed. "The theater is *my* true calling."

". . . and the other heroes of the world rejoice at hearing your decision," piped in Harper Nordhoff, who had just joined the two in their cabin. "I just came by to wish you both luck on your journey. Remember, Passepout: It takes all kinds to make a world, and a hero is as a hero does."

"Amen," said Volo.

The two travelers shook hands with Nordhoff, left the cabin, which would now return to being an above-deck storeroom, and disembarked from the ship to the harbor of Arrabar.

# THE GOLDEN ROAD
# AND BEYOND

## OR

### Farther South to the Shining South

Centuries ago, Chondath had been one of the leading trade empires of all Faerûn, and Arrabar had been the golden apple of its eye. Opulence led to decadence, and decadence to decline. Soon war was followed by war. First, foreign predators lay siege in hopes of sharing in the bastion of wealth. This was followed by petty disputes from within, culminating in numerous civil wars. War was accompanied by famine, plague, pestilence, and the sisters of ruin, leaving the once golden apple a mere husk of its former self.

Arrabar was now in a period of rebuilding, and its streets were a bit more sleepy and subdued than Passepout would have expected of the capital of the allied city-states of Chondath. New construction was underway, and traders and merchants flocked the harborside to claim their recently delivered goods, and engage in commerce. (The *Amistad's Bounty* had undergone a discreet name change before heading into port so as not to incur the wrath of the intended recipients of its former— living—cargo, and was now called the *Balding Quaestor*.)

"Where to now, Mister Volo?" Passepout asked.

"Farther south," Volo replied. "I just haven't figured out how yet."

The two travelers took a room for the night at an inn just beyond the city wall. During years prior, the building had been a plague house for those denied entrance to the city during its self-imposed quarantine. None of the city dwellers ever stayed there, and few travelers stayed for the second night of the inn's two-night minimum upon finding out about the building's heritage. As a result, the proprietor always had rooms to spare, and figured that he was making twice the profit for half the bother on each guest. He sometimes liked to joke that the only second-day boarders in the history of the inn were those waiting to be carried off by the plague cart.

As luck would have it, the inn was also boarding a group of mercenary adventurers who were headed south to Ormpetarr in hopes of finding work. Volo and Passepout entertained the band with tales of travelogue, adventure, and tourism from Volo's vast catalogue of experiences, and numerous monologues and jokes and mercifully few songs from Passepout's ever-growing repertoire.

As the entertainment lasted late into the night, a deal was struck whereby the gazetteer and the thespian would be allowed to travel with the mercenary band as long as they paid their own way and treated the band with a bit of entertainment each night. The travelers agreed, and the following morning Volo and Passepout joined the long roll of one-night-stand guests of the inn.

The mercenaries were a fun bunch, led by a former captain in Azoun's Purple Dragons who deserted after finding the peace that followed the successful routing of the Horde invasion too boring. The others in the group included a dark-skinned half-giant with a bad attitude, a good-looking elven marksman who was also a bit of a con artist, and a wayward cleric halfling who fell prey to bouts of chaotic madness. All four were on the run from someone (Azoun, the Lords of Waterdeep, the Zhentarim, whatever) and fiercely loyal to each other, or whomever they accepted employment from.

All along the way Volo treated the heavily armed band of protectors to descriptions of the wonders of Faerûn, stories of various encounters, and legends and lore of days gone by. He had just finished relating the tale of Shandaular, the legendary city outside time, when the group noticed that they had reached their destination of Ormpetarr, where his and Passepout's path would diverge from theirs.

Hannibal, the former captain in the Purple Dragons, shook hands with the two travelers who had provided them with so much entertainment.

"I love it when a plan comes together," he said, "and never have I felt so well compensated for merely sharing the road with other travelers."

"And never have I felt so well protected," replied Volo.

"Nor I," added Passepout.

"I'm expecting mention in one of your upcoming guides," Hannibal quipped.

"Guaranteed," replied the grateful gazetteer.

"And you, Passepout, what can I say? Don't give up your day job," the mercenary jibed, then added, "Just kidding."

The mercenaries and the travelers waved farewell and parted company. Volo and Passepout entered the city of Ormpetarr, leaving the familiarity of the Vilhon Reach, for the Shaar, the northern boundary of the Shining South.

From Ormpetarr, the two travelers joined an ever-changing caravan that was headed south along the Golden Road. Initially, it had been composed primarily of merchants from Nimpeth and farther north but now seemed to be composed primarily of nomadic herders and their families, going south in search of greener pastures. Volo and Passepout had made a few acquisitions before joining, including a change of clothing into more suitable 'native' gear, and a few beasts of burden to support the provisions that they would require for the journey farther south.

Passepout was amazed that Volo never seemed to run out of gold, no matter how many purchases he made. No matter where they were he always had the appearance of a man of means, and initially the thespian thought that perhaps he was exercising some magical power that had been left untouched by the dampening spell. After the pre-caravan shopping trip, Passepout finally asked him about his curious abilities at procurement.

"There really isn't anything to explain," Volo replied. "My travelers' guides have been popular all over, and most merchants are more than willing to allow me the use of a certain ration of their supplies in exchange for some goodwill, advertising, and an occasional mention in print."

Passepout accepted this as an answer that pertained to the merchants, and acknowledged that the master traveler was also a master of persuasion and self-promotion, but wondered what he would do if such perks failed.

Passepout then recalled the two-dragoned coin back in Cormyr and chuckled to himself, thinking, *I guess no matter what the situation, Volo will think of something.*

Five days later, Passepout's assessment of Volo's non-magical abilities was once again put to the test.

The latest group to join the caravan southward was a quartet of wizards returning to Halruaa after a long trip abroad. Though magically powerful, the four magic-wielders were also rather old and infirm, with wits slightly feeble. They soon became the laughingstocks of the caravan until Volo and Passepout intervened, declaring themselves the quartet's bodyguards in order to discourage future attacks, either verbal or physical, on the wizards whose only wrongdoing was to grow old.

The caravan had made camp for the night in a mountain canyon. The sun was setting, and dinner was being prepared at a half-dozen campfires when the roar of thundering hooves split the peace and quiet of the approach of twilight.

Out of a cloud of dust in the distance roared a gang of bandits who had been lying in wait for a caravan to settle for the night, boxed in by the canyon wall.

The leader of the band was a tall halfling, balding and badly in need of shave, with a wide-brim hat that had been blown off his head and now rested against his back, held in place by a string at his neck. He quickly dismounted from his horse and began to strut around their camp.

"I am Eli of the Wallachs," he announced, "and you have entered my territory. But that is all right, for I am a reasonable man and not the vicious bandit that rumor has promulgated. I know you have no wish to cause trouble, and you will therefore be more than willing to pay tribute to me for permission to pass through my land."

With that the other bandits dismounted and began to raid the caravan of its valuables.

"We have no desire to kill anyone," Eli continued, "and we greatly appreciate your cooperation."

Passepout thanked Eo that the gems were safely obscured from view by the bag that Storm had provided, and since both he and Volo had been traveling light, didn't really anticipate any great losses since the bandits seemed interested only in objects of value rather than supplies of provisions.

The caravan members all complied with the bandits' wishes, until one of the old wizards refused to give up an amulet that he wore around his neck.

"No!" he screamed. "I will never give it up!"

This wanton act of defiance infuriated Eli, who prepared to backhand the wizened old magic-user. Volo intervened.

"Eli of the Wallachs," Volo begged, "please forgive this old man. He is an enfeebled mage, as are all of his fellow travelers, and they are all poor, but honest, men of learning."

Eli laughed a fiendish laugh.

"Mages!" he crowed. "We don't need no stinkin' mages, particularly old and senile ones." The bandit leader drew out a dagger and prepared to throw it at the enfeebled old man who wouldn't give up his amulet.

Volo dove to try to intercept Eli's hand before he could throw the dagger, only to fall against an invisible wall that separated him from the bandit. Momentarily stunned by his collision with the invisible obstacle, the master traveler shook his head to try to clear the haziness from the concussion, and looked up in time to see the bandit Eli, dagger still in hand, burst into flame. In less than ten seconds, Eli had been reduced to a pile of soot and ash.

The other bandits panicked, dropped their loot, and took off for the hills, leaving their steeds and the ill-gotten gain from previous extortions back at the caravan's camp.

Slowly Volo got to his feet and turned around to face the wielder of the fireball that had taken out the fiendish bandit. There stood the other three wizards with their arms folded, stern expressions on their faces as they watched the rest of the outlaw gang heading for the hills. In the meantime Passepout had helped the mage with the amulet to his feet, and was now leading him back to the rest of his group.

The youngest of the four elderly wizards approached Volo.

"I would like to thank you for your kindness and heroism, but as you see, it really was quite unnecessary. It would have been rude for us to turn down your offer to be our bodyguards, but under no circumstances could we allow you to unnecessarily risk your life on our behalf. As you can see, we can more than take care of the whole caravan, let alone ourselves."

Passepout had now reached Volo's side and queried the youngest of the mages, "But why did you stand for the others' insults and allow yourselves to be thought of as feeble old men?"

"It is true that we are not as young as we used to be, but no one is," he answered. "Insults are cheap, and when you get to our age, one sometimes gets selectively hard of hearing so as to make it easier to ignore the callous remark that is occasionally thrown our way. Daggers, however, are another matter entirely, and require a much different course of action, as you have just observed."

The youngest wizard offered his hand in thanks to Volo and Passepout for their unnecessary but appreciated assistance, and gave each of them a medallion that had been forged in ancient Netheril.

"Please accept this as a token of our gratitude," the oldest wizard, who had refused to give up his amulet, said. "Tomorrow we will leave the caravan to travel on our own. It is not meant as insult, but I'm afraid that the rest of you will slow us down. The medallion will protect you and the others until you reach your destination. If you are ever in Halarahh, please look us up at the Porter's Shop, at the corner of William and Henry. If not, just think of us kindly whenever you remember the gift mages."

The following morning, when Volo, Passepout, and the rest of the caravan arose from a sound night's slumber, the four old mages were nowhere to be seen.

Though Volo undoubtedly picked up numerous details and anecdotes to be used in some later *Volo's Guide to the Shining South*, the rest of their journey southward continued uneventfully, and the caravan was disbanded upon reaching Halarahh.

"So let me get this straight," said Passepout. "This is a city of wizards, right?"

"Well, not quite," answered Volo indulgently. "It's a city that was originally settled by wizards."

"Big difference," the thespian replied. "I guess I better count my fingers after shaking hands with any of the citizens."

Volo scratched his head, puzzled at his companion's blind prejudice.

"I really don't understand why you feel this way toward wizards," he said, vocalizing his confusion. "You know that I have magical abilities . . . well, uh, . . . at least I used to."

"But for every kindhearted Mister Volo," Passepout said, "there is a dastardly Lord Khelben just waiting to take advantage of his powers, and take advantage of you."

"What about the four mages on the way here," Volo countered. "What about them?"

Passepout just shook his head and refused to listen to reason.

"I think the old sage said it best," the thespian replied. " 'To trust is good, but not to trust is better,' and as far as I'm concerned, that goes double for mages!"

Volo chuckled.

"Despite your prejudice," the master traveler countered, "you have a lot in common with the people of Halruaa. Why, I remember reading somewhere that someone once referred to it as the most paranoid country in all of the Realms, and that you couldn't walk three feet without some sort of divination spell being cast over you. It's a nation rampant with courtesy and politeness based on fear, and a strict set of laws to insure order, with justice and punishment meted out faster than a lich can lurch."

"Which reminds me," the thespian interrupted. "Just exactly why are we here?"

Volo resumed his strut through the city streets, calling back to his companion, who was scrambling to catch up.

"If one shortcut fails, try another," the master traveler answered. "Surely we don't expect to walk all the way to Kara Tur, do we?"

The Porter's Shop was an inn located at the corner of William and Henry. The four mages who had been part of the caravan resided there between trips abroad for study.

"Welcome! Welcome!" said the eldest of the four, his much-prized amulet still hanging around his neck. "We are so glad that you could drop by. One never knows when one might need two burly bodyguards such as yourselves."

The other three mages laughed at the absurdity of the fourth's joke.

Passepout became offended, but, as per Volo's direction, kept his mouth shut.

"The pleasure is all ours," Volo replied, using his best reviewer-at-large persona. "Do you own this inn?"

"Of course, and for helping us in the Shaar, we are more than willing to offer you, without charge, accommodations for the duration of your stay. Let me call our porter to fetch your things to a room. Oh, Henry!" the youngest of the four called.

"That won't be necessary," Volo replied before he could repeat the appellation. "I'm afraid that we are in a bit of hurry, and I was hoping that you might be able to point us in the right direction of where we could possibly rent an airship."

"An airship," the eldest repeated, scratching his chin whiskers.

"An airship!" Passepout exclaimed, remembering in terror Volo's query of the cleric who cured his motion sickness, about its effectiveness on airsickness as well.

"An airship," Volo repeated. "You see, we have to cover a great deal of land in the least time possible."

"How much land?" inquired one of the previously silent wizards.

"All of Toril," Volo replied. "I agreed to a foolish bet out of pride and vanity, and must now live up to my part of the bargain."

"From what I understand," the youngest replied, "the airships are only supposed to travel within Halruaa airspace. They are the property of the archmages and require frequent recharging."

"I realize that," the master traveler pressed, "but I have also heard rumor of a supposed black market of mages who have, shall we say, fallen from grace, who might be willing to rent out one if it were made worth their while."

"I'm afraid that we can't be of any assistance in those sorts of matters. We of the city of Halarahh are an honest and orderly citizenry," said the youngest.

"The place you want to go is farther south," the eldest interrupted. "Khaerbaal. It's a wild town."

"Hush!" the youngest scolded. "We don't want to lead these young men astray."

"We realize that we would be taking a risk," Volo countered.

"We do?" Passepout interrupted.

"We do," Volo repeated, "but we also realize that we have very few options."

"Then try Khaerbaal, and go with Mystra."

"Go with Mystra," all four mages said in unison.

"We shall," Volo answered, and taking the still-stunned Passepout by the hand, led him out of the inn.

No sooner had they turned the street corner when they ran into the eldest of the mages, who had teleported there to intercept them in private.

"Don't ever tell my brothers that I told you this, but try the deserted shipyards down by the Bay of Taertal. Occasionally an archmage will junk an old airship there when he's acquired a new one. In many cases, it is still charged enough for a few more months of flying. Go with Mystra."

Upon completing his blessing, the old mage disappeared, leaving Volo and Passepout looking at each other on the street corner.

"Well . . . " Volo announced to his companion.

Passepout interrupted.

"I know," the thespian replied, "we're burning daylight. On to the Bay of Taertal."

"Yes!" Volo agreed enthusiastically, "On to the Bay of Taertal!"

"Eo save us," Passepout muttered, following the master traveler to the harbor, where they would book passage to their next destination.

It was a rocky ride southward along Lake Halruaa. The ship hugged the shore out of necessity as the wind and strong current continually threatened to throw it off course. The experienced crew was more than a match for the elements that continually confronted them, and the voyage went off as usual, without any mishap. What the crew did not lack in skill, they made up for in lack of hospitality. Volo and Passepout were booked in steerage, and locked below deck for the entire trip so they would not get in the way of the busy sailing experts. Food was passed down to the two travelers by means of a hatch in the deck, which also afforded them their only glimpse of sunlight for the entire voyage.

With three voyages under his belt, Passepout was unsure which he preferred the least: the one with seasickness, the one with pirates, or the one in steerage. He prayed that this would be his last seagoing venture and that the dreaded upcoming airship journey would be easier . . . but of course, he doubted that it would be.

As the two travelers finally enjoyed the luxury of standing upright, feeling direct sunlight on their faces and firm ground beneath their feet, Passepout decided to query the master traveler on his plans.

"So we are going to try to rent an airship?" the thespian remarked.

"It will make things much easier, and our journey much quicker," Volo replied. "Look at it this way: We've already determined that our sole restriction is that we can't *set foot* on the same place more than once. Therefore flying over it shouldn't be a problem. Our sea voyages have also shown that the gems will still mark the passage of distance, even when they are not on land."

"I think I've probably thrown more gems overboard than I've dropped on land so far," commented the thespian, who felt the bag of gems getting progressively heavier as time went on, despite the reduction in the number of gems.

"I'm sure you're mistaken, dear son of Idle and Catinflas," Volo corrected, taking a quasi-parental tone with the thespian/novice traveler.

"Whatever."

"Don't be discouraged. Once we rent an airship, we'll be flying east in no time. Just think of the sights we'll see. We could pass over Dambrath. True, men aren't exactly welcome there, but who says we have to land? We can always view the legendary Bay of Dancing Dolphins with its entertaining inhabitants from above . . . or perhaps you would prefer stopping by Luiren, the land of the halflings. We could pick up some of their remarkable cheese and stout. I've sampled both, and paid a pretty penny for the pleasure, too. I ordered them through *Aurora's Whole Realms Catalogue* and . . . "

"Stop," Passepout insisted. "You're making me hungry."

"Then we shall eat," Volo replied.

"Just so long as it's *not* fish!"

"I guess the lack of variety of the steerage menu has gotten to you, my friend," Volo replied. "So let's go find us some real *land-lover* food!"

Volo and the thespian discovered a tavern, not too far from the shipyard, that boasted good food, strong ale, and accommodating hostesses. The manager of the establishment recognized the master gazetteer by his reputation and needed no prodding to roll out the red carpet in the hope of securing a good review in the guide that the master traveler claimed to be working on.

Well-supped and entertained, the master traveler and his thespian companion planned to enjoy a few tankards of ale before turning in, and perhaps secure a few leads on an airship available for rental.

# KHAERBAAL AND ON
# INTO THE AIR

## OR

## Up, Up, and Away Off Course

"I understand that you are looking for a slightly used skyship for charter," a dwarf whispered to the two travelers, who were just about to turn in for the night.

"Maybe we are," Volo replied.

"Another round of ale," Passepout bade the serving wench.

"I think I have something that might interest

you," the dwarf continued, taking a place between the two travelers. "Mind if I join you?"

"Be our guest; care for a drink?" Passepout replied, fully cognizant that their tab was being comped in exchange for possible good review consideration.

"Don't mind if I do," the dwarf replied. With the dwarf sitting between them, the two travelers quickly noticed the aroma of dwarf body odor that comes when one chooses to ignore common sense and normal dwarf hygiene.

Passepout quaffed another tankard of ale, hoping it would dull his olfactory senses.

"Been working hard?" Volo inquired, seeking possible justification for the dwarf's body stench.

"Nope," replied the dwarf, downing a tankard and wiping the foam from his beard-and-moustache-framed mouth with his soiled shirtsleeve. "That is, unless you consider making deals to be hard work."

"What type of deals?" Volo pressed.

"Oh, just deals," the dwarf replied, helping himself to a refill on his tankard. "Now, your company and hospitality are wonderful, and I'm sure both of you are truly great fun to be around, but time is money. Are you interested in a skyship charter or not?"

"Well, maybe we are," Volo replied.

"It will cost you," the dwarf interjected.

"We will be willing to fairly compensate the skyship's owner for the charter."

"Good!" the dwarf replied. He quaffed the last of the ale and jumped to his feet, tossing a piece of parchment on the table. "Come to that address tomorrow at precisely midday . . . and come alone. If I see more than the two of you there, I will leave."

"We'll be there," Volo assured.

"Tomorrow, then." And with that, the dwarf left.

"I hope he bathes tonight," said Passepout.

"So do I," agreed the master traveler, "but somehow I doubt it."

The two travelers slept late the following morning, but left the inn with more than enough time to reach the appointed place of their rendezvous with the dwarfish airship broker.

" '*Meet me at the abandoned boathouse at the farthest end of the Hale shipyard, signed Jonas Grumby*' " read Volo from the parchment that had been left on the table. "I guess Jonas Grumby is our aromatic dwarven friend."

"Aromatic nothing. He just plain stank!" said the thespian. "I don't know if I'll be able to stand being cooped up with him for an around-the-world flight."

They arrived at the shipyard with time to spare. With the exception of a teenage barefooted beachcomber who was feeding the sea gulls, no one seemed to be around for miles. Likewise, no airship was in sight either, only the broken-down boathouse, which looked as if it were ready to cave in on itself.

"Hey! Over here!" Jonas yelled from the door of the boathouse. "Get inside! Quick!"

"All indications point to Captain Grumby here not necessarily being a businessman used to doing things on the up and up," Volo whispered to the thespian as they approached the boathouse. "We'll have to be careful. We can't afford to buy a pig in a poke."

"*No!*" Passepout replied in mock shock. "I thought he was as honest as Cadderly the cleric."

"Enough of your whispers," Grumby scolded. "An airship is what you want, an airship is what I have. See!"

Grumby pointed inside the door. The ramshackle boathouse was only a front, with walls propped up by poles in the sand. Inside, resting on the broad beams of its hull, was a two-masted airship with the name *Minnow* painted on the side.

Volo ventured farther into the pseudo-boathouse and walked around the ship with a critical eye.

"As I recall," Volo commented, "Halruaan airships have three masts of flexible wood to hold their windsails in place. This, uh, ship has only two masts, and no sails at all."

"That is true," Jonas replied, as if his answer sufficed.

"Now, I realize that the ship is powered by the spell rod, which seems to be in place, and not the sails, but, again if I remember correctly, weren't the sails used for steering?"

"Yes," replied the dwarf, whose odor from the night before had not improved.

"So," Volo persisted, "how do you steer it?"

"All of that can be explained later. Do you think she suits your needs?"

"Is she airworthy?"

"I guarantee it!" the dwarf assured.

"Mister Volo," Passepout interrupted, taking his former master aside, "I don't trust him."

"Neither do I," the master traveler replied, "but we don't seem to have much of a choice."

Just then a new voice joined the conversation within the boathouse.

"Excuse me, I was wondering if perhaps there were any openings for a mate's position. I have sailing experience."

The voice belonged to the young beachcomber who had been feeding the sea gulls at the shoreline. He was human, of indeterminate mid-teen age, with skin the color of an acquired tan. His clothes were ragged, his frame thin, probably from too many missed meals, and his feet were calloused and dirty from having gone without shoes for a fair amount of time. He was also quite handsome in a rugged sort of way and physically fit, with the bright blue eyes of a person who did not overindulge in ale or any other intoxicating or debilitating substance.

"Scram!" Jonas yelled. "This is a private matter."

"No, stay." Volo countered the obstreperous dwarf's order. There was something vaguely familiar about the lad, Volo thought, and another body to help on the ship might come in handy if Grumby tried anything. Even if the kid didn't have enough experience to fly the ship, he could probably take care of the tasks that the dwarf no doubt expected his passengers to tend to.

"Do you want the charter or not?" the dwarf persisted. "I don't care what you do with the overgrown urchin. He can come along or stay behind. My price is based on slag commission."

"Slag commission?" Volo queried.

Passepout again took the master traveler aside.

"He thinks we're smugglers," the thespian replied. "Slag commission means he can lay claim on one third of the revenues from the sales of whatever we are transporting."

Volo thought for a moment and went back to the dwarf. "That seems reasonable," the master traveler replied, "but what will we do for a contract?"

"No contract is necessary. I'm a shrewd judge of character, and I can tell you must be smuggling something real dear," Grumby replied, taking out a gunnysack that was inscribed with various glyphs. "Just grab hold of the sack, and agree that I am entitled to one third of the proceeds of whatever you are smuggling. Agreed?"

"And you in turn agree to fly us for an indeterminate period until our, uh, transaction is completed. Agreed?"

"Agreed," replied Grumby.

"Then I agree, also," replied Volo, taking hold of the gunnysack.

The dwarf and Volo were bathed in a black aura, which quickly dissipated.

"There," the dwarf replied, "we have a contract, enforceable by the god of thieves, Mask himself. If either of us backs out, he forfeits his life. Now, what will I be hauling?"

"Just us," Volo replied.

"No," Grumby answered, losing patience, "the loot, the slag. What are you smuggling?"

"We're not smuggling anything," Passepout answered.

"But we agreed to slag commission!" the dwarf persisted.

"Yes," Volo agreed, "and one third of our ill-gotten gain is now yours. Unfortunately, as we lack any *slag*, I'm afraid that your take for this charter is therefore nothing."

"No!" the dwarf screamed, horrified that he had been swindled.

"And by your own devices, you are now bound to fulfill our charter or risk the ire of Mask," added Volo.

"No, I mean it can't be . . . aaggh," the dwarf raged, and then all of a sudden regained his composure. "You win. You got me, Wands. Where are we going?"

"Wands?" Volo replied, shocked to hear the name of the imposter who was indirectly responsible for his current plight.

"Yeah," Grumby replied, "that's your real name, isn't it? I mean, I heard the fat guy call you Volo back at the inn. Volo, also known as Marco Volo, also known as Marcus Wands, scoundrel, scalawag, rogue, smuggler, and thief."

"I'm afraid that you're mistaken," the master traveler replied. "I am Volothamp Geddarm, the master traveler of all Faerûn and gazetteer author of the best-selling Volo's Guide series."

"Never heard of you," the churlish dwarf replied.

"I am the original Volo, the one whom Wands was impersonating."

"You don't say," replied Grumby, scratching the ill-kept thatch that was his beard.

*Well, that explains a lot of things,* Volo thought to himself. *Maybe Wands has enhanced my reputation in ways that are beneficial in the right circumstances, and circles.*

"So, Giddyup . . . "

"That's Geddarm, . . . but just call me Volo."

"All right, Mister Just-Call-Me-Volo," the dwarf replied with a malicious gleam in his eye, "so where are we bound?"

"First to Kara-Tur, and from there farther east," Volo replied.

"Well, a bargain is a bargain for as long as it's a bond," the dwarf replied, resigned to the arrangement. "Just give me few minutes to get things ready, and we'll be off."

"We're leaving today?" Passepout asked, shocked that things were moving so fast.

"No time like the present," Grumby replied, continuing to fiddle with his preparations.

"Kara-Tur, here we come," Volo stated with a sense of confident victory over the way things worked out.

"But now?" Passepout persisted, having hoped for at least another night spent in the comforts of an inn.

"As Captain Grumby said," Volo replied, "no time like the present."

Volo then turned his attentions to the eager-to-work teenage urchin, who had been waiting silently and patiently within hailing distance.

"Come here, boy," Volo hailed as he imagined a sea captain might address a cabin boy.

"The name is Curtis, sir," said the lad, obviously taking offense at the boy moniker without wishing to seem insubordinate to his desired superior.

"You say you have sailing experience?" the master traveler inquired.

"Yes, sir," Curtis replied. "I interned with the Cormyrean Freesails for a while after leaving school. You see, I'm really the son of a Cormyrean nobleman. I've set out on my own to see the world before returning to university and then accepting my proper place in the family business. I know my way around a ship and would relish the opportunity of joining you on your journey."

Volo sized up the youth. He was in good shape and told a good story. The master traveler could not help but remember a certain other young traveler, who may have lied about his roots years ago, before gaining the prestige and acclaim of a master traveler and gazetteer.

Passepout joined the interviewer and interviewee, and popped in with a question.

"You say you have sailing experience," inquired the thespian, throwing the lad a piece of rope.

"Well, here then, tie me a sheepshank knot."

In ten seconds flat, Curtis tossed the knotted rope back to the chubby thespian.

Passepout just stared at the knot in his hands.

"Is there something wrong?" Curtis asked.

"No, my bo—, I mean, Curtis," Volo answered. "The knot you made is fine, not that Passepout would know a sheepshank from a box twist."

Passepout pouted. "I never said I was an expert," the chubby thespian muttered. "I just asked him to tie me one. I wanted to see what it looked like, that's all."

"Sure," said the master traveler, and then, turning back to the lad, added, "Welcome aboard."

The master gazetteer and the teenage urchin shook hands, sealing the lad's appointment.

Volo returned his attentions to Grumby. Behind him, he heard Passepout ask Curtis to tie the knot again, but this time slower.

"So, Grumby," Volo pressed, "now that we're working together, what is the story of this ship? You really don't look the part of an archmage, if you know what I mean. No offense, of course."

"None taken," the dwarf replied, still bustling with what appeared to be a large canvas bag. "But for that matter, now that I get a good look, you don't look like much of a smuggler, either. No offense."

"None taken," the gazetteer replied.

"Good," Grumby replied, taking a break from his prep work to smoke a bowl full of his pipe and tell the tale of the ship. "You see, she wasn't always my ship. She wasn't even originally called the *Minnow*. Originally she was christened the *D. Niven*, and she was the property of an archmage named Ffogg. Like yourself, he once planned on making a sky journey all around the world. Claimed he could do it in less than eighty days, too. You see he designed this ship himself, utilizing what he called a bag sail, that canvas thing over there, claiming that it would increase the speed and staying power of the ship's enchantment."

"So what happened to him?" Volo inquired.

"Just before he was going to take off, he was arrested for embezzlement. The world tour was just a scam to mask his getaway. As you may have heard, justice around here is rather swift when certain people set their minds to it, and there is nothing like the memory of someone's hand in your purse to set your mind to it."

"I can well imagine."

"So," the dwarf concluded, "he was swiftly and fairly dealt with."

"Come again?" Volo queried.

"Let's just say that he wasn't in any condition to lay claim to the ship that was waiting for him in the harbor at Halarahh, a ship that someone had—how shall I say?—accidentally set adrift."

"That's where you came in," Volo noted.

"Exactly," the dwarf replied. "The law of the sea clearly states that an abandoned vessel is fair game for salvage. I just extrapolated that law to airships as well and moved her down here to Khaerbaal for a new paint job and a rechristening."

With that, the dwarf finished his pipe and climbed aboard the *Minnow*, did a few last minutes of fiddling with the bag sail, and announced, "Okay, we're ready to go. Bag's in place, pantry filled. Climb aboard."

The two travelers and their recently acquired "mate" Curtis climbed aboard in wonderment.

"But," Passepout interjected, "shouldn't we be

outside? I mean, we can't go very far inside this boathouse."

"Observe," the churlish dwarf replied, with a knowing twinkle in his eye.

Grumby manned the main wheel and pulled a lever that was attached to the two main masts. That set off a chain reaction that threw open the main hatch, centered on the deck between the two masts, and started to inflate the bag sail, which expanded and lifted the *Minnow* slowly off the ground. The roof of the boathouse collapsed backward, folding over the sides of the external walls by means of huge hidden hinges, and the airship rose up into the air, unfettered any longer by the boathouse's confines.

Grumby chuckled at the openmouthed amazement of his passengers. "Kinda neat, huh? I rigged the boathouse myself. Feel free to explore the ship. I'll be busy until we get out of Khaerbaal airspace, but by then we'll be smooth sailing. Don't mind the scorch marks on her bow. She had a slight altercation with a red dragon on the way down here. Didn't do much damage. Only lost two crewman. Oh, well, easy come, easy go."

And with that the dwarf began to sing an old sea chantey about seven castaways, from which Volo, Passepout, and Curtis quickly sought relief in the confines of their cabin.

On the main deck of the airship, in addition to the two masts and the centralized hatch, were two cabins, one at the fore and one at the aft. The aromatic delights of Grumby dictated that he have the fore cabin, closest to the ship's wheel, for himself, while Volo, Passepout, and Curtis shared the aft one.

The legendary walls of Halruaa, which succeeded in boxing in the nation with mountains, dictated that their course bear due south first, out over the Bay of Taertal, before turning eastward toward Dambrath and beyond. Grumby was reluctant to give up the helm to anyone else but appeared confident in his own navigational skills, and this confidence soon infected the rest of the ship's crew, who gradually settled into a routine. Curtis, indeed, did know his way around a ship and was a great help in keeping the riggings straight and the bag sail unfouled. True to the cleric's word, Passepout avoided any bouts with airsickness, but he was plagued with vertigo any time he thought to look overboard. He also vigorously complained of the cold, a condition exacerbated by the wind whipping around the deck. Volo, for his part, contented himself with taking in the scenery below and reminding the chubby thespian to cast over the necromancer's gems at the appropriate locations.

"This is boring," said the disgruntled thespian, having lost count of the amount of gems that he had dropped since they had left Suzail.

"That's only because you have been unwilling to enjoy the sights. There are numerous citizens of Faerûn who would give their right arm for the aerial view that we have been enjoying these past few days . . . at least those of us who are willing to enjoy the view."

Passepout blushed. "I can't help it if I'm scared of heights," he answered. "Maybe I'll try again when we come to that place with the flying fish."

"You mean the Bay of Dancing Dolphins," Volo corrected, then paused. "Now that you mention it, we should have passed it by now."

"We're going the wrong way for that," Curtis answered, joining the two travelers at the rail.

"Oh, really?" Passepout skeptically retorted.

"Sure," the lad replied. "We're heading northwest."

Volo panicked. "Where is the sun?" he demanded.

"There." Passepout pointed.

"No!" responded Volo in a fit of anger. "Grumby! Get down here!"

The dwarf swung down from his place at the helm to join the group at the rail. "What do you want?" he growled.

"We're off course!" Volo screamed.

"Says who?"

"The kid," Passepout replied.

"He's mistaken," the dwarf countered.

"No, he's not!" Volo contradicted. "We're heading west."

"No, we're not," the dwarf maintained. "If we were heading west, we'd be over Chult by now."

"What's Chult?" Passepout inquired.

"It's a land of jungles on the western edge of the Shining South, believed to be inhabited by giant thunder lizards," replied Curtis, further fueling Passepout's conception of him as a know-it-all brat.

Volo looked overboard for a moment and then refocused his attention on the aromatic dwarf. "Chult is bordered on the west and the south by low, mountainous hills and lakes, and on the southeast, the direction from which we would be coming if I am correct, by savannahs," the master traveler stated.

"Savannahs?" the dwarf queried. "What are savannahs?"

"Grasslands," Volo replied. He gestured over the side, "like those."

"Oh," replied the dwarf, once again scratching his rat's nest of a beard. "I guess this isn't a good time to bring up a few things."

"Like what?" Volo demanded, barely holding his anger in check.

"Like we're heading toward that volcano over there, and, uh . . . "

"Spit it out!" the master traveler screamed.

". . . and, uh, we seem to be losing altitude."

"You mean . . . " Passepout pressed.

"Yup," the dwarf replied. "We're going down."

# CHULT

## OR

## Passepout Becomes a Master of Hot Air

The *Minnow* continued its gradual trip downward toward the slope of the volcano they were approaching. Though the ship was falling at a reasonably safe speed, all crew members had immediately switched to emergency stations. Curtis took control of the wheel, trying to steer the ship toward a plateau that seemed to jut from the side of the volcanic mountain, while Volo alternated between throttling Grumby and trying to control Passepout, who was in an advanced stage of panic.

"We're all going to die!" screamed the chubby thespian. "Man was not meant to fly!"

"Shut up, you coward!" screamed the dwarf, barely managing to remain out of arm's distance of Volo

"Calm down, son of Idle and Catinflas!" Volo ordered, sternly yet calmly, then, switching to a tone of total belligerence, turned to Grumby and screamed, "If we get out of here alive, I'm going to beat you within an iota of your smelly hide!"

"Promises, promises," the dwarf retorted.

The airship's passengers could feel the hot and humid air wafting up from the jungle below.

Curtis yelled back to Volo from the helm, "We're still going down!"

"Why are we losing altitude?" Volo demanded of the dwarf.

"Well, I guess the rod that causes the ship to levitate might have lost its charge," the dwarf replied, again scratching his beard.

"You guess?" the enraged Volo retorted.

"We're all going to die!" the chubby thespian repeated.

"I'll try to bring us in for as smooth a landing as possible," Curtis called back as he tried to maintain control of the helm.

"I guess we'll just have to walk home from here," the dwarf taunted, enjoying the prospect of mixing it up with Volo, as only a dwarf could really enjoy a fight.

"Why, you . . . ," Volo replied.

"We're all going to die!" Passepout reiterated.

"Land ho!" Curtis announced.

*Thud!*

All of the ship's passengers were thrown off their feet as the ship came to rest on the very edge of the volcanic plateau. Curtis had barely managed to steer the ship away from the uneven surface of the mountainside, which no doubt would have smashed the ship to bits.

"Safe at last!" Passepout announced, jumping to a conclusion that would soon prove to be erroneous.

*Kwaaaahk!* An unearthly scream pierced the humid mists of the mountainside.

"What was that?" cried the thespian, ready to resume panicking.

"Sounds like a pteradon," Volo replied, "one of the thunder lizards."

*Kwaaaahk!* The scream was repeated, its owner still obscured by the humid mists.

"Sounds awful," the thespian cried.

"I think they are herbivores," Volo answered.

"Come again?" Grumby queried.

"Noncarnivorous, plant eaters," the master traveler explained.

"Wonderful," Passepout replied.

Curtis swung down from the helm to join the other passengers of the now-landed airship. "Sorry for the rough ride," he apologized.

"I could have brought us down safely," Grumby grumbled, "if any one would have let me."

"The way you knew how to navigate this ship?" Volo replied.

"So I made a wrong turn," the dwarf muttered.

Volo realized that to act on his anger would be futile and would only succeed in wasting precious minutes that could be applied to solving their current predicament. They could not afford to remain precariously balanced on the mountainside, nor could they really walk home as Grumby had laughingly suggested. And even if his memory was right, and pteradons were vegetarians, he was more than aware that many of Chult's inhabitants weren't.

"We have to come up with a plan to get out of here," Volo announced.

"You have a keen grasp of the obvious," Grumby retorted. "I guess that's why you're a big-shot author, or so you say."

"Quiet!" Volo ordered, taking command of the ship away from the incompetent dwarf. The master traveler paused for a moment to survey their position and the condition of the ship. It was hot and humid; the bug-infested jungle that surrounded their mountainside clearing hardly made for a comfortable resting place.

"Curtis," he ordered, "check out the condition of the ship, masts, sail bags, levitation rod, etc."

"Aye, aye, Captain," replied the youth, tossing a mock salute before he scurried back to the helm.

"Passepout, check out the ship's stores. If Grumby lied about his ability to navigate, we can't assume that he didn't lie about the extent of our provisions."

"Yes, Mister Volo, but do you mind if I grab a bit of lunch as I take inventory?" the thespian answered, once again aware of the rumbling in his stomach. "Crash landings always give me an appetite."

"Later," Volo ordered. "And also let me know what nonfood supplies we have below."

"Aye, aye, sir," Passepout replied half-heartily, his own groans over not eating joining the involuntary chorus of rumbles from his stomach as he went below to follow orders.

"Now you," said Volo, trying to retain control of

his temper as he addressed the dwarf, "what do you really know about how this ship works?"

"Just what I told you," the dwarf grumbled. "No more, no less."

The two adversaries just stared at each other until they were rejoined by Curtis and Passepout.

"The masts, helm, and sailbag seem to be intact," Curtis reported, "but the levitation rod seems to have split a hole in the bottom of the hull. Good thing we weren't over water when we started to drop. She would have sunk for sure."

"Who cares?" the dwarf chided. "I can swim."

"Probably the way you can navigate," Passepout replied, trying to mask a mouth full of food. "Our provisions should do us for about a week and a half."

"There's at least four months' worth down there!" Grumby argued.

"Maybe for you," Passepout replied with a burp. "There are also several casks of glue and paint."

"All part of giving the *Minnow* a face-lift," the dwarf volunteered.

"Well," Volo observed, "whatever let out that screech seems to have gone away, so I guess we are safe for the time being."

*Rumble. Rumble.*

"Excuse me," Passepout apologized.

"I'm afraid that that wasn't your stomach," Volo corrected. "I think it was the volcano."

*Rumble. Rumble.*

"She's going to erupt!" Grumby screamed.

"We're all going to die!" Passepout chimed in.

"Not just yet," Volo countered. "Curtis, ever take any geology classes?"

"No, sir," the lad replied sheepishly.

"I thought not," Volo said, confident that he had

indeed seen through the story of the lad's education, "but I did, and before a volcano blows, there are numerous rumblings and other geological manifestations that may never culminate in an actual eruption."

"Geological manifestations?" Passepout queried.

A hot-air geyser sprang up from the rock of the plateau beneath the ship, fortunately escaping through the existing rupture in the hull.

"Like that," Volo replied. "Lucky for us there was the break in the hull, or the sheer force of the hot air escaping from the ground could have lifted us up and over the side of the plateau, or at least unseated us from this fairly firm base."

Passepout became extremely excited, but couldn't quite get his explanation out. "Look!" he finally screamed.

All eyes turned to him.

"Not at me," he cried. "At the sail!"

The other passengers of the Minnow turned around to behold the object of the thespian's excitement.

The geyser's hot air was inflating the sailbag, which was beginning to lift the ship.

"Quickly!" Volo ordered. "Throw down a hook to keep us in place!"

"Aye, aye," said Grumby. He released a lever that activated the lowering of anchorlike grapples to the ground below. "That was a close call; we would have gone over the side for sure."

Passepout looked at the inflating sailbag and had an idea.

"Mister Volo," the thespian offered, "I remember when I was once working on a show with my parents, Idle and Catinflas, the famous thespians, that I helped out with some of the set decorations.

The set designer was an elf, and he used hot air to inflate bags of colored paper, which would then float in the air around the stage. Perhaps we could do something similar here."

"If we can get the ship aloft and on an even keel," Curtis asserted, "I'm sure I can helm her back toward the east."

"Capital idea!" Volo exclaimed. "Curtis, you and I will unfoul the rigging so that the sailbag can continue to inflate evenly. Once it appears to be full, we can use the paint and glue that Passepout found below to make a sealing paste to take care of any slow leaks or ruptures in the sail skin."

"What do you want me to do?" Passepout asked, instantly regretting that he had spoken up.

"I want you and Grumby to find something to cover that hole in the hull. Once the sailbag is inflated, we have to be able to stopper it. So scout around the immediate area . . . and hurry. I might have been overly optimistic about the amount of time we have, volcanically speaking, that is."

The thespian and the dwarf grumbled as they took off for their assignment, as much about their assigned companion as about the duty itself. Passepout decided they should follow a path through the brush that would circle around the ship so that at least he would not fall prey to retracing his steps.

"Superstitious, are you," the dwarf commented upon hearing the thespian's concern about doubling back.

"Something like that," he replied, not wanting to further explain. He did not trust the dwarf and had no desire to supply him with any information that could be used against him or Volo.

"You know, that kid Curtis is pretty smart," the dwarf continued, purposely trying to provoke the overweight and out-of-shape thespian, who was having a difficult time getting though the hot, humid rain forest brush that occupied the jungle side of the volcanic mountain.

"Well, I was the one who figured out about the sailbag, and the hot air!" the thespian contended indignantly.

"I would have expected you to be an expert on hot air," replied the belligerent dwarf, "since you are so full of it."

Passepout was about to reply with a similarly discourteous remark about the dwarf's body odor when he heard the approach of footsteps in the brush.

"Quiet!" the thespian whispered, then, indicating a break in the shrubbery, ordered, "Let's hide here."

The fat thespian and the foul-odored dwarf crammed into the small break in the foliage that, despite the mutual discomfort of the two explorers, nevertheless managed to safely hide their combined bulk while providing them with a clear line of vision at the source of the overheard footsteps.

"Look!" Grumby ordered.

"Hush!" Passepout replied.

Walking along the path they had taken no less than seconds before were several lizard men. Obviously native to the jungle, the four in the lead were at least ten feet tall, with tiny scales covering their bare, olive-green torsos; they trudged along on talon-clawed feet. They were carrying what appeared to be the appendages of a recently slaughtered thunder lizard, the meat still left on the bone for the upcoming meal causing their razor-toothed mouths to water. Bringing up the rear was the runt of the litter, only six feet tall, who was struggling with the silvery-gray hide of the recently slaughtered prey.

"Lizard men," Passepout whispered to his cramped companion of the moment.

"Kinda funny-lookin', though," Grumby responded in a similar tone. "Where are their tails?"

Passepout, ignoring the dwarf's question, whispered as the hunters passed, "I bet we could use that hide to both seal the rupture in the hull and reflect the sun's rays upward to keep the air hot in the sailbag itself."

Grumby couldn't control himself, and started to laugh. "I've never heard such rubbish," the dwarf howled.

The runt of the lizard men stopped in his tracks and, without notifying his brethren but still bearing the skin, returned to the spot he thought he heard the laughter coming from.

Both the dwarf and the thespian hushed. Unfortunately, Passepout had to sneeze and couldn't hold it any longer. "Atchoo!" he roared, scaring the native, who dropped the thunder lizard's skin and took off after his comrades.

"Well, that was easy enough," the thespian commented.

"Oh, yeah," the dwarf retorted. "I bet he's just gone to bring back company."

Grumby was right, and by the time the two novice explorers, the thunder lizard's skin carried between them, could see the inflated sailbag floating above the plateau clearing before them, they could hear the footsteps of the lizard hunter and his buddies in hot pursuit.

The incline of the terrain, the humid climate, the bulky lizard hide, and the less-than-athletic physiques of both Grumby and Passepout all succeeded in slowing the duo. With the balloon in sight and with one last thicket blocking their way back to the ship, the lizard men had almost caught up with them.

*Rumble! Rumble!*

The ground beneath them began to shake, and Grumby and Passepout were pitched forward into the clearing.

*Barooooom!*

The humid mists that enshrouded the plateau instantaneously cleared as the volcano above started to erupt, spewing flames, molten rock, and clouds of ash down the mountainside.

Volo leaned over the side of the ship to help Passepout aboard. "Back in the nick of time," Volo gratefully professed.

"Hope so," the out-of-breath thespian replied. "The lizard skin . . . we can use it to stop the hole . . . "

"Perfect," Volo answered. "Curtis, take the skin and seal the hatch above where the rupture is."

"Skin . . . shiny side up," Passepout panted.

"As he says," Volo ordered. "Grumby take the helm, and get us out of here!"

"Aye, aye, you . . . " the dwarf replied, mumbling an inaudible curse.

In the time it took for the patch to be fixed in place and for Grumby to take the helm, the tailless lizard men, having regained their balance after the initial tremor, broke into the clearing.

"Take off now!" Passepout yelled.

. . . and the *Minnow*, with Grumby at the helm, responded, leaving the plateau surface, which was quickly cracking in two, volcanic fissures reaching out from the spot where the first geyser had appeared.

Looking down at the plateau below, Volo noticed the scrambling forms of the lizard men, who were trying to avoid falling into the recently formed crevices. "Who are they?" he asked his quickly recovering companion.

"The owners of the thunder lizard's skin that we borrowed," Passepout replied.

"Borrowed?"

"In a manner of speaking," the thespian answered. "It's not like we stole it or anything. The runt dropped it, and we appropriated it."

"I see," the master traveler replied, looking back at the plateau's surface. "You mean the smallest one of the group—the one who is only now sprouting wings to join the others, who are flying after us."

"What?" the shocked thespian responded, ignoring his vertigo and joining Volo in staring back from whence they came.

The lizard creatures, having recovered from the shock of the volcanic eruption, had taken to the air, and in the process had polymorphed into a form for flying, with wings that stretched fifteen feet from point to point.

*Kwaaaahk!* the leader screamed.

"Those weren't lizard men," Volo yelled. "They were pteramen. Grumby, get us out of here as fast as possible. Everyone else, battle stations."

Passepout and Curtis joined in a chorus of aye-ayes, while the disgruntled dwarf could be heard grumbling something about being suitable to navigate the ship under these circumstances.

Passepout and Volo armed themselves with oars and proceeded to bludgeon any of the pteramen who tried to board the ship in midflight. The lizards' bodies were surprising light, easily thrown back over the side of the ship, where they fell to the ground. Curtis had armed himself with one of the ship's anchors, which he proceeded to throw through the air, conking the approaching flyers in midair and throwing them off-course.

The battle was going fine until three pteramen reached the deck at the same time. The master traveler and the thespian did their best to fight off the intruders. Volo managed to throw one overboard, but another had locked the chubby thespian in an embrace and was threatening to drag him over the side as well.

Thinking quickly, Curtis lassoed Passepout with the anchor rope seconds before he and his attacker went overboard. When the rope went taut upon reaching its end, the vibration separated the two attackers, and the pteraman fell to the ground below, while the thespian hung, panicking, in midair. "Help! Help!" the thespian screamed. "The rope is going to break."

The rope held fast while the battle with the final attacker on board continued.

The last of the pteramen, the runt, had polymorphed back to his terrestrial form and was trying to reclaim the hide, which was being used as a plug. Curtis threw a net over him, as Volo subdued him with the last remaining oar.

The pteraman, wrapped in the net, passed into unconsciousness.

"I'm glad that's over," Curtis remarked.

"Good flying, Grumby," Volo called to the dwarf, who muttered something unintelligible in return.

"Help!" Passepout cried, still hanging a good fifteen feet below the boat.

"I guess we should drag him in," Volo replied.

"Yeah," agreed Curtis, "but you should have seen

the one that got away."

The master traveler and the teenage urchin continued to laugh as they hauled in their heavy shipmate.

No sooner had he reached the deck than Passepout passed out, only to open his eyes moments later to find himself staring into the eyes of the net-bound pteraman.

Once again he screamed . . . and passed out.

By nightfall they had put the subcontinent of Chult well behind them, as they proceeded to fly farther eastward and to the north.

Passepout was cheered for his heroic exploits. Not only did he procure the reflective thunder lizard skin, assist in the defense of the ship, and hold on to the anchor line until the others were able to haul him in, but he also took the time, while suspended in midair, to fling one of the recently turned gems into the mouth of the erupting volcano. He had earned a tourist's rest and was taking advantage of it.

Curtis was a fast learner and soon was a better master of the helm than Grumby.

Volo charted their progress over the deserts, towns, and cities of Faerûn by posting the enchanted map that Khelben had given them, so as to notice if they veered off course at the earliest possible dropping of a gem (a maneuver that would have saved their side trip to Chult had he thought of it earlier).

Grumby, surprisingly, spent all of his time either practicing macrame or conversing (if it could be called that) with the captive pteraman, who had settled into a quiet existence of a prisoner on board ship. Grumby also took responsibility for the caring and feeding of the creature, who, without the support of its allies, was extremely docile and well-behaved.

"Now, eat this, little buddy," Grumby would instruct it at feeding time. "Do what Grumby says."

The pteraman was also the only one on board who didn't seem to mind the dwarf's odor, and during times of rain, it was allowed to share the dwarf's cabin.

One morning, Curtis, who was scheduled for morning duty, woke Volo and Passepout with a start. "Mister Volo, Mister Passepout!" he shouted. "Grumby and the pteraman are gone."

The master traveler and the thespian rushed to the side to see if they could see the missing duo. Volo spied a moving dot in the distance. Using his traveler's spyglass, Volo focused on the dot.

Flying through the air in the distance was Grumby, astride the pteraman, a makeshift harness and bridle fashioned from the dwarf's macrame.

"Son of a golem!" Volo exclaimed in disbelief.

"He left this note," Curtis revealed.

Volo took the note and read its contents out loud. "Volo (if that is your real name) and deadweight, I've trained the pteraman as my mount and plan on flying it to Tantras, where I can put it on exhibition. With the loss of the ship's magic, our bond is null and void. So long, suckers. You'll never make it to Kara-Tur."

"A charmer to the end," Passepout commented. ". . . but how did he manage to train it? I thought dinosaurs were wild and untrainable monsters."

"Not true," Volo replied. "I remember reading about a race of albino dwarves who spent their lives mining in the mountains of Chult. Perhaps it was in the writings of Artus Cimber . . . "

"But what does that have to do with . . . " the impatient thespian demanded as the dot grew smaller and smaller to the naked eye.

"I was getting to that," Volo replied. "These dwarves supposedly had domesticated smaller dinosaurs to do hauling work in and out of the mines. Perhaps dwarves just have some sort of ability in this area."

"Well, good riddance," the thespian replied.

". . . and nothing but more fragrant air space ahead," concluded the master traveler.

# FLYING OVER FAERÛN

## OR

## Watch Out for That Fireball!

Life on board the eastbound airship *Minnow*
quickly fell into an agreeable routine for all concerned. Curtis manned the wheel, maintaining a
northeasterly course over Faerûn as charted by
Volo, who used the enchanted map, with its illuminated trail that maintained the path of their journey. Volo also made use of his handy portable
charts and maps, the very necessary kit pack of a
master traveler. Passepout became the nominal

cook of the trio, spending most of his time preparing (and consuming) a variety of tasty dishes from the rather bland stocks and stores of the ship. Occasionally he would also go fishing for fowl with the net that had formerly confined the pteraman of Chult; he would scoop up an occasional member of a flock that ventured too close to the side or below the passing airship.

Across the Shining Plains, over the Sea of Fallen Stars, and far above Aglarond, the party made their way eastward with the occasional gem thrown overboard to mark their path on the enchanted map and on the surface of Toril far below. With high winds at their backs and a semi-regular current of thermals below, Volo anticipated smooth sailing ahead. Next stop: Kozakura in Kara-Tur, where provisions could be gathered before they continued their aerial journey eastward across the uncharted Eastern Sea. Unless, of course, Passepout had consumed their seemingly inexhaustible stores of foodstuffs prior to their arrival at their expected destination.

As time passed, Volo witnessed a gradual change in the young beachcombing urchin, Curtis. Though still maintaining a certain degree of respectfulness toward the master traveler, the lad quickly became a thorn in Passepout's side, playing tricks on him, joking about his girth, and in general acting like a kid. Passepout responded in kind, promoting a misplaced sibling rivalry between the two for the attention of the well-traveled father figure.

Curtis was also revealed to be quite knowledgeable about numerous subjects: not just geography, and navigation, but history, politics, and theater as well. Though Volo still doubted the veracity of his claim to noble birth, he nonetheless accepted the evidence that the youth was indeed the recipient of an incomplete education that was probably not indigenous to his beachcomber abode. The master traveler's skepticism only drove the lad to be more insistent on proving the veracity of his claims, particularly if he also succeeded in showing up the proud thespian son of Idle and Catinflas.

One evening, somewhere over Westgate, Passepout was reminiscing about his exploits on the stage and treating his two companions to a few saucy tidbits about his past. "Why, I even kept company with the legendary bard Olive Ruskettle," the proud thespian boasted.

"You mean Olav Ruskettle," Curtis corrected.

Passepout ignored the correction and continued his tale.

"Though only a fair singer and musician, her gift for the gab, glib tongue, and saucy red hair and hazel eyes worth dying for more than made up for her lack of true theatrical talent," the thespian pointed out. "Of course, I was willing to give her a few pointers and show her the old stage ropes, if you know what I mean. Normally, I'm not much fond of halflings, particularly tiny ones like her, but let it not be said that Passepout, the favorite son of the legendary thespians Catinflas and Idle, wasn't willing to make an occasional exception."

Curtis became quite indignant.

"I don't know who you were talking about," the teenager interjected, "but it sure doesn't sound like any legendary bard I've ever heard of, let alone Olav Ruskettle."

"Well, then," the haughty thespian responded, "I guess that just goes to show how really little you really know, doesn't it?"

"I know enough not to mistake some halfling guttersnipe pickpocket for the famed bard Olav Ruskettle," the youngster countered.

Passepout—ignoring the fact that, now that he thought about it more clearly, he did recall having his pocket picked that night—nonetheless retorted, "Takes one to know one!"

"Are you calling me a thief?" the youngster asked, getting very hot under the collar. He was more than willing to throw the chubby thespian over the side just to prove a point, as young men whose pride lacks the tempering of maturity are wont to do.

"Well, now that you mention it," the thespian continued with his taunts, "it's not as if you really are the son of some noble or millionaire merchant from Suzail or some other highfalutin society town, now, is it?"

"That's enough from both of you," Volo interrupted with a tone of finality. "Who cares if it's Olive Ruskettle or Olav Ruskettle? Perhaps there are two bards by that name. Perhaps one of them moonlights as a pickpocket. Who knows, and frankly, who cares? I'm sick and tired of your bickering and your one-upmanship. Men of the road such as ourselves have to live by our own code of honor. Accept another fellow traveler's tale with a discriminating grain of salt . . . but never call him a liar to his face or a charlatan to his crowd unless you are willing to risk not being the one to walk away in a one-on-one mortal match. Now shake hands and apologize."

Begrudgingly, the pudgy thespian extended his hand and apologized. "I'm sorry that I implied you were a thief and a liar. I myself have been accused of such things at no other place than the gate of

Suzail, where I first met Mister Volo."

"I also apologize," the youngster agreed, accepting the offered handshake, "and am equally sorry that I corrected your mistake."

"What mistake?" Passepout asked, wondering if he had once again been insulted.

"Doesn't matter," said Volo, quickly trying to derail the argument that once again threatened to come barreling down the track. "Does it? Of course not," he continued, trying not to leave enough time for a response from either of the hotheads. "I'm sure that Passepout here is more than willing to share his worldly wisdom with an eager young student such as yourself. You know, the type of education you left university for."

"Well, I *have* led a rather sheltered life," Curtis conceded.

"Of course you have," Volo agreed. Turning his attention back to Passepout for a moment, he added, "And you, good son of Catinflas and Idle, have previously admitted to having occasional, shall we say, lapses in memory and judgment, particularly around young ladies, if I'm not mistaken."

"Well, I guess, sort of."

"Of course," Volo agreed, and continued to divert the conversation away from the trouble spot by telling a story. "Which reminds me of a tale I once heard about a huge and hungry fish that was troubling the people of the Moonshae Isles, around old Amity town. The townspeople all chipped in to hire a crusty old sea dog to catch him. A young cleric fresh out of university, probably not much older than you, joined him in case there was a need for any ministering or healing or such—provided the fish didn't eat the old coot whole, that is. There was another guy with them, too, a constable from the town guard if I remember correctly, who was reluctant to join them at first, even recommending that they get a bigger boat . . . "

Volo, a not bad showman and entertainer himself, continued to spin the rest of the fish story off the top of his head until the sun had begun to set. His two companions had long forgotten their silly disagreement.

The next morning, all was forgiven, and the three travelers returned to their daily routine. Passepout mentioned that he particularly liked the part where the old sea dog was swallowed whole by the maneating devil fish, and recommended that they swap "fish stories" among themselves more often.

Curtis and Volo agreed, and tale telling became a regular part of their evening meal . . . the only requirement being that there was an unstated agreement that the veracity of the stories was never questioned, commented on, or corrected, which was particularly difficult for Volo to refrain from, or even to keep a straight face while Passepout related to the wide-eyed Curtis the story of how he heroically became the scourge of the Sea of Fallen Stars.

*I bet Ahib Fletcher is rolling in his watery grave now*, thought Volo, stealing a quick look far below to the crashing waves.

"By my calculations," Volo observed, "we are somewhere in the area of either Thay or Rashemen."

"What's the difference?" Passepout inquired.

"Not much," the master traveler replied. "Rashemen is a land of berserker barbarians and witches, while Thay is the land of the infamous Red Wizards."

"Great," replied the sarcastic thespian. "Just what we need, more sorcerers with sour dispositions."

"Like that one over there?" Curtis inquired, pointing over the starboard bow at a wizened old codger in red robes who was apparently resting on a nearby mountaintop.

"I guess we're in Thay, then," Volo observed. "Good eyes there, Curtis."

Not to be outdone, Passepout seized the opportunity to show off.

"Sure, he has good eyes, but I bet my aim is better," the thespian boasted. "Watch this!"

Before Volo realized the intentions of the boastful thespian, Passepout had already extracted a red gem from the pouch at his belt and had pitched it overboard, beaning the old wizard on the top of his noggin.

"Good shot!" Curtis complimented.

"I don't think that was such a good idea," Volo commented.

"Why not?" replied the proud thespian, revelling in sure aim and quick arm. "It's not like the old geezer saw us or anything, . . . and if he did, so what? It's not like he can do anything about it."

The crackling of flames in motion ripped through the sky around the ship as a fireball made its presence known.

The Red Wizard on the mountain was none too amused.

The first fireball had barely missed the ship, and the mage was now readying a second one that he was sure would meet its mark.

Volo quickly took command. "Curtis," he instructed, "take the helm!"

"Aye, aye, Captain Volo," Curtis responded, "but

I don't think she can dodge those fireballs. This ship was not cut out for bobbing and weaving."

Volo quickly came up with a plan.

"Curtis, you just hold her steady, laying a course that will get us out of here as fast as possible. Passepout," the master traveler instructed, turning his attention to the direct cause of their current situation, "I want you to run from stem to stern as fast as you can, back and forth."

"Back and forth," the frantic thespian complained, "how many times?"

"Until I tell you to stop," the master traveler shouted. "Now!"

Passepout responded just as the evil mage let loose with his second fireball and started preparing a third.

The radical shifts in weight and balance on board, caused by Passepout running back and forth, succeeded in causing the ship to tip and bob as if it were gliding along rough and tempest-ridden seas. The fireballs just missed the ship, passing over its bow and under its stern as the ship continued its rapid exit away from the mountainside, bobbing, jumping, and weaving in tune to Passepout's laps back and forth along the deck.

When the last fireball failed even to come close, Volo shouted, "That's it! We're out of range. You can stop running now."

An exhausted Passepout sank to the deck in exhaustion.

"I will never throw anything at a wizard again," he huffed and puffed.

"For as long as you live?" Volo queried.

"Longer," the thespian conceded, adding, "but what's that smell?"

"What smell?"

"Smells like smoke," the exhausted rotund thespian observed.

"Fire!" Curtis yelled down to his two companions and pointed to the hull below.

Though they had managed to avoid any direct hits, one of the fireballs that had passed below had ignited a section of the hull with its flaming streamers.

Volo and Passepout spent the better part of an hour trying to contain the flames, while Curtis held them on their course. The fire finally put out and their course stabilized, all three travelers hit their bunks, exhausted beyond description.

They slept through the night, only to be awakened by the morning sun and the observation that everything seemed to be back to normal.

It was a few days before they even realized they were losing altitude.

# TAAN

## OR

### Hostage to the Horde

"What do you mean, we're going down?" said the on-the-verge-of panic Passepout, whose aforementioned fear of heights now seemed to have been replaced by a fear of vertical sudden impact.

"The balloon seems to be tearing at its seams," replied Curtis, whose bravery did not mask his realization of their possible doom. "The strain of maneuvering around those fireballs and the constant changes in air pressure are finally taking their toll."

"Well," replied Volo, fingering his beard while thinking out loud, "she wasn't really constructed to hold the ship aloft."

Curtis continued with the bad news at hand. "I also fear that we can no longer steer. The strain of the ropes pulling on it will only hasten the wearing of the inflated material."

"Well, then," Volo replied, "we seem to have only two choices. We can let the ship steer itself until eventually the balloon deflates or breaks, at which point we will surely crash, or we can try to continue to steer her, thus accelerating the damage to the balloon, and the resultant crash."

"Great," replied Passepout, rolling his eyes, and wondering why they were wasting time examining two equally lethal alternatives, "but what's the difference where we crash?"

"A plain is always better than a jagged mountainside, and a gradual descent is much better than a freely accelerating plummet. Remember, when falling it is much better to emulate a feather than a rock—unless, of course, you want to make a hole in the ground or to be a pancake."

"Mister Volo," Curtis interjected, "meaning no offense, of course, but I really don't think this is a good time for pithy epigraphs from some Kara-Tur fate biscuit."

"Point well taken, lad," the master traveler replied. "On to the course of action. We must control and delay our descent for as long as we can, or at least until our chances of surviving a landing have increased dramatically. First, we must find something either to patch the leaks or at least cushion the balloon's surface from the abrasion of the ropes during steering. Might I recommend using the thunder lizard's skin as a cushion against the ropes? Its value as sun reflector is now outweighed by the matters at hand. And we can use the remaining paste and paint as a temporary sealant on those areas where the balloon has already worn thin."

"Aye, aye, sir," replied Curtis, who immediately hopped to the task at hand.

"We must also reduce the strain on the balloon's buoyancy itself," Volo continued. "Therefore Passepout, you and I must get rid of anything that is not an absolute necessity, to lighten our load . . . and that includes food."

"Aye, aye sir," replied Passepout, who oddly enough also immediately hopped to the task at hand and set off for the food stores.

"Mister Volo," Curtis asked, while tending to the removal of the patch from the hull, "what next? I mean, this won't really solve the problem."

"No, lad," the master traveler replied, "but it will buy us time."

Volo left the lad to his task and followed Passepout's lead to the ship's stores, but instead of finding the thespian busy casting the supplies overboard, he instead found him gorging himself with all of the provisions at hand.

"Passepout, what are you doing?"

"*Oonk, ooff, sputter, foo,*" the thespian replied, which Volo's keen ear easily translating as "getting rid of the food."

"That doesn't help us one bit," the master traveler scolded. "The food weighs the same inside you as it does inside the stores."

"But we can't just throw it overboard," the pudgy Passepout protested. "What will we do for supper?"

"Supper will only concern us if we survive that

long," Volo corrected. "Now move it!"

The thespian's grumbling retort was interrupted by the arrival of Curtis, whose flustered manner seemed to indicate that his task was also not going as well as expected. "Mister Volo," he implored, "it won't work."

"What won't work?"

"The thunder lizard's skin. I got it up from the hull all right, but I can't cut it down to a manageable size to line the ropes. The skin is too tough, and now the hull seems to be cracking as well."

The two older travelers left the stores and accompanied the young beachcomber to the site of the former patch. The skin had been loosened and pushed to the side, now revealing two ever-widening cracks that reached out from both sides of the hole in the hull, threatening to bisect the ship lengthwise.

"The strain of dodging those fireballs must have been too much for her," the master traveler observed.

"Well, don't just stand there, Curtis," Passepout ordered. "Replace the patch! Put the skin back!"

"It's too late for that," Volo replied. "The hole's gotten too big."

Suddenly the ship lurched to the left, setting the deck askew.

"What happened?" the frantic Passepout demanded.

"The ropes holding the balloon to the boat must have shifted," Volo replied. "She's deflating faster than I thought."

"We have to do something," Curtis implored.

Volo climbed up top to check the riggings, his two crew mates in tow. As he feared, the balloon was deflating, the ship descending at an ever-increasing rate. Volo was at a loss, but both of his crew mates were looking to him for guidance and inspiration.

"Well," he said out loud, trying to defuse their impending panic, "too bad Grumby cut out with the only available Chultian air support . . . wait! That's it! It just might work!"

Passepout and Curtis were shocked by the sudden change in the calm conduct of their airship captain, who was quickly undoing ropes and rushing around the deck like an ant on the edge of the abyss.

"Here!" their animated leader instructed. "Tie these ropes to each of the four corners of the lizard skin. Fast!"

"Why?" the two crewman replied, while simultaneously following orders.

"I remember reading in the papers of the explorer Artus Cimber on some of the obscure customs of some of tribes of Chult. I think it was the Tabaxi who had some sort of manhood ritual whereby the young males, upon reaching maturity, would have to throw themselves off a cliff with only an umbrella-shaped blanket to slow them down. You see, the warm air currents would slow their descent just like the geyser that inflated our balloon, thus allowing them to survive the fall. Supposedly it was done in honor of three Tabaxi who saved their king by helping him escape from the Batiri goblin tribes. I think their names were Gherri, Aahnnie, and Modesti."

"But how does this help us?" Passepout implored.

Volo pointed to the ground that they were approaching.

"There!" he instructed. "If we stay on board at our current rate of descent we will be bashed to our deaths on those rocky ridges. Ergo, we must abandon ship before we reach there."

"So we can be bashed to our deaths on the plains below?" Passepout asked.

"Maybe," Volo replied, "but hopefully not. Good, that should be secure enough. Curtis, pass me my pack."

The lad complied without thinking.

"Good," the master traveler responded, hoisting it into place on his back, with the shoulder straps. "Now quickly, take the other end of one of the ropes, and attach it to the front of your belt. On second thought, Passepout attach an end on each side."

Both complied, unaware of the rhyme or the reason for their actions, and ever aware of the approaching doom of the rocky mountain cliffs.

"Good, now one more rope, tied around us, holding us back to back to back," the master traveler continued. "Better make it twice around. Good."

"But I don't understand," Curtis queried, while still complying.

"We're all going to die," the thespian replied in resignation.

"I hope not," Volo responded, shifting their bound, three-person bulk toward the ship's bow. "If it works for the Tabaxi, it might work for us."

"What did you say those guys' names were?" Passepout asked.

Volo checked the security of the ropes and straightened out the unfurled thunder lizard's skin as he replied. "Gherri, Aahnnie, Mo . . . "

Once again the ship lurched. The hull cracked in two. The three bound travelers were thrown backward over the bow, the lizard skin following at a rope's length.

Falling.

Falling.

Falling . . . lurch upward.

The skin caught the wind and became inflated, slowing their descent drastically.

"It's working!" Curtis replied.

"We're going to die!" Passepout cried.

"Hold the ropes!" Volo shouted. "Use both hands! We should hit the plains in seconds."

True to his word, they did.

Volo managed to extricate himself first from beneath the lizard skin that had landed on top of them, and managed to catch one last look at the airship *Minnow* as it crashed into the rocky ridge and tumbled down the mountainside, breaking into unrecognizable splinters and shards of airbag and wood.

Under his breath, and unheard by his crew members, Volo breathed a sigh of relief, saying, "I honestly didn't think we'd make it. I guess I owe Artus Cimber one."

The master traveler then turned his attention back to Passepout and Curtis, who were having trouble extricating themselves from the rope-and-skin contraption that had saved their lives.

"My aching body," Passepout complained, "and we forgot the food."

"We made it!" Curtis announced in disbelief.

"Of course," Volo replied. "Was there ever any doubt? Let's make camp here. The sun is setting, and our makeshift sky sail will also make a perfect windbreak and blanket to protect us from the evening chill."

Few words were spoken, and the exhausted threesome were at rest before the sun had fully dipped below the horizon.

Fatigue had won out over caution, and the night passed uneventfully despite the lack of a guard on watch.

As the sun made its appearance on the opposite horizon, Curtis and Passepout awoke to muscles and joints that were now just beginning to make known their complaints about the activities of the previous day.

"Good morning," greeted Volo, who had obviously been up since the first crack of sunlight had started to illuminate the shadow-ridden plains. He was contemplating the enchanted map, which he had luckily placed in his pack at the first sign of trouble with the Red Wizard. "As best I can estimate, we're somewhere around here, in the northern part of the Quoya Desert, around the Horse Plains."

"Huh?" Passepout replied, wiping the sands of slumber from his eyes and yawning.

"The Horse Plains, also called the Hordelands, or Taan as it's known in the native tongue," Volo elaborated. "Not too bad, considering the alternative."

"What alternative?" the thespian groaned, the complaints of his joints drowned out by the rumblings of his stomach.

"Death," the master traveler succinctly replied.

"Oh," the thespian acquiesced.

"But aren't the people of the Hordelands hostile?" Curtis asked. "And didn't King Azoun and his Purple Dragons defeat them and their savage and barbaric ways during the Horde Wars?"

Volo chuckled.

"Well, I guess we found an area that your alleged education is lacking in. Sure, Azoun and his boys managed to turn back the Horde invasion . . . but savage and barbaric ways? I don't think so, that is unless you happen to be one of the merchants whose caravans were plundered of their wealth and wares. From what I understand, Yamun Khahan, leader of the Tuigan (that's what they call themselves; the Horde is a western moniker) would even offer his captives the choice of joining him and his raiding party on their invasion westward."

"What if a prisoner declined the offer?" Curtis asked.

"If he or she was of value as a hostage, they were ransomed. If not, they were killed, not unlike any other civilized culture engaged in the uncivilized practice of making war. Savage and barbaric? No more than any other special interest group of our own fair Faerûn."

"I'm hungry," Passepout grumbled to no one in particular.

"So I hear," Volo replied, pointing to the thespian's ample abdomen, whose rumblings were hard to miss. "As are we all."

"So what do we do now?" Curtis inquired.

"Just wait right here until that cloud of dust on the horizon catches up with us."

"Oh, great! A dust storm! Just what we need," commented the sarcastic thespian.

"Not a dust storm, my friends," Volo corrected. "That cloud is too self-contained to be a manifestation of nature's wrath. No, if I don't miss my guess, I'd say that's a Tuigan *minghan*—or, shall I say, raiding party—coming our way. No doubt they saw our rapid descent of yesterday and are on their way to lay claim to anything that has survived the crash. So the real question, gentlemen, is whether we prefer to be dead, new recruits, or hostages. Any questions?"

The horse-borne raiding party arrived within the hour and were shocked to find survivors from the ship that had fallen out of the sky. Volo, Passepout, and Curtis were taken prisoner, bound, and led on horseback back to the camp of the party's leader under armed guard, while the rest of the party proceeded to the mountainside to pick among the rubble of the *Minnow* for something of value.

The Tuigan camp was not far from the crash site, and in less than two hours, the three travelers found themselves in audience with the Horde leader Jamign, or as he preferred to be called, Aleekhan.

Aleekhan was a typical minor Horde warlord who had come to power after the western campaign. His *minghan* was composed of fewer than a thousand members, and his store of wealth was even less impressive. Like many other small-time warlords, he was just another tribal bully who managed to be in the right place at the right time to be named Khan. Dumb, maybe . . . but also dangerously lucky, as the numerous now-dead rivals for the khanship had found out.

"I am Aleekhan, Master of the Wastes, successor to the realms of Yamun Khahan, greatest of all Tuigan, and plunderer of the West," he bellowed in the common tongue used by most of the merchants of Faerûn. "All who approach, cower in my wake. All who oppose me, die!"

Passepout, weakened from hunger, having not eaten in more than twelve hours, fainted as if on cue.

"We cower in your wake, O great Aleekhan,"

replied Volo in his most fawning tone, nudging Curtis to quickly drop to his knees. "We have traveled far to join the greatest of all *minghans*."

"You are the men who were dropped out of the sky?" the warlord inquired.

"Yes, O great Khan," Volo answered. "We have braved both air and sea to arrive in your presence."

"Well," replied the warlord, his ego fueled by Volo's blandishments, "you are now here. What do you have to offer your Khan?"

"Our undying gratitude, and our lifelong service!" Volo responded with as much enthusiasm as he could muster.

Aleekhan stood up and approached the three travelers.

"What's the matter with him?" the Khan queried, poking the still unconscious Passepout with the toe of his slipper.

"He is the great warrior Passepout, bloodthirsty buccaneer of the Sea of Fallen Stars. No doubt you have heard of him," Volo replied.

"No doubt," replied the Khan in a noncommittal tone, "but why is he unconscious?"

"He was consumed by awe, almighty Khan, having never been in the presence of a warrior even mightier than himself."

"Quite," replied the Khan, returning to the makeshift throne upon which he had been seated before. "But enough about him. Tell me more about why you've come to join me on my quest for glory."

"Well," Volo replied, trying to think fast.

"No doubt, you have heard of my latest hostage," the Khan interrupted.

"But of course," Volo answered. "Further proof that you are indeed the heir to the glory of Yamun Khahan."

"But unlike him, I shall make the West cower at my feet. Even now, my name will inspire terror throughout Cormyr. What other warlord would have in his possession one of the most respected daughters of their greatest trading company, the Seven Suns?"

"You mean your hostage is the daughter of Lord Gruen Bleth of the Seven Suns Trading Company of Cormyr?" the master traveler answered. "I am in awe."

"But of course," the Khan replied. "Rouse your friend, and let us dine. Let it not be said that Aleekhan mistreats his minions."

With that, Aleekhan clapped his hands and was borne in his throne out of the reception tent, and into another even more tackily lavish tent, where a feast already seemed to be underway.

Volo and Curtis quickly roused Passepout with the promise of food and followed the Khan to the feast.

"Your friend the great warrior has the appetite of a dragon," commented the Khan.

"And the fearsome bravery to match, O great Khan," Volo replied.

Volo's fawning blandishments had secured himself and his companions places of honor at the great Khan's side during the afternoon's feast, which they learned was the daily occurrence that accounted for the Khan's massive bulk, which far exceeded that of Passepout, Curtis, and Volo combined.

"So how did you plan on serving me?" the Khan inquired. "What talents do you have to offer?"

"I am learned in the ways of many nations," Volo replied. "In addition to warfare, I can also advise you on politics, customs, cultures . . . "

"Can you help me get a better price on my hostage's ransom?" the Khan interrupted.

"Sure," Volo replied, "but . . . "

"Good," the Khan interrupted. "Then tomorrow we head westward to Cormyr."

"No!" Volo exclaimed, then adding quickly, "almighty Khan."

Aleekhan began to become enraged, his bloated body turning red in fury. "You dare to contradict your Khan?"

"No, almighty Khan," Volo obsequiously replied, trying to backpedal as fast as possible. At the same time, he plotted to discourage the Horde leader from causing him and Passepout to double back and risk the mortal consequences that had been promised. "What I meant to say was that perhaps you should consider another destination."

"Why?" the Khan demanded. "Would not her value be the greatest in her homeland?"

"In most cases, almighty Khan, yes," Volo conceded, adding, "but because she is a merchant's daughter, perhaps a higher price can be fetched by selling her to a rival merchant house, like those that exist beyond the Dragonwall in Kara-Tur."

"I know of no such rival merchant houses," Aleekhan interrupted.

"But I do," Volo countered, "and I am sure Lord Gruen Bleth's rivals would pay a handsome sum to keep him in check by holding his daughter ransom."

Aleekhan fingered his beard the way he had seen Volo do, in hopes that it would make him appear to be as intelligent as the quick-witted master traveler appeared to be.

"You may have a point," the Khan said. "Originally I had contemplated making her my consort, my *Reeta*. That is why I originally bought her from my cousin Sammhie."

"You bought her!" Curtis exclaimed in disbelief. "I thought you had . . . "

Volo gave Curtis a sharp elbow to the ribs that more than succeeded in hushing him.

"Of course I bought her, and at the time I thought it was a bargain. We had just seized a caravan laden with feed for horses. Sammhie's band had fallen on hard times. He lacks the necessary qualities to be a great Khan and busies himself with collecting tapestries and sculptures."

"Sort of a Khan artist you might say," Passepout offered before being encouraged to silence by the master traveler's inconspicuous pinching of his portly rump.

"Exactly!" the Khan agreed. "He was never much of a warlord, and now his mounts were starving, so I agreed to trade a supply of hay, which I now had in excess, for the lovely hostage he had picked up on one of his bazaar raids. I intended for her to be my bride. All were to know the price I paid for her. She was to be known as my *Reeta-hayworth*. Unfortunately, she turned out to be more trouble than she was worth. I mean who wants to lie down with a raging wildcat? You see these scars?"

The Khan pointed to a series of scabbed rake marks on his cheeks.

"I thought they were a sign of bravery," Volo answered.

Aleekhan laughed. "No," the Khan retorted, "they are the sign of an uncooperative consort. That's when I decided to ransom her."

Volo sensed that the feast was coming to an end, and decided to make his move.

"O great Aleekhan, I and my companions are at

your disposal. Why don't you let us proceed to Kara-Tur to make the arrangements for the ransom? With four of your best-fed steeds at our disposal, we will be back in no time, with arrangements made and booty in hand. Then both east and west will know of the great exploits of Aleekhan, the Khan who dared to ransom the daughter of Lord Gruen Bleth, causing all of Cormyr to quake in his wake."

"Catchy," Passepout commented to his former master, adding, "and don't forget to ask for food."

"All we will require is provisions for two weeks, and the horses."

The Khan briskly rubbed his hands together in anticipation of his upcoming booty.

"So let it be said, so let it be done," the Khan replied. "You will leave at first light."

The Khan then clapped his hands, and the banquet was over.

For the rest of the afternoon, the three travelers went about putting together the provisions for their trip eastward. At sunset they convened at the outskirts of the camp.

"Once the camp is asleep, we will leave," Volo instructed.

"Do we have enough supplies?" Passepout asked.

"The four fastest stallions of the tribe, each packed with provisions," Curtis replied.

"Perfect," Volo commended, adding, "but did you say four?"

"Of course," Passepout answered. "One's just for my lunch, right?"

"Wrong," Curtis replied. "I just assumed that we would also rescue the daughter of Lord Gruen Bleth. Right, Mister Volo?"

Volo shrugged. "Why not?" he agreed. "And now that I think of it, I have a plan in mind, too."

"But why do we have to?" Passepout whined.

"We are just following orders," Volo replied.

The three travelers had arrived at the tent where the Bleth heiress was being held captive.

"She'll just slow us down," Curtis interjected. "Couldn't you talk the Khan out of it?"

"The Khan's will is our command," Volo replied, then turning to the guard who stood at the tent's entrance, added, asking for corroboration, "Right?"

"Khan's will be done," the guard replied in the high voice that bespoke a eunuch.

"Uh, right," Volo replied. "You see the Khan instructed us to take the hostage with us so that we could get a better price for her." The master traveler then elbowed the guard in the ribs. "I think he also wants to be rid of her as soon as possible. I understand that they didn't really get along."

"Khan's will be done," the guard replied.

"Uh, right," Volo answered. "Now, if you will just fetch her for us, we will be on our way."

"No," the guard replied.

*Okay, now what?* Volo thought. *The ruse hadn't worked.*

". . . I have no desire to dance with that wildcat," the guard continued. "Fetch her yourselves. I'll watch your horses."

"Of course," Volo answered, and the three travelers entered the tent.

The young woman was the perfect synthesis of eastern and western beauty. Dark eyes, auburn hair, and ample curves and calves, she was bedecked in the silks of a Tuigan princess, which did little to conceal her obviously pampered beauty.

Her full and luscious lips were interrupted by a silken gag, and she was bound both hand and foot.

"We've come to rescue you," Curtis said, as he undid the scarf that bound her mouth.

"Well, it's about time!" she scolded in none too discreet a tone. "Do you know who I am? I've been—"

"Quick! The gag!" Volo ordered, and Curtis immediately complied.

"*Mmphgh!*" she protested indignantly.

"Do you think that's a good idea?" Passepout inquired. "I mean, ticking off an heiress and all. What if she tells her father, and he gets mad, and decides not to give us a reward . . . "

"Later," Volo instructed, silencing the thespian. "Curtis, escort the lady out."

"Aye, aye, sir," Curtis replied absently, forgetting that they were now off the ship. With that, he hoisted the young woman over his shoulder as if she were an extremely well-proportioned sack of potatoes and carried her out of the tent.

"Good luck," the guard bade them as they bound their burden to one of the fleet-footed steeds.

Volo mounted his horse, and replied, "Khan's will be done!"

The three travelers and their "guest" headed eastward under the cover of night.

# ON THE ROAD
# IN KARA-TUR

## OR

### Three Men, a Woman, an Old Coot, and a Baby

True to the words of Aleekhan's horse master, the purloined steeds were indeed the fastest that the encampment had to offer, as evidenced by the noticeable lack of a similarly mounted party dispatched by the enraged Khan to bring back the turncoats and his hostage. By noon the following day the travelers felt reasonably safe that they would not be further pursued. They had skirted the edge of a sandstorm, and warring dust devils had succeeded in crossing the path from whence they had traveled numerous times, thus obscuring any tracks or trails that they might have left.

As of noon that same day, they had also attempted no less than three times to remove the gag from the mouth of their rescued heiress, only to quickly replace it each time as she refused to listen to reason. The travelers realized that they needed to cover the greatest amount of distance between themselves and the Khan's Horde, and had no time for conciliatory explanations or deflections of insults. As a result, when the group finally stopped to eat later that afternoon (much too much later to suit the rumblings of the stout thespian's stomach), the heiress Bleth was still bound and gagged, and really quite ticked off about it, having now ridden more than twenty hours in a manner more suited to a merchant's pack than a lady of breeding.

In his own mind, Passepout had quickly resolved that the heiress Bleth would be his ticket to easy street, once his commitment to world travel was fully resolved, and therefore he committed himself to ingratiating himself with her as soon as possible—and what time could possibly be better than mealtime?

"We can't afford to tarry too long," Volo instructed, "so therefore, let's eat, be quick about it, and back in the saddle, and on our way."

"I hate rushing a meal," Passepout remarked sadly. "It's usually my favorite part of the day."

"If you had your way," Curtis jibed, "mealtime would be the whole day."

Passepout ignored the teenager's comment and

began to press his case for getting on the heiress's good side with the master traveler.

"Mister Volo," he requested in as angelic a voice as possible, "don't you think we should offer some food to our new, uh, companion?"

Volo was stunned. Never before had he seen the pudgy thespian willing to share a meal with an extra mouth that might result in the diminishment of his own portion. He suspected Passepout had an ulterior motive and quickly decided that the situation might indeed prove to be quite amusing, particularly in view of his dubious success with the young lady from the Company of the Catlash.

"Good idea," Volo replied. "Curtis, why don't you bring a bowl over to our reluctant rescuee and see if her manners have improved any?"

Before Passepout could protest, Curtis had already objected.

"Meaning no offense, Mister Volo," the teenager replied, "but I'd rather not. Last time I tried to remove her gag, she almost bit off my fingers."

Passepout interjected himself into the discussion.

"Poor boy," he said, "obviously your, uhm, schooling has left you grossly ignorant of the ways and needs of the gentler sex. Allow me to take care of her, Mister Volo."

"As you wish," Volo replied, and with a wink added, "just make sure you come back with all your fingers . . . and if she puts up a fight, feel free to accept her portion for yourself. It's the least reward you deserve for so hazardous a mission."

Passepout took the bowl and proceeded to the shade where the heiress now lay, still tied and gagged. Setting the food aside, he contemplated the girl, and then the bowl, trying to decide which was more important to him at the moment.

*Possible future wealth*, he contemplated, *or an immediate second serving. Decisions, decisions.*

His quiet contemplations were rudely interrupted by a quick kick upward by the heiress, who had managed to free one leg from its thong imprisonment, and whose contact with one of the rolls of the thespian's abdominal bulk threw him off balance, causing him to almost fall on top of the bowl he had brought to feed her.

"Now that wasn't very nice," he barked, and then in a gentler tone added, "don't you want something to eat?"

She hesitated for a moment, her beautiful, dark eyes filled with apprehension.

"We're not going to hurt you. I mean, we rescued you, and all," the thespian explained.

Her gaze darted to the bowl of food, then back to Passepout.

"Sure, you can have food," he surmised. "Just don't try to kick me again. The food's not bad. Of course, if we had time I could fix you a real feast." Passepout paused for a moment to pat his substantial stomach, and then continued, "You might say I'm sort of an expert on the science of the gastronomy, and culinary cuisine . . . but Mister Volo says we're in a hurry . . . "

Her eyes blinked in recognition, interrupting his chain of thought.

"Oh, you've heard of him. Yes, he's that Volo, author of the Volo's travel guides, and master traveler of the Realms. I'm Passepout, his trusted advisor. He asked that I come along on this trip. Needed my help, actually. Of course, I agreed. Anything for Volo, after all. He has a reputation to live up to. I do too, just not as a traveler. Oh, here; let me undo that."

Carefully, the chubby thespian undid the gag that blocked her mouth.

"You see, I'm an actor," he continued, seemingly oblivious to the fact that his removal of her gag hadn't really changed her situation. "I am Passepout, favorite son of Catinflas and Idle, famed thespians of the Realms, and . . . "

"The food," she interrupted.

"Oh, yeah, sure," Passepout replied, offering her the bowl, and only then realizing that her hands were still bound together. "Oops, sorry," he apologized, and began to undo her wrist bonds.

"Well, it's about time," she began to harangue, but then thought better of it, adding courteously, "Thank you."

"You're welcome," Passepout answered.

Having undone the wrist thong, he handed her the bowl.

"Now that I think of it, I really must apologize for the food," he continued. "An heiress such as yourself is obviously accustomed to better."

"Yeah, sure," she responded between mouthfuls that were none too dainty or delicate.

*She's probably just real hungry,* the thespian thought. *I know how I get when I haven't eaten in a while. I guess rich people are no different than poor people when they are really starving.*

"What are you staring at?" she asked haughtily.

*Oh, dear!* Passepout thought, *I offended her!*

"Why, your regal beauty, of course," he replied, quickly trying to think on his feet. "I mean, I've never been this close to an heiress before, I mean, never when I wasn't giving a command performance, that is."

"Well, okay," she replied, "just try not to be too obvious about it."

*Thank Eo she doesn't offend easily.*

Putting down the now-empty bowl, she began to massage the cramped joints that had been bruised by the thongs that had bound her.

"So your name is Passepout," she stated.

"Yes," he replied, "the son of Idle and Catinflas, the noted ... "

"Yeah, I know," she interrupted. "The thespians."

"Exactly," he replied, adding, "and what is your name?"

"Shurleen Laduce," she replied absently, her concentration still focused on relieving her aching joints.

"Excuse me," Passepout inquired, desperately trying not to appear insubordinate or dense, "but aren't you the daughter of Lord Gruen Bleth? Meaning no disrespect, but shouldn't your last name be Bleth?"

"Oh, yeah," she corrected, "my full name is Shurleen Laduce Bleth."

The thespian began to become skeptical, until with a bat of her eyes she added, "but you can call me Shurleen."

"Oh, thank you, Miss Bleth, I mean, Shurleen," he fawned, "and if there is anything I can do for you or your fabulously rich father, just let me know."

"Yeah, sure," she replied, back to her previous mood of indifference. "So I guess you're going to tie me up again."

"Oh, no," he assured her. "I wouldn't dream of it."

"What about the other guy?"

"Mister Volo? Oh, I don't think so ... "

"Not him," she countered, "that guy who wouldn't untie me back at Ali's place."

"Oh, you mean Curtis," the thespian answered. "You don't have to worry about him. He takes his orders from Mister Volo and me. I must speak to him about his abhorrent behavior back there, and I assure you it won't happen again."

Shurleen batted her eyes at the moonstruck Passepout, saying sweetly, "My hero."

"Yes, ma'am, I mean Shurleen," the thespian fumbled, "but I think we have to be hitting the road again."

"Good!" she replied eagerly. "I can't wait to get back to Cormyr."

Passepout shook his head in resignation.

"I think you had better talk to Mister Volo about that," he replied.

"What do you mean, we are heading due east?" Shurleen screamed. "Cormyr is back to the west!"

"I am aware of that," the patient master traveler replied, "but unfortunately, our path back west is due east."

"But why?" she whined with all of the grating intensity of a spoiled princess.

"Because that's just the way it is," Curtis interrupted, "and you're just going to have to accept that!"

Volo was shocked at the lack of tact Curtis showed toward their pampered guest, and even more surprised at the guest's response.

"How dare you talk to me like that!" she ranted. "Wait till my father finds out! He's Lord Gruen Bleth, you know, and he could buy and sell your sorry little hide, so you better watch out. Who do you think you are?"

Curtis bit his tongue to hold back an equally vitriolic response, mindful of the keen eyes of Volo that were concentrating on his behavior. Passepout, on the other hand, decided to jump in and answer her question.

"He claims to be the son of some wealthy merchant off to see the world before settling down to the family business," the thespian replied with more than a bit of sarcasm in his voice.

"Oh, really," she retorted. "Well, I know all of the eligible bachelors on the Faerûn society registry, and I don't recall anyone on the list by the name of Curtis."

"My thoughts exactly," Passepout added. "Why he's never even seen the lovely halfling bard Olive Ruskettle in concert. I, of course, have performed with her."

"Really," Shurleen answered. "Personally, I've always preferred the bardic charms of Danilo Thann, but Olive is not without her merits. I guess you could say I've always had a thing for bards . . . "

Passepout's ample bulk shrank as his heart began to break.

". . . and other thespians, of course," she added.

Passepout reinflated.

"All of these discussions are well and good," Volo responded, "but unfortunately, due east is where we are heading. You are more than welcome to join us, or if you prefer, you can help yourself to a quarter of the provisions, and the horse you rode in on, and set your own course due west, but I would advise against it."

Volo began to repack his stallion in preparation for breaking camp and resuming the journey. Curtis did the same, trying very hard to ignore the spoiled heiress.

Shurleen was in a quandary, and looked to her only ally, Passepout.

"Passepout," she implored, "surely you will . . . "

Passepout held up his hand to halt her request.

"I'm afraid that I've given Mister Volo my word, and a gentleman's word is his bond. Sorry," he explained as he began to pack his steed as well. "Due east it is."

Shurleen, having no desire to be left alone in the desert, stomped her foot, and demanded, "Well, then, east it is. Now who will help me pack my horse?"

"Curtis," Volo instructed, "help her, and lend her your blanket. Those silken pantaloons weren't really cut out for traveling."

Curtis left his own mount and began to pack Shurleen's steed as the spoiled heiress harangued him.

Passepout discreetly joined Volo at his steed's side. "Isn't she something?" the thespian said.

"That's one word for her," Volo replied.

"I think she likes me," he professed, as only a moonstruck victim of a crush could.

Volo just rolled his eyes and resumed the setting of his packs.

The ride eastward was reasonably uneventful.

Deserts gave way to hills, to mountain passes, and back to plains.

The four travelers' journey was reasonably comfortable with ample water, and food for themselves, and their steeds.

Even Passepout's usual vocal protestations of hunger, starvation, and gastric deprivation seemed to be held in abeyance by the presence of the newest member of their traveling party.

Shurleen, unfortunately, more than made up for his moony agreeableness with a continuous stream of protestations about her comfort, their destination, and the time it was taking getting there.

Volo himself began to consider the desirability of ditching her in one of Kara-Tur's numerous seaports, leaving her to find her own means of getting home from there. But then common sense would intervene, and he would have to dismiss such plans. He had no desire to get on the bad side of the Bleth family, nor did he wish to upset Passepout, who was lavishing an unseemly amount of unconditional acceptance of her bad behavior.

As they passed just to the north of Kara-Tur's famed Dragonwall, Volo mused to himself that it was just one less wall for Shurleen's whining to echo off.

Shurleen's cacophonous drone of complaints was interrupted by a question. "What's that smell?" she asked.

The travelers reined in their stallions and paused to evaluate.

"Smells like smoke," Curtis answered.

"And where there's smoke, there's fire," Passepout added, not wishing to be upstaged by the younger man.

Volo fingered his beard in contemplation. "It's fire and smoke, all right," he observed. "Bamboo, I think."

"It seems to be coming from over there," Shurleen added, pointing toward a nearby ridge that blocked a valley pass.

"We should proceed with caution," Passepout declared, trying to sound officious to conceal his own growing fear.

"Agreed," the master traveler answered. "Let's proceed on foot."

The four travelers dismounted in unison, Curtis taking the reins of Volo's and Passepout's mounts so that they could discreetly proceed ahead and do reconnaissance.

As the two traveling companions reached the ridge, Shurleen called, "Do you see anything yet?"

"Quiet!" Curtis hushed, none too sweetly.

"Why?" she pouted.

"We might not want to give our presence away!"

"Oh," she answered softly, for the first time really noticing that Curtis cut a fine figure for a young fellow of the itinerant classes.

*Too bad he's not rich,* she thought to herself, *I really might be able to go for his type. Still, a dalliance on the road might not be too bad, provided no one finds out.*

"Uh, Curtis," she said sweetly, "now that we're alone, I . . . "

"Quiet!" he hushed again, not paying attention to anything she had to say, only to the amount of noise she was making. "I told you to be quiet!"

*Well that settles it,* she fumed. *Never in a million years, not even if he was the richest man in all Toril. I'd sooner marry that blimp of a thespian Passepout than keep intimate company with this young rogue. At least the fatso minds his manners.*

"You know, I really think she likes me," Passepout commented, as he and Volo sauntered around the ridge.

"Quiet!" Volo snapped. "We might not want to give our presence away."

"Oh, yeah, right," the thespian agreed, dropping to a whisper, while falling into line behind the master traveler.

The smoke from smoldering bamboo was coming

from the remnants of a small merchant caravan that apparently had been attacked by bandits. After they had finished ransacking it of all that was valuable, they had inexpertly set it on fire, which resulted in many clouds of pungent smoke but very little fire damage, as the flames quickly smoldered instead of spreading.

"Let's take a closer look," Volo suggested, immediately drawing closer to one of the overturned wagons.

"Do we have to?" protested the chubby thespian, who nevertheless followed the master traveler to the scene of carnage.

No fewer than ten bodies had been hacked to pieces at the attack site. Most of the victims were old men and women whose possessions were probably of little value to the raiding party of bandits.

It was apparent that in lieu of an expected windfall of booty, the thieves had chosen entertainment in its place, much to the misfortune of their innocent victims.

Volo shook his head in disgust. Once again he decided that no matter how wide his experience or far his travels or extensive his knowledge of the way of the world, he would never get used to the cruelty and inhumanity that man brings to bear on his fellow man.

"I guess we're too late to do any good here," Volo muttered in resignation.

"Good," Passepout answered out of relief. "I mean, yes, uh, too bad, a real shame."

The two travelers turned to rejoin the rest of their group on the other side of the ridge, when Volo swiveled back, cocking his ear to the wind.

"Wait," he instructed. "Did you hear that?"

"Hear what?" Passepout answered, anxious to

rejoin Shurleen, and not trusting her alone with that arrogant beachcomber, Curtis.

A soft wailing seemed to be coming from the ambush site.

"That," Volo replied.

"It's probably just the wind," Passepout replied hopefully, adding, "We should be on our way."

"In a minute," Volo replied, and turned his attentions back to the site of the ambush.

The wailing grew louder as they approached one of the overturned wagons, which though light in construction nonetheless covered a large amount of the plain in its rubbled and wrecked form.

Volo began to pick through the rubble as the wailing persisted. Lifting up the remnants of two bamboo screens, he uncovered the bodies of two men, one of whom had been beheaded. The shifting of the screen further revealed the missing head, a face mask still in place.

"Obviously this guy put up a fight," Volo commented, gesturing to the intact body, "and managed to behead one of the bandits before the others managed to do him in. See here, in addition to killing him, they gave him a haircut."

"Why?" asked the slightly bewildered Passepout, who really wished that he was still back with the horses.

"They cut the topknot of his hair that indicates that he was a samurai."

"Strange souvenir."

"Sure was," Volo replied.

Passepout turned to leave and stumbled over another piece of the rubble. The wailing quickly changed to a loud crying.

"Quickly," Volo ordered. "Help me move this. I think something is trapped under here."

The two travelers pulled back the piles of bamboo screen, and uncovered the top of a cart that had been buried in the ground, and covered with the screens. The cart was bedecked with all sorts of throwing knives and swords, a veritable portable arsenal for a wandering samurai. In its center, completely at home among the weaponry but crying from the pangs of hunger from not eating for several hours was a very small child, probably less than two years old.

Carefully Volo and the chubby thespian extracted the child from its highly lethal bower of martial arts, and returned to Curtis and Shurleen, who were just beginning to get worried.

"A baby," Shurleen cooed. "Where did you find that?"

"He's the sole survivor of a bandit's ambush of a very poor merchant's caravan," Volo explained. "See how his hair is tied back into a knot. He is probably the son of the samurai who tried to defend the caravan and wound up giving up his life. We found his body back there, too."

"What are we going to do with him?" Curtis inquired.

"He's precious," Shurleen cooed, taking the child into her arms. "Look, he even has some toys tied to his belt."

"Those aren't toys," Volo replied. "They're throwing stars. Very pretty, but also very deadly."

"Sounds like a few women I know," Curtis jibed.

"Me, too," Passepout agreed, "present company excluded, of course."

"What will we do with this little angel?" Shurleen inquired.

A new voice joined the conversation, one that

was very old and dry, with a touch of the whimsical.

"He must be brought to the school for warriors on the Isles of Wa off the coast of the Fouchu Peninsula."

The four travelers turned toward the newcomer: a five-foot-one oriental man in a ragged kimono that seemed to be at least a hundred years old— and at that only half the age of its wearer. The parched skin that covered his head was bald save for five strands that drooped across his weathered face, two in the place of eye brows, two in the place of a mustache, and one in the dead center of his chin acting as a poor excuse for a mandarin beard.

"Who are you?" Volo asked, coming forward, mindful that rarely were those who appeared so unthreatening really as they seemed.

"Gracious travelers," the old man replied, "I am Chiun de Lao, last surviving adult of the caravan whose remnant you have seen around the ridge. It is I who hid the child, which you now possess, so that I might go in search of help. As the gods would have it, help found us."

"What happened to the rest of your party?" Volo inquired.

"Slaughtered by bandits. Only the child and myself survived," Chiun answered. "The child's father was a brave warrior who gave his life protecting his son. It was his final wish that his son be sent to the Warriors' school that he himself attended."

"Well, we will be happy to allow you to travel with us until we reach a town where you will be able to book passage for yourself and the child," Volo offered.

"No," the old man insisted. "You must accompany us on this journey so that you might guard the child. His father was an honorable samurai of a dishonorable shogun, and assassins are lying in wait for us at every turn. His enemy will not rest until the legacy of this warrior who died defending our caravan has been erased from the world."

"Why didn't they kill the kid with the others?"

"Father hid son," Chiun replied. "When father was killed, bandits assumed like father like son. Their patron will be very angry."

"I guess it's hard to find good help these days," Passepout offered, taking a moment to noticeably glare over at Curtis.

"How did you survive their attack?" Volo inquired.

"I was away from the others when the attack came," the old coot replied. "I had to relieve myself, and such things take time."

"I see," answered Volo, not wishing to hear any further details on the matter. "Well, once we arrive at a sizeable town, I am sure that you will be able to hire sufficient protection for your journey. If not a powerful ward, perhaps a mercenary who happens to be heading your way."

"Mad Monkey say, 'You don't loan a wolf a cub if protection is what you want,'" replied Chiun.

"What?" replied the befuddled Passepout.

"Mad Monkey also say, 'The young should pay attention to the elderly so as not to tire them out by making them repeat what they have already said,'" replied the old man, then insisting, "you must take the child to the Isles of Wa."

Volo fingered his beard, partly in amusement at the old man, partly to evaluate the situation at hand.

"I think we will have to talk about this among ourselves before we come to a decision, Mister

Lao," Volo said finally.

"Chiun," the old man corrected. "You may call me Chiun."

"Would you mind holding the child while we discuss this?" Volo asked, indicating to Shurleen to hand the babe to the old man.

"No," he replied. "No can do. My arms are old and frail, and my skin ravaged by the diseases of age. A child as pure as this must not be placed in the arms of the incompetent. Mad Monkey say . . . "

"No," interrupted Volo, holding his hand in a symbolic gesture to halt the onrush of epithets, "that will be fine."

"Chiun will fetch his staff from the caravan while you talk among yourselves," replied the old coot, who proceeded to scramble around the ridge with greater ease than either Passepout or even Volo had been able to manage.

Volo motioned for the rest of the party to draw close together to discuss the matter at hand while they were alone save for the child.

"Well, what should we do?" Volo asked to no one in particular. "We can't abandon either the child or Chiun. There are bandits and other dangers around, and if there are assassins lying in wait for this child, all the more reason to get it to a safe haven like that school on the Islands of Wa."

"It's not like we had another destination in mind," Passepout offered, "but who will take care of the child?"

"Why, Shurleen, of course," Curtis proclaimed. "Child care is women's work."

"How dare you talk to me like that?" Shurleen protested, coincidentally without giving up the child, who had fallen asleep in her arms. "Woman's work, indeed."

"It's not like you've ever done any work or anything," Curtis sniped, throwing fuel on the fiery rage of their female companion.

"Why, you . . . " she sputtered.

"I think you'd make a *wonderful* mother," Passepout offered, trying to calm her down, though his comment fell on deaf ears.

"That's enough from all of you," Volo commanded, taking control of the situation. "Since no one seems to have another plan in mind, it's now settled. We will escort the child and Chiun to the Isles of Wa, and we will all take turns tending to the child."

"Thank you," replied Chiun, who appeared behind them, having fetched his staff from the caravan, and rejoined the group at just the right moment. "Mad Monkey will bless you all."

"By the way," Passepout inquired, "who is this Mad Monkey that you always quote?"

"Oh," explained Chiun, "Mad Monkey is a powerful demigod and free spirit who protects those who follow his school of martial arts, such as the one located on the Isles of Wa which will be our destination. He is also the author of many pithy epigraphs."

"Like what?" the chubby thespian inquired.

"Man who have yen for success in baking business may have to amass a fortune in cookies. Too tight a top knot tangles many a comb. Man who forsake the fire of cookery to eat raw fish may find himself with flames in his bowels and belly. Dwarf who enlists in the army of titans often comes up short. Dragon who . . . "

"Enough," the thespian interrupted. "I get the idea."

"Some are quite funny," Chiun concluded, "but

all are insightful."

"Uh, right," Volo replied, trying to get the show back on the road. "Chiun, why don't you ride with Curtis?"

"You are most kind," the old man replied.

"Uh, yes," Volo continued, "and Shurleen, would you mind taking the first shift in child care?"

"No problem," she replied agreeably, the addition of the child having a wonderful effect on her disposition. "I can feed him as we ride."

"We can do it together," Passepout offered.

"I pity the poor horse if you do," Curtis sniped.

Passepout was about to retort with a full measure of vitriol, when Shurleen intervened.

"No, that's all right," she offered. "I'm sure I can manage on my own . . . but thank you for offering," and with another bat of her long lashes, she returned her attention from the chubby thespian to the child.

Passepout helped her mount her horse with the child in her arms and rejoined Volo, who was holding the reins of his steed for him.

"You see," the chubby thespian insisted, "I told you she likes me."

Volo turned away so that no one could see him rolling his eyes, and turned his steed toward the one bearing Curtis and Chiun.

"Well, Chiun," he inquired, "where do we go from here?"

"To the sea," he replied, then adding, "thataway."

They journeyed at a varied pace to accommodate the needs of the child and the bowels of the old man, whose age and diet had left him with little self-control, particularly after a long day of horseback riding.

If one was to believe Chiun, Mad Monkey was indeed smiling on them, as it never rained when they couldn't find shelter, nor did they ever run out of food when generous farmers weren't around to restock their supplies.

Their paths did not cross with bandits, or other disagreeable sorts, and in relatively no time they arrived at the shore.

From there they traveled south to the first available harbor where they could trade their horses for a boat to take them to the Isles of Wa.

They finally came to rest at a harbor inn called the No Bull House. It was run by an old sailor from the Moonshaes by the name of Blackthumb, who agreed to put them up for the night and introduce them to a dealer with whom they could trade their horses for a boat on the following day.

After an unusual but tasty meal of seaweed salad and Moonshae stew à la Shou Lung, prepared by the innkeeper's wife from her own recipe, and all washed down by several flagons of imported Moonshae ale, the inn was closed for the night. The travelers were escorted to a common room equipped with enough beds for the entire party, where they settled in for the night.

All had grown quiet, and the travelers were on the verge of a peaceful night's rest when the silence was shattered by an ear-splitting cry.

"Waaaaaaaaaaa!"

The child, who had fallen asleep while the rest of the group was still finishing dinner, had awakened and was making its presence known.

"This is just great," Passepout grumbled. "My first night in an inn in I don't know how long, and I have to be on baby duty."

Passepout swung his legs over the side of the

bed, wiped the sleep from his eyes, and was about to go to the makeshift crib that housed the crying infant when he noticed four shadowy figures in the room with them.

"Hey, who are you?" he shouted loud enough to wake the whole inn.

A flash of steel was barely glimpsed in the candlelit room. A katana was removed from its scabbard and brought in a sweeping arc toward the unprotected neck of the chubby thespian.

*Craaaaaak!*

The chubby thespian fell to the floor as the side of the bed upon which he had been lying caved in from the unbalanced strain of his tarrying too long while sitting on its edge.

The katana's blade embedded itself in the now off-kilter bedpost that came crashing to hit the foundering thespian on the bed, barely deflecting the blade from its lethal course.

Blackthumb appeared at the door, torch in hand, illuminating the intruders. They were dressed in black from head to toe, with only a slit in their masks to reveal eyes of elven gray. By this time, all had drawn their swords and were choosing their targets.

"Assassins!" Blackthumb yelled, cudgeling the closest one with his shillelagh of Moonshae briar.

Silent except for the whistling and whooshing of displaced air, the masked intruders sprang into action.

Shurleen screamed and threw herself on top of the makeshift crib, intending to protect the child, only to find that it was no longer there.

"The baby!" she cried. "He's gone!"

"No, he isn't," Curtis called, having thrown himself on the child, who had managed to climb out of the crib and crawl toward the beachcomber's bed.

Volo threw his trusty dagger, catching one of the approaching assassins squarely between the eyes.

Curtis dispatched another with remarkable accuracy, using the throwing stars that the child still carried.

The fourth assassin, who also had set his sights on the crib, was about to skewer the shaken Shurleen, when Passepout, having only partially recovered his equilibrium from the fall, came lumbering into him, throwing him off-balance and succeeding in delaying his recovery long enough for Shurleen to stab him with his own sword. She and the thespian were doused with a spray of bloody gore from the newly opened hole in the assassin's chest.

The entire battle had lasted less than a minute.

Volo undid the black hood from the assassin nearest him, the one who had been cudgeled by Blackthumb, to reveal its oriental elven facial features.

"Well," said Passepout, regaining his balance, "that was easy enough!"

As if on cue, the assassins began to stand up, ready to resume their attack.

"It can't be!" Shurleen screamed.

"Undead elven ninja assassins," Blackthumb exclaimed. "Recently raised from the dead, I might add."

Slower this time, as the element of surprise was gone and counterattacks realized to be ultimately futile, the assassins regrouped, and prepared to resume their business, quickly and efficiently.

The smell of corruption, decay, and death pervaded the room, and the way to the door was clearly blocked by the assassins.

There was no escape, and everyone knew it.

*"Rots ah Ruck!"*

Chiun had appeared at the doorway, once again having evidently left the room prior to the attack in order to relieve himself, and, with trusty staff raised, was now invoking some ancient incantation.

*"Nough tee que knoe shur tay!"*

The ninjas immediately burst into flame, incinerating to dust in seconds without harming anyone in the room or even singeing the floor upon which they were standing.

"Nice work, Chiun," Curtis complimented.

The old coot bowed. "Mad Monkey say, 'Sending undead assassins to do a man's work is cheating.'" Chiun replied.

"I take it you are a priest of this Mad Monkey," Volo responded, taking a moment to give the frail old man a gentle pat on the back.

"You might say that," Chiun replied, "but now I must sleep if you will be so kind. 'Mad Monkey say, 'Early to bed, early to rise . . .'"

"'. . . makes a man healthy, wealthy, and wise,'" Blackthumb completed.

Chiun was taken aback for a moment.

"Are you a disciple of Mad Monkey?" he queried.

"No," the innkeeper replied, "just here to defend my guests, and clean up after messy attacks."

"Mad Monkey say, 'Good innkeepers are hard to find.'"

With bare minimal rearranging, the room was restored, and the innkeeper and the travelers once again prepared themselves for bed.

Volo, Chiun, Blackthumb, and Curtis had once again turned in for the night, and the child was soundly sleeping back in his makeshift crib.

Shurleen had decided to clean herself up after the bloody attack, while Passepout had decided that a few more flagons of Moonshae ale was in order to steady his nerves after the evening's excitement. After a while, Shurleen returned to the room.

"Hi," she greeted, sitting next to the portly thespian. "Mind if I sit here?"

"Not at all," he sputtered, his eyes consumed by the wonderments that lay beneath the new silken kimono that Blackthumb's wife had lent her.

"My hero," she purred. "You saved me from that horrible assassin."

"Nothing to it," the proud Passepout replied, trying to regain his self-control by taking another drink. "Nothing any other full-fledged hero wouldn't do."

The tavern room in which they were sitting was almost silent. Only the sounds of Volo's snoring from the adjoining common room disturbed the peace.

"I'm glad we have this chance to be alone," she pressed.

"So am I ," he replied, trying to tear his eyes away from her physical charms.

"You're not really an actor, are you?" she queried.

Passepout was dumbstruck. "What do you mean?" he replied, regaining control of his words and his eyes.

"Well, I've never known a rich actor," she replied, "and you are obviously rich. Not that I mind, of course."

She pressed herself closer to him, and the chubby thespian felt peculiarly uncomfortable.

"Why do you think I'm rich?" he inquired, surprised to find himself drawing back from her overt advances.

"Well, you're also rather careless," she replied. "You seem to have been dropping these rubies all along the way since you rescued me. I only really noticed since the site of the caravan attack. Here."

In her hand were clearly a half-dozen of the necromancer's gems.

# THE WAY TO WA
# AND BEYOND

## OR

### Mad Monkey's School for Boys

Passepout was shocked, scared, and panicked all at once, and at any moment expected something horrible to happen. He put his hands up to cover his face and cried, "No!"

"Now, don't be silly," Shurleen cooed. "You see that I'm giving them back to you. After all, no matter how rich you are, rubies aren't just something that you want to throw away. Right?"

"No!" Passepout cried, now shaking his head from side to side, his hands still covering his face.

"That's what I thought," replied Shurleen, oblivious to the rotund thespian's panic. "So why don't you put these gems back in your pretty little pouch, and then you and I can get to know each other a little better."

"No!" he repeated, once again, his eyes now darting to the inn's door, expecting at any moment for some purveyor of doom to make his entrance.

"Don't be shy," she purred. "I really like actors, especially rich ones. So just give me your hand, and leave the riding to Shurleen."

Passepout's sputtering and Shurleen's purring were just then interrupted by a voice emanating from the previously silent darkness.

"Excuse, please," Chiun announced, now illuminated by the tavern table's candlelight. "Did not mean to interrupt. I am only on my way to the outhouse."

Chiun stopped by the table, where Shurleen was almost on Passepout's lap, the gems that had previously been in her hand now spread on the table to allow her fingers to attend to other matters. He looked down at the red gems that were causing Passepout his grief, and passed his hand over them, saying, "Oh, necromancer's gem. All go away."

The gems disappeared from the table as if they had just faded into thin air.

Chiun then continued on to his elected duty.

"Stop him!" Shurleen replied. "He's taken the gems."

Chiun popped his head back in for a moment, replying, "Gems now back where they belong," and ducked back out again.

"It's for the best," Passepout replied, still uneasy about the whole thing but relieved to be rid of them once again.

"But what about the gems?" she insisted, growing agitated at the thespian's immediate acceptance of the old man's actions.

"They're not important," Passepout replied, trying to steer the conversation back in the direction he thought she had been going. "You were saying something about us getting to know each other."

"You're crazy," she said, pushing him away. "That was probably a fortune in rubies."

"But they're not important," he persisted. "We ..."

"Get this straight, mister," Shurleen corrected. "Now, there is no 'we.' An actor, okay, I can accept that. Fat, you can lose weight, I accept that. But someone who is crazy and throws away a fortune in gems, that I cannot accept. I am going back to bed. Alone!"

"Shurleen," Passepout begged, as she left the tavern room for a room next door.

"Let her go." Chiun, who had miraculously just materialized, stood at the thespian's side. "She is more interested in the gems than in your happiness."

"I guess you're right," Passepout answered dolefully. "I guess heiresses are like all other women."

"You speak the truth," Chiun replied, patting the thespian on the back, as Volo had done to him earlier in the evening, "but maybe not as you see it now."

"Wait a minute," Passepout replied. "How did you know that they were necromancer gems?"

"Chiun knows many things," Chiun explained, "and since you didn't touch them after you discarded them you have nothing to worry about. It is as you left them. They are back along the path upon which you dropped them."

"How did you do it?"

"Priest of Mad Monkey know many things, especially how to undo that which someone else has done," he replied.

"Can you remove the spell that has bonded Volo and myself together, or at least remove the bond that exists between us and the gems?"

"No can do," Chiun replied. "Spells are tricky as are magical gems. It is much easier to just put things back in their proper place. Nothing is changed except for the location."

Passepout just shook his head, not really comprehending what he had just heard.

"Now back to bed," Chiun instructed.

The frail old priest helped the slightly inebriated and more than slightly depressed thespian next door, and back to his mattress on the floor, the repairs on the damaged bed having to wait for morning.

The events of the previous evening and the resultant surprises created an invisible bond between the travelers, with the sole exception of an apparent glacial rift between Shurleen and Passepout.

Blackthumb reminisced over breakfast with tales of his mercenary adventures in the marine trade. There was much mutual patting on the back, and a newfound respect for the ancient priest of Mad Monkey who suffered from irregular bowels.

Volo took Passepout aside and inquired after the cause of his depression.

The thespian was torn. He didn't want the group

to know of the ineptitude with which he handled Shurleen, for that would surely ruin his all-important reputation as a lady's man, while at the same time he felt a certain obligation to tell Volo of the incident involving the gems, and Chiun's remedy for the problem.

In the end, Passepout only confessed to a Moonshae ale hangover, and Volo accepted it at face value.

After breakfast was over, Blackthumb led the group to a harborside establishment where they could trade their horses for a boat that would take them to the Isles of Wa. According to the innkeeper, Pan's Sampans was the most honest establishment in the area, and the owner was a good friend of his.

"Fellow travelers of Faerûn," Blackthumb introduced, "I'd like you to meet my good friend Tai, the most honest shipbuilder on the Celestial Sea."

The honorable shipbuilder bowed graciously, and, in a very Western manner undoubtedly influenced by Blackthumb's company, proclaimed, "Okay, guys. What do you wanna buy, and what do you have to sell?"

Chiun leaped to the front of the conversation.

"We want the best junk available to take us to the Isles of Wa," the old priest proclaimed, "and in exchange we will trade you the four finest steeds from all of Taan."

Tai examined the horses one at a time, scowled, and acted as if he weren't interested in the deal. "Gee, I don't know," the shipbuilder considered out loud. "I know that you're friends of Blackthumb and all, but if you ask me, these horses aren't even worth the price of a dinghy."

Chiun responded.

"Mad Monkey say, 'Honesty is the best policy' and 'A fair deal is a square deal.' "

"I guess you're right," Tai agreed. "You just bought yourself a junk."

Passepout whispered to Volo, "What do we need a junk for?"

Volo answered, "To bring us to the Isles of Wa. A junk is an oriental sailing ship."

"Oh, great," the chubby thespian responded, hoping that the cleric's cure for motion sickness was still in effect.

Though overtly rickety and obviously in need of a good coat of paint, the junk that Tai provided was more than suitable for the next leg of their journey eastward, with ample room under cover as protection against the spray of the surf.

Shurleen's iciness toward Passepout continued. Upon seeing him once again discard a red gem into the depths of the Celestial Sea, she began to rant publicly. "Do you believe that half-wit?" she fumed.

Passepout tried to ignore her, turning his attention to their young charge, who was badly in need of a change of diapers.

"Why don't you leave the guy alone?" Curtis scolded. "It's not like he's ever treated you like anything less than a queen."

"Position in society has its privileges," she countered. "Royal treatment is no less than I deserve after the way I've been treated."

"I'm sick of your wining, your complaints, and your insults," Curtis responded. "A simple thank you to us for rescuing you from the Horde, let alone to him for saving your life last night would be a pleasant change."

"How dare you!" she sputtered.

"Yes," he agreed, "how dare I!"

Curtis turned his back on Shurleen and took a seat by the chubby thespian. He proceeded to apologize for his unkind remarks of the past and to compliment Passepout on his bravery of the night before. Shurleen turned her back on the two, and fumed to the waves.

Chiun was standing by Volo at the junk's helm, the Isles of Wa just coming into view.

"Chiun, last night you said something about 'sending undead elven assassins to do a man's work is cheating,'" Volo commented.

"Yes," Chiun responded. "Elves are not native to Kara-Tur. Training them as ninjas is abhorrent. Involving them in Kara-Tur affairs is even worse."

"Who is involving them in Kara-Tur affairs, and how?"

"The corrupt shogun who desires the child dead has a patron who goes by the name of Dragon Claw, who is in reality a petty fiend. He is the arch nemesis of Mad Monkey, and the one responsible for the cheating."

"Why are he and Mad Monkey at odds?"

"Many years ago they fought a contest of fighting styles. Mad Monkey won, and an agreement was reached whereby the Mad Monkey school on the Isles of Wa would be considered a sanctuary for those wishing acceptance."

"I see," said Volo, fingering his beard.

"There are rules, of course," Chiun said, adding pointedly, "not unlike the ones you must follow in your eastward journey."

"Rules?" Volo asked innocently. "Us?"

"Requirements such as the dropping of the necromancer's gems along the way while never retracing your steps."

Volo was taken aback. "Did Passepout tell you about this?" the master traveler inquired.

"No," Chiun replied. "I saw the gems in his possession, and recognized them."

Volo was still slightly uneasy.

"Don't worry," Chiun explained. "Mad Monkey will watch out for you."

Volo was still unsure and wanted to pursue his inquiry when the old priest pointed to the largest isle.

"There is the harbor for the school. It is our destination. The place where the child will be safe."

The junk made port at an unattended dock, as per Chiun's instructions.

"You must take the child to the school at the end of the path," he instructed.

Curtis asked, "Won't you be going with us?"

Chiun shook his head, and said, "Mad Monkey say 'The needs of the young may precede the concerns of the elderly.' I will meet you there later." The old man then set off down a different path along the shore.

"Well," Volo instructed, "no time like the present to get things started. The sooner we get the kid to the school, the sooner the kid's safety will be assured."

"Mad Monkey say," Passepout jibed, " 'can't we have lunch first?' "

The entire group groaned, ignored the suggestion, and headed down the path.

After an hour's walk along the carefully slated path, the Mad Monkey school began to appear in the distance.

"Looks like we've got this kid home free!" Shurleen declared, nuzzling her charge and beginning to miss him already.

A sulphurous explosion erupted before them, blocking their path.

When the smoke cleared, they were standing face-to-face with the dreaded fiend Dragon Claw.

Dragon Claw was repulsive—fatter than Passepout, covered in scales, with the head of a dragon, and four arms, each ending in a tightly gripped hooked sword, which was the signature weapon of his school of fighting.

The scent of fire, sulphur, and brimstone was heavy in the air. The fiend let loose with four fireballs as a show of force. Each one exploded right before the travelers, leaving a scorch mark at their feet.

"Give the child to me!" the Dragon Claw demanded.

"No!" Shurleen screamed. "Over my dead body!"

"No," cried the fiend with a laugh, "that comes later, for all of you."

Dragon Claw began to bear down on the group, swords slicing through the air with lightning speed as the fiend showed off his skill before going in for the kill.

"Hey," cried a familiar but frail voice, "over here, you pustule on the Celestial Bureaucracy's rear."

Chiun had appeared, once again seemingly out of nowhere, to challenge the demon.

Chiun raised his staff, and declared, "The son of the samurai has achieved sanctuary. You can harm him no longer."

Dragon Claw laughed at the frail mortal.

"The son of the samurai will be my appetizer. You will be my supper," the fiend replied.

"You have violated the terms of our agreement by interfering with the quest of these mortals.

Their bravery has saved them, even after your otherworldly interference has threatened them. The child will receive sanctuary, and the travelers will have their journey vouchsafed."

Dragon Claw continued to laugh and crow, bolts of fire and lightning framing his awe-inspiring figure.

"I have made no agreements with mortals," the fiend replied.

"I am not mortal," Chiun replied, and with a flash of blue light, the old coot became transformed into his demigod form, even more awe-inspiring than that of Dragon Claw. "I am Mad Monkey!"

Dragon Claw growled, smoke emanating from its ears. Quickly the growl turned into a roar and the smoke into flames of purple fire. Like an onrushing dragon, the fiend let loose a bellow of sulphurous gas and sprang at the demigod.

Raising his staff, which was also revealed now as *the iron bar of power*, the demigod struck the lesser fiend across its infernal countenance, knocking it out and allowing the travelers to pass with the child.

Carefully the travelers stepped around the prostrate body of the denizen of the abyss, their nostrils assaulted by the noxious fumes that emanated from its unconscious form.

On the other side of the brush behind the petty fiend was the door to the school. As the group approached, several priests came out, and took the child from the hands of Shurleen; without saying a word, they carried it into the inner sanctum of the school.

"Wait," Shurleen called. "I just wanted to say good-bye."

The demigod Mad Monkey reappeared at their side.

"They do not understand you," the demigod explained. "Common is not spoken here. It is only because I am part of the Celestial Bureaucracy that I have been able to communicate with you."

"I should have known that," Volo volunteered.

"You had other things on your mind," the demigod offered. "Though I am prohibited from transporting untried acolytes to my school, I am allowed to assist them, provided they prove themselves worthy, as indeed you have."

Mad Monkey continued his proclamation.

"The child will be safe. He will be trained as a samurai, and his father's legacy will be secured. He will not be allowed to leave the sanctuary of this citadel until he is able to protect himself. You who are not disciples of Mad Monkey cannot receive the sanctuary of my school."

"Great," Curtis replied unenthusiastically.

"Dragon Claw will awake soon. He will be angry, and though he cannot hurt Mad Monkey or his disciples, he can hurt you," the demigod confessed.

"*Wonderful,*" Passepout remarked, thinking about just what else could go wrong at this point.

"I cannot protect you from him," the demigod explained, "but I can see that you are safely escorted from the lands in which he dwells before he awakens. I could offer you a shortcut to the east, you might say."

Mad Monkey gave Volo and Passepout a wink, overlooked by the others, to assure the two travelers that he realized the needs of their arrangements. Then with a wave of his staff, the demigod opened a hole in the fabric of reality that was the Isles of Wa.

"Go quickly," the demigod instructed, "and follow the path that lies ahead of you. Observe whatever you want along the way, but stop to talk to no one except each other. There will be a light at the far end. Go to it."

"Where will that be?" Volo asked.

"A place farther east," the demigod replied. "Now go! Time is short. Already that petty fiend Dragon Claw is drifting into consciousness."

One by one, the travelers entered the pitch-black portal until only Passepout remained with Mad Monkey.

The chubby thespian hesitated.

"You are braver than you believe," the demigod encouraged.

"Is this shortcut dangerous?" Passepout asked.

"Of course not," the demigod replied, giving the heavyset thespian a push that sent him hurtling through the portal. "It is only through the land of the dead."

The last thing Passepout heard before the darkness enveloped him was the laughter of the demigod known as Mad Monkey.

Then all went black.

# THE PORTAL TO THE EAST

OR

## A Shortcut Through
the Land of the Dead

"Well, it's about time," Shurleen reproved. "What took you so long?"

"I had to say good-bye to our most gracious host," Passepout responded, brushing past her to take his place at Volo's side.

"Well, if that's all of us," Volo observed, taking the lead, "onward, then."

The four travelers started walking farther into

the darkness.

The darkness was of a strange quality. It was pitch black, as if one were buried alive, yet there seemed to be enough illumination so that they could see each other, as well as certain details of the passage around them.

The passage around them was also curious. At one point it seemed to be an infinite universe of darkness stretching out in all directions around the narrow path upon which they walked, dwarfing them in its infinity. At other times it seemed to close in on them as if it were a mine or a cave through some Underdark lair or mountain cavern, with the only space existing a hairbreadth above their heads and even less than that at their sides. It was both an agoraphobic's and a claustrophobic's nightmare at the same time.

Though none of the party had yet to see anything that might pose a threat, uneasiness pervaded their midst, a palpable fear of the unknown that seemed to be tightening its grip on them the farther they went.

"Remember," Volo reminded, "don't talk to anyone we come across."

"What is this place?" Shurleen asked, a none-too-slight tremor audible in her voice.

"Mad Monkey said it was the Land of the Dead," Passepout replied.

Shurleen shivered at the mention of the word "dead," and quickly grasped the hand of the person nearest her as a secondary reinforcement that she was not alone. Curtis looked down at his hand firmly grasped by the heiress, her lacquered nails reflecting the darkness while framed in the creamy whiteness of her pampered hands. His urge to pull away was overridden by his sense of the needs of his companion, no matter how disagreeable she could be.

Gradually, parts of the passing landscape became clearer as they passed. Exotic beasts, horned beings, and mindless husks that once might have walked among the living seemed to pass them by as if they were unaware of the travelers' presence.

"Who are they?" Shurleen whispered.

"Beings with whom we do not wish to speak," Curtis succinctly replied, urging her to move faster so their group would not become more stretched out.

After what seemed like hours of treading through the darkness, the group decided to rest for a few minutes to catch their breath.

"Mad Monkey didn't say anything about not stopping along the way, did he?" Volo queried of the rotund thespian.

"No," Passepout replied. "Stopping seemed to be all right as long as we didn't talk to anyone. I even remember he said we could observe what we wanted, though, quite frankly, I really haven't seen anything worth writing home about."

"Let's hope it stays that way," Curtis interjected. "I prefer boring and dull to dangerous and deadly any day."

"I wouldn't call the walking dead and fiends of the underworld boring and dull," Shurleen argued, without relinquishing her grip on Curtis's hand.

"Hey, if they don't bother us, we won't bother them, and that's fine by me," Curtis replied, beginning to enjoy the feeling of feminine digits between his rough-skinned fingers, calloused by the bristles of splintering ropes and abrasive surfaces.

Passepout saw a rocky, mushroomlike growth off to the side which he thought would make a good seat to rest his weary bulk, and decided to remove himself from the group to take advantage of it.

*Eo, that feels good,* Passepout thought, his thoughts beginning to drift as his body began to relax.

"Hi! Remember me?" a voice purred.

There, now sitting next to him, was the inviting figure of Shurleen dressed as she had been that night at the No Bull House, silken kimono open almost to the waist, her hair freshly scented with lotus blossom shampoo.

"I want you!" the voice purred.

Once again Passepout was at a loss for words, his desires and fragile ego riding a runaway mining car down a steep-sloped tunnel.

"Now!" the voice demanded.

"Hey, Passepout, time to get the lead out. We'd be burning daylight if there were any light to be had," called the voice of the master traveler.

Passepout was pulled back, jerking his head back toward Volo's voice. The rest of the group had taken to their feet and were preparing to leave . . . Shurleen included, now attired in the traveling clothes he seemed to recall she had been wearing when they entered the portal.

*But if she's over there, then who's over here?* the chubby thespian thought. He turned his head back to the source of the amorous purring, but nothing was there now, not even the lingering scent of lotus blossom shampoo.

Passepout got to his feet and rejoined the group.

*Oh, well,* he thought to himself, *at least I didn't talk to her. That would probably have been a bad thing. I think I'll stick to the path with the others from now on.*

With a quick glance back at where he had been

sitting, a quick thought of regret at what might have been, followed by a quick thought of terror at what *really* might have been, he proceeded with the others down the path.

"You know," Passepout declared, "I think it's probably a good idea for us to stay on the path, and not wander too far to the sides, and, above all, remember not to talk to strangers."

"Good advice, well said," Volo agreed, wondering what had instigated the advisory recap from the young thespian, but then quickly returning to the matters at hand.

"Onward," he urged. "Mad Monkey assured us that there would be a light at the end of this tunnel. We just haven't reached it yet."

"And remember," Passepout interrupted, once again with a warning tone, "sometimes the darkness plays tricks on the mind. There's no telling what you might see—or at least think you see."

Volo did a double take at his overly cautious companion, shook his head, and pressed on.

The path began to wind more, and the sights became more bizarre. They saw an ashen tapestry of what appeared to be crying mouths, hanging from a spear, frozen in mid-decay as if to have been preserved at precisely the moment before total disintegration occurred. Maniacal laughter could be heard from the shadows, though the source of the jocularity was noticeably absent.

Farther on, they came upon a rubbled site, as if an entire palace had been destroyed. The wreckage from the site seemed to have been made of bone and human flesh, both now reduced to shards and tatters.

"The bone palace of Cyric has been destroyed," Volo whispered. "There were rumors of this among the Lords of Waterdeep and the College of War Wizards, but I never thought I would ever actually see it, at least not while I was still alive."

"Wasn't Cyric the God of Strife and Lord of the Dead?" Curtis asked. "Who could have done this?"

"Even the mad Prince of Lies himself has powerful enemies," Volo replied.

Much farther down the winding path, Volo halted the group.

"Listen!" he whispered urgently.

A steady murmuring of a single monotonous voice could be heard in the distance.

*The truth is there.*

*They will understand it.*

*Am I not the true King of the Dead?*

*It must be true.*

The Cyrinishad *said so.*

*Yes.*

*Yes.*

"Who is that?" Shurleen whispered.

"The Prince of Lies himself probably; we must avert our eyes so as to not be taken in by his trickery," Volo instructed.

The travelers hooded their eyes with their hands, focusing only on the next step in front of them.

Only Passepout dared to look up for a fraction of a second, but common sense intervened, and he quickly rehooded his eyes. Concentrating as he walked, he vaguely remembered a glimpse of some underworld castle but couldn't really remember if it was a tower, a pyramid, or a mansion of bone, and despite the murmuring, no one seemed to be home.

*Am I curious enough to look back?* he thought, then quickly dismissed the idea. Even if he was as brave as Mad Monkey seemed to think, bravery alone was a silly justification for foolhardiness.

In the distance behind them, they could hear a new ream of maniacal laughter.

They pressed on down the path faster, hoping that a light would soon appear in the distance.

At last a glimmer of sunlight seemed to be emanating from a crack in the darkness in the distance.

"There," Volo declared. "That must be the way out."

"Just like he promised," Passepout agreed. "And no harm has come to us since we stayed on the path and kept to ourselves."

"I'll be glad when we're out of here," Curtis confessed. "I can't wait to feel daylight again."

Though the crack of light was still a good distance away, their journey toward it, now that it was visible, passed quickly. Along the way, they could barely make out the gleam of lights reflected off shiny faceted surfaces. As they drew closer to the shaft of light that was their exit, the surfaces became more distinguishable, revealing that the tunnel surface that seemed to surround them was entirely composed of loose gems of indefinable value.

"Maybe we should pick up a souvenir, sort of a very valuable keepsake," Curtis suggested. "It's not like there are any armed guards around or anything."

"I wouldn't do that," Volo advised. "I remember the story of a mortal who, like ourselves, was granted a trip through the nether realms. She was warned to eat nothing, talk to no one, and stay on the path. She stuck to the rules with one exception

—she ate three pomegranate seeds. When it came time to leave, her way out was blocked by an invisible wall. No one ever heard of her again."

"That sounds like a fairy tale," Shurleen scoffed, "and besides, Mad Monkey didn't say we couldn't pick something up along the way."

"Mad Monkey didn't say a lot of things," Volo replied, "and I don't think he felt compelled to tell us not to steal, if you know what I mean."

"Oh, phoo!" Shurleen complained. "Let's just get out of here."

The four travelers hurried to the crack of light that was the passage back to the surface world.

"Ladies before gentlemen," Volo offered, giving a mock bow, and indicating that Shurleen could go first.

"It's about time," she answered, about to barge through the crack.

"Wait a minute," Passepout interrupted, blocking her way. "I don't think letting her go first is such a good idea." The chubby thespian had just recalled his own close encounter with a beholder on the other side of the Myth Drannor portal.

"What do you mean?" the spoiled heiress demanded.

"Who knows what is on the other side? Mad Monkey only guaranteed us safe passage. He didn't mention anything about safe arrival," Passepout replied.

"Passepout is right," Curtis agreed. "Who knows what could be lurking out there? I'll go first."

"Agreed," said Volo, making way for Curtis to pass.

Curtis stepped forward into the light and seemed to disappear.

"All clear," he yelled, seemingly from afar. "Nothing here except a dark-skinned halfling, and he seems to be agreeable enough."

"Satisfied?" Shurleen asked sarcastically.

"Next," Volo instructed, indicating for her to pass.

Shurleen barged forward into the light but wasn't able to pass through.

"It's closed," she screamed in a panic, backing away from the light. "I can't get through."

"Empty your pockets," Volo instructed.

"Why?" She pouted.

"Just do it!" the master traveler demanded, growing very impatient.

Shurleen turned out her pockets.

They were empty.

"Let me see your hands," Volo demanded.

"Why?" she protested, hiding her palms.

Faster than a pickpocket at the Westgate fair, Volo grabbed her wrist and turned her hand over, revealing the palm of her hand.

A red ruby seemed to be stuck to it.

"It won't come off," she protested. "I picked it up back at the ruined castle, and it sort of got stuck to my hand. Now it won't come off."

"Maybe there is some truth to that fairy tale," Volo remarked.

The gravity of her situation dawned on her.

"No," she cried. "I can't stay here. What about Dragon Claw? What about Cyric? You can't just leave me here."

Volo was troubled. Though she was no picnic in the Dales, and a regular pain in the South, he knew he couldn't just leave her behind in the netherworld. He also noticed that since Curtis had passed into the light, the portal had indeed become smaller, and was shrinking as he watched.

"Let me try again?" she pleaded.

"It won't work," Volo replied, frantically fingering his beard.

"Wait!" Passepout exclaimed. "I have an idea!"

The chubby thespian looked into his pouch, smiled, and pulled out one of the necromancer's gems that had just turned red.

"Let's see if the guards of this portal, or whatever is holding her back, will take a substitute," Passepout said, lobbing the necromancer's gem back the way they came.

The gem bounced twice, and then proceeded to roll away from them.

"Now try," Passepout instructed.

"Hurry!" Volo urged.

Shurleen rushed forward and passed to the other side.

"Good thinking," Volo complimented, "now quickly, the portal is closing."

The two travelers rushed forward into the light, the portal closing behind them.

When their eyes had adjusted to the new infusion of sunlight, they noticed that they were standing on a sandy mountainside. The heat was oppressive, and the terrain was rocky.

Blinking his eyes, and then squinting until he could see clearly, Volo noticed the halfling that Curtis had been talking about, who had now been joined by a man of normal height.

"Look boss," the halfling told the man, who was apparently his master. "The planes . . . they are visitors from the planes."

The man strode forward, and said, "My friends, welcome to Maztica."

# THE LAND ACROSS THE SEA

## OR

## Viva Maztica!

"Maztica," Volo repeated.

"Yeah," Curtis interjected, "that's what the man said."

"Somehow I didn't think we were in Kara-Tur anymore," Passepout added.

"Maztica?" Shurleen repeated the place's name, though this time as a question. "Where is Maztica?"

"It's on the whole other side of the world," Volo explained. "It's on the other side of the Trackless

Sea, farther than fabled Evermeet. It was colonized a few years ago by conquerors and settlers from the Empire of the Sands and the island kingdom of Lantan."

"I see you have heard of our fair land," the man who welcomed them replied in impeccable Common.

"And you are originally from Faerûn, the Empire of the Sands, I would guess," Volo continued. "A former soldier, I would say, though apparently one who hasn't seen much action or physical work in the last year or so."

"You are a most excellent master of the powers of observation," the man replied. "What is your name?"

"I am Volothamp Geddarm, master traveler of all Toril," Volo announced proudly.

"I have heard of you," the man replied, "and your guides, but surely you are not writing one on the continent of Maztica."

Volo chose his worlds carefully.

"No, not at the present time, though I'm sure I will get around to it one of these days. At the present time, I and my friends are engaged on a world tour, you might say," Volo explained. "We sort of made a wrong turn in Kara-Tur, passed through a portal, and came out here."

"Uh-hum." Shurleen cleared her throat.

"Oh, I'm sorry," Volo apologized. "This is the lovely Shurleen Laduce Bleth."

"Charmed, I'm sure," Shurleen said to the handsome gentleman, offering him her hand.

He graciously accepted and kissed it. "The pleasure is mine," the man replied.

"And this is my good friend, Passepout," Volo continued.

"The thespian," Passepout clarified, "son of the famed thespians Catinflas and Idle."

"Honored," the man replied, giving the thespian a firm handshake.

"And our traveling companion, and jack of all trades, Curtis," Volo concluded the introductions.

"Curtis," the man repeated, with a faint nod of his head to the young beachcomber.

"And you are . . . ?" Curtis inquired, a trace of insolence in his voice.

"I am Rurk," the man replied. "The, um, governor of Phantasia. That is what we call this settlement."

"What settlement?" Curtis asked. "All I see is the edge of a desert and a rocky ridge."

"True, true," Rurk replied, "but beyond that ridge lies Phantasia, a land worthy of your wildest dreams. Come. You shall be my guests. Herve, run ahead, and tell the servants to ready the guest quarters."

"Yes, boss," the halfling replied, scurrying ahead through a pass in the rocky ridge.

"Herve is my right-hand halfling, you might say," Rurk explained. "Part interpreter, part manager, he helps me keep things running smoothly and minimizes the troubles with the natives."

"He is a native?" Volo asked.

"Well, yes and no," Rurk explained. "He is a native of Maztica, but from the lands north of here, where I first landed when I came here. He was hired at our camp to take care of certain menial duties and took quickly to the Common tongue. I hired him as my interpreter, and when duty called for me to come south, well, obviously he came along."

"I see," Volo replied. "What was the purpose of

your mission, coming south, I mean?"

"Questions, questions," Rurk replied, shaking his head in dismissal. "There is plenty of time for questions later. Even the loveliest desert flower will wilt if left in the sun too long, and I have no desire to subject Miss Bleth to such a risk. Follow me. It is only a short walk to my humble dwelling, where shade and refreshments await. We can continue our getting to know each other a little better later." Rurk then brushed off some seemingly imaginary trail dust from his perfectly tailored doublet of light, gauzy material, and offered his arm to Shurleen, saying, "Miss Bleth, if you will do me the honor."

"Charmed, I am sure," she replied, accepting his arm and falling into step beside him as he set off along the path that Herve had taken a few moments ago.

Volo looked to the others, and inquired, "Shall we?"

"Charmed, I'm sure," Curtis replied in a tone meant to mock Shurleen.

"You know, I can't put my finger on it, but there's something about that guy that I don't like," Passepout offered.

"I know," Volo replied, "but right now he's the only game in town."

The three fell into step and followed the route Rurk had taken.

The settlement known as Phantasia was little more than a few clusters of huts and hovels around a large estate manor house that Rurk referred to as the governor's palace. The natives of the area were of a darker color, similar to that of Herve the halfling, and were for the most part short, with muscular builds and intense black eyes.

As Rurk would pass, the natives would bow, saying, "Mis Ta Rurk," their tone highly respectful.

"That is what they call me," Rurk explained. "They once overheard Herve calling me mister, and they assumed that was my title. I've seen no reason to dissuade them."

Along the way to the mansion they also passed an arenalike structure composed of a playing field between two high parallel walls. They also passed several boiling works where fruit was distilled into a sort of wine juice, and where sap from nearby rubber trees was melted and molded into strips for weaving and tying. Several native women were in the process of weaving the strands into a hammock. The mansion itself had a Tethyrian flavor to its architecture: a large verandalike porch where several woven thrones had been placed, each framed by two servants, one holding a tray with a pitcher and a cup, the other holding a huge plumed fan.

"Here we are," Rurk announced. "Take a seat and be comfortable."

Rurk escorted Shurleen to the throne on the farthest right, and then seated himself immediately to her left. The others followed suit, Volo next to him, Passepout next, and Curtis on the end.

Curtis, however, did not remain seated long, and preferred to sip from his drink while walking back and forth on the porch, causing the servant holding the fan a great deal of difficulty. The servant continued to follow at a respectful distance but had to be close enough to still cool the guest of his master, Rurk.

Curtis quickly became frustrated at running into the plume fan every time he turned around, and finally said to the servant, "Will you just leave me alone?"

A look of mortal terror passed on the servant's face.

Rurk clapped his hands, and Herve appeared at his side. The two exchanged whispers, at which point Herve said something to the servant, who immediately responded with a relieved look and left the porch.

"There is no reason to be uncomfortable or nervous, Curtis," Rurk explained. "The servants are solely here for our comfort. And I *do* hope my guests are comfortable."

"Why, sure," Shurleen replied, having a peeled grape popped into her mouth.

"And we greatly appreciate your hospitality," Volo offered. "So how many are you?"

"Excuse me," Rurk replied, not quite sure about the question.

"Others from Faerûn in this settlement," Volo clarified, "in the province for which you are governor."

"Oh, I see," Rurk replied carefully. "I came down from the North with twenty of my best men. Ten are still here in similar accommodations along the ridge. The others fell victim to the hazards of this paradise known as Maztica. Disease, accidents, you know the risks."

"That flag over there," Volo pointed out. "I don't recognize it."

"It was our divisional flag."

"I see," said Volo, seemingly dropping the conversation.

Rurk stood up.

"My newfound friends from Faerûn, accommodations have been made for you in my humble abode.

It is now siesta time, and I am sure that you will all want to rest. Herve will escort you gentlemen to your room, while I will personally escort the lovely Shurleen to her private accommodations."

"Charmed, I'm sure," Shurleen responded, once again taking Rurk's arm.

"Mind if I tag along?" Curtis asked, a feeling of uneasiness in his voice.

"Yes, I do," Shurleen replied brusquely. "It's about time I was treated to some privacy."

Rurk and Shurleen continued down one veranda passageway, while the three male travelers followed the halfling down the other.

"I think there's something rotten in this province in Maztica," Curtis whispered churlishly, "and I don't like it."

Passepout, his heart gradually recovering from being broken, tried to lend a sympathetic ear to the young beachcomber. "I don't like the way that Rurk has his arms all over Shurleen, any better than you do, but you have to admit he's a hospitable host."

"For now," Volo interjected, "for now."

The room that they were escorted to was a more than adequate common room with three beds for reclining, three more woven thrones, and a bell cord to summon servants.

"If you require anything, please feel free to ring the bell. These are your room servants," Herve instructed, indicating three heavyset women standing in the hall. "They don't speak Common, but I am sure that you can make your desires known to them."

One of the servants Volo recognized as one of the hammock weavers from the rubber plant. She was as wide as the chubby thespian, though not as tall, and possessed a face that might have been attractive for a warthog. She gave Passepout a knowing wink and a smile as she closed the door behind Herve.

"I think she likes you," Curtis said to Passepout.

"Not if I can help it," replied the chubby thespian, a shiver of revulsion passing through his entire body.

"Isn't it strange that with such a large mansion available, Rurk would seemingly situate us at the complete opposite end of the building from Shurleen?" Volo pointed out.

"I noticed that," Curtis agreed. "That is why I offered to tag along, to at least see where he was putting her."

"I'm sure that was the only reason," Passepout jibed.

Curtis did not respond, and Passepout thought better of pushing the issue. He changed the subject. "And what was all that business about the flag, Volo?"

"Indeed," Volo replied. "I'm afraid that we are in the hands of a renegade Tethyrian mercenary warlord who has deserted his unit to the north and set up his own fantasy kingdom in this remote settlement."

"That's why there is only the division's flag, his flag," Curtis agreed.

"But what does that mean to us?" Passepout asked.

"It means," Volo replied, "that for the time being he can do anything he wants with us."

A little over an hour later, Herve returned to the quarters of the three travelers to take them down to dinner in the room behind the main veranda where they had been sitting earlier that day. Rurk was already seated at the head of the table when they arrived, and indicated that they should join him, leaving the seat by him free for Shurleen, who had yet to arrive for the meal.

"The lovely Miss Bleth informs me that you will probably be wishing to resume your travels eastward as soon as possible," Rurk said, then resumed sipping a cup of distilled fruit wine.

"Yes," Volo replied, not wishing to give too much away, "we have pressing business awaiting us in Suzail."

Just then, Shurleen entered the hall, or rather more correctly floated into the hall, her pampered, beauteous body held aloft a foot off the ground by the gown of feathers she was wearing.

Passepout and Curtis's jaws dropped.

"Isn't she angelic?" Rurk commented.

None contested his observation, as Shurleen floated to her place.

"Plume magic?" Volo asked.

"But of course," Rurk replied. "The natives here are particularly adept at it. I've even seen them constructing veritable rafts of enchanted plumes to lift their dwellings off the ground during times of flood. The floating power in these feathers seems inexhaustible."

"Quite," Volo agreed. "I bet your patrons back in Faerûn are making quite a pretty coin in profits on your exports."

"Their interests are no longer any concern of mine," Rurk replied, a touch of deadly seriousness apparent in his tone. "No doubt you realize I no longer claim allegiance to my patrons, as you call them. Your observation about the divisional flag, or shall I say that the lack of any other, made that clear to me, so let's drop the facade."

"Agreed," Volo replied. "All we want is to continue our way eastward. We have no desire to expose your private kingdom to the scrutiny of other concerns here or in Faerûn. So with your blessing we'd like to resume our journey tomorrow, giving you our word of honor that as far as anyone is concerned, we've never met a Mis Ta Rurk, nor come across a settlement of plumeweavers, camouflaged by a ridge of rocks that obscures them for miles."

"I'm afraid things are not quite that simple," Rurk replied. "Of course, I desire your discretion, but I also desire one of your companions."

Shurleen dropped her cup and looked up in amazement and fear.

Rurk looked to her the way one might look at an uneasy child.

"Yes, my dear," he replied. "I have no illusions that your flirtations masked anything except your girlish ego, and that if given the chance to choose, you would undoubtedly desire to continue along your way with your companions. Fortunately for me, I hold all the cards, and I think it will be better if you stay."

"Why, you!" Curtis yelled, jumping to his feet, and about to rush to Rurk's end of the table.

Rurk clapped his hands, and six Tethyrian mercenaries appeared, fully armed with bows and arrows fletched with enchanted plumes.

"These are some of the men who joined me on my excursion. I wouldn't advise causing any trouble as their arrows are fletched for accuracy by means of enchantment."

"Curtis, sit down!" Volo ordered. "What do you want, Rurk?"

Curtis resumed his seat as Rurk made his pitch. "Sometimes it's boring being a god for these primitive savages," Rurk said. "Sometimes I need a little challenge."

"Get to the point," Volo pressed.

"Of course," Rurk conceded. "Of course I would love to take the lovely Miss Bleth as my mistress, but I'm sure you wouldn't stand for that."

"Right," Volo agreed.

"Not that you can really do anything about it. One of my men is a rather powerful chemist who could undoubtedly come up with a potion that will make her my slave in a matter of moments . . . but that wouldn't be sporting. What I suggest is that you three take part in a game against three of my best athletes tomorrow. It's called the ball game. You might have heard of it."

"I have," Volo replied.

"Good," Rurk continued. "If you win, you are free to go, if not, the lovely Shurleen becomes my mistress."

"No!" Shurleen screamed, bursting into tears. She was quickly spirited away by several of Rurk's more attractive female servants, evidently his other mistresses.

Volo fingered his beard for a moment and thought.

"How about this?" the master traveler counteroffered. "If we win, you will have your plumeweavers weave us a raft that will be capable of flying us back to Faerûn."

"One already exists," Rurk interrupted, "you never know when you will have to make a fast getaway. Sometimes even peaceful and stupid savages like these get restless."

"One might say that this would be fairer compensation for our efforts," Volo pointed out.

"Agreed," Rurk assented. "The game will be to-morrow at midday out on the field we passed getting here. You three against my champions, those tall fellows over there."

Volo and his companions turned to see the individuals that he was referring to. Each was a good foot taller than any of the natives they had seen so far, and all were built like oxen.

"Don't let their bulk fool you," Rurk pointed out. "They have the reflexes and speed of jaguar men."

"*Wonderful*," Passepout replied, sensing imminent doom.

"And one more thing," Rurk added. "My home court has a particular rule attached to all games. You lose, you die. Death before dishonor."

Passepout fainted, and Curtis revived him with a cup of water.

The three companions ate the rest of their meal in silence, all along Volo fingering his beard in thought, as if trying to come up with a plan.

As the meal was brought to a close, Rurk stood up and said, "I assure you that no harm will come to Miss Bleth tonight. I am more than willing to wait to collect the victor's spoils."

"That goes without saying," Volo replied, adding, "One thing, though. I understand that the game is played in sandals. Would it be possible for us to obtain three pairs in the morning, so that we can break them in for the game?"

"But of course," Rurk replied. "What kind of host would I be not to grant such a simple request?"

Once again Rurk clapped his hands, and Herve appeared to lead Volo and the others back to their room.

19

# THE BALL GAME

## OR

### How a Little Ingenuity
### Can Make Up For
### a Lack of Athletic Prowess

True to Rurk's word, the following morning
three pairs of sandals were delivered to the challengers' room.

"What are we going to do?" Passepout pleaded.

"Call your servant," Volo instructed.

"Why?" the chubby thespian asked. "Did you see
the face on that one? I hate to think that was the

last female on my mind when I meet my maker, which is apparently going to be way too soon for my tastes."

"Just do it!" Volo ordered, continuing to finger his beard in nervous contemplation.

"And what about Shurleen?" Curtis demanded. "We can't let Rurk enslave her!"

"And there is nothing we can do about it if we happen to be dead, right?" Volo countered. "Therefore, our main objective at the moment should be staying alive."

"Here she is," Passepout said, having returned with his warthog-faced, would-be paramour.

"Good," Volo replied. He took her aside, making his needs known to her in sign language. She continued to nod in agreement, occasionally tossing a glance and a wink in the chubby thespian's direction.

Volo and the servant began to leave. "We'll be right back," Volo called. "We have a bit of sandal customizing to do."

With that they left.

"Well, I never heard it referred to as that," Passepout commented.

"Somehow I wouldn't have thought of her as his type," Curtis agreed.

"By the way," Passepout asked, "what is this ball game in which we are supposed to meet our deaths?"

"I haven't the foggiest idea," Curtis replied.

Volo returned with the sandals in a little less than an hour.

"Well, it's about time!" Passepout said sarcastically.

"You sound a bit jealous," Curtis jibed the chubby thespian. "I thought she wasn't your type?"

"Can it!" Volo ordered. "Time is short, and we have a plan to work out. The odds are against us, and the deck is stacked in their favor, but with a little luck, I think we can bounce our way to victory. Now listen."

The ball game, as Volo explained, was the major accepted form of entertainment for all Mazticans. Though on the surface it appeared to be only a contest or sport, the human cultures of the continent had invested in it a great deal of significance as a religious ritual and as a means of dispute arbitration through divine intervention. The game was usually played with a hard, round ball roughly six inches in diameter, made from the congealed sap of a rubber tree. It was the object of opposing team players to maneuver the ball without the use of their hands or feet through the opposing team's goal line. The first team to score three goals would win.

There was, however, another option for winning. Midway down the walls that line the court was a stone ring roughly fifteen feet above the playing field. The first team to score a goal through the ring would win.

"Just looking at the opposition, I can tell it is their intention to bulldoze their way down the field each play to pummel home a shot on our goal," Volo explained.

"And there doesn't seem to be much we can do to stand in their way," Passepout observed.

"Almost," Volo replied. "The first thing I have to do is to get Rurk to up the ante. Normally, victory is only attained after a match is won, and three games make a match. I need to have him agree to a one-game match."

"Sure," Passepout interjected, "no reason to postpone the inevitable."

"Our only advantage is the element of surprise, and we will only have that once."

"Surprise about what?" Curtis queried.

"These," Volo replied, holding up the newly customized sandals.

Volo, Passepout, and Curtis arrived about ten minutes before the sun was at its apex. Rurk and his team of brutes had already arrived and were eagerly waiting in anticipation of an easy victory.

Shurleen had arrived as well, bedecked in the skimpy garments of a high-class courtesan, a profession she feared soon awaited her.

Curtis walked over to her with his, Volo's, and Passepout's packs cleverly disguised as ornate, overstuffed pillows. He was amazed at how much the strident, demanding heiress now resembled a very scared child who just wanted to go home despite her seductive attire.

"Don't worry kid," Curtis consoled. "Mister Volo has a plan. When he gives the word, grab the packs and run."

"I know you may find this hard to believe," Shurleen choked in a whisper, "but I think I would prefer to share in your fate. Death seems almost desirable to the alternative."

Curtis patted her, and in a moment of mad inspiration kissed her on the forehead. "If things go according to plan, no one will have to face death or a fate worse. Wish me luck."

"Good luck, Curtis," she whispered, "and to the others as well, and . . . " She halted in midsentence, placed her two hands on the sides of his face, and drew him closer to her, kissing him long and lovingly on the lips.

Curtis returned to the others feeling as if he were walking on air, and grateful that Passepout had not seen their little interaction.

"Now remember," Volo instructed, "everything hinges on none of us getting hurt while they score their first two goals."

"No problem," Passepout replied. "The ball comes this way, I go that way."

"No," Volo corrected, shaking his head. "We can't make it look that easy. If Rurk catches on that we're throwing the game for the first two goals, we're sunk."

"We'll do our best," Curtis replied, his heart filled with a new shot of confidence.

"We have to," Volo replied, then yelled to Rurk, "Hey, let's get this show on the road."

"Hey," Passepout yelled, "that's my line."

"Whatever," Rurk responded. "Don't you want to put your sandals on?"

"Later," Volo replied curtly. "I'd like to see our prize before we start."

"Whatever," Rurk said dismissively. He clapped his hands and watched as the plume raft was flown in by Herve. It would fit the four companions and the three packs with room to spare.

"Ready," Volo announced.

"Good," Rurk replied. "A ball game match. Three games make a match. To the winner: freedom, life, and this plume barge. To the loser, the usual: death. Let the games begin."

The ball was thrown into center court, and the opposing team of brutes stampeded down the field. The one-eyed monster who led their pack reached the bouncing ball first, and butted it with his head farther down the field, where it was elbowed by a team mate to the side, where the third member took a shot on goal. While the masters of menace were continuing their rampage down the field, Volo's team tried to put on a good show. Curtis threw himself in front of the oncoming ball, barely missing it. An oncoming goon tried to skewer him on its abnormally long claws (though the rules prohibited the use of one's hands with the ball, nothing had been mentioned about their use against an opponent). Curtis easily dodged its oncoming thrust, his exceptional reflexes more than compensating for the goon's superior strength and bulk.

Volo made a great show of trying to get under the ball as it sailed back to earth, having been head-butted by the opposition with such force as to surely concuss the master traveler. As with Curtis, the traveler narrowly escaped the mortal blow.

Passepout ran back and forth in the goal, trying to put on the appearance of blocking the ball, while actually just trying to stay out of the way. The oncoming team didn't even bother with him as a target of aggression; some prey are just too easy to kill and therefore not worth the effort.

The goons quickly decided that the pleasures of violence and pain-giving could be safely deferred to game end and refocussed their attentions on simply scoring.

Rurk's team easily scored their two goals, and Volo called a time out.

"What is it now?" Rurk asked, impatient to see the slaughter end, so that the slaughter could begin.

"We're going to put our sandals on," Volo announced, making a great show of huffing and puffing.

"Tired, huh?" Rurk chuckled.

"Can't wait till it's over," Volo puffed.

"My feelings exactly," Rurk replied. "Why don't we dispense with the facade of two more games? Game equals match, so that we can get on with it."

Volo huffed and puffed, fingering his beard in tired contemplation.

"Okay," the master traveler replied, "but I think we deserve a handicap."

"Like what?" Rurk replied.

"Could we start from a third of the way down?" Volo offered. "It might give us a chance to get our hands on the ball, so to speak."

"Not that it would do you any good," Rurk countered, then added, "Why not? Let's get on with it."

Rurk stood up and announced to the crowd as Herve translated.

"New rules," he announced. "Challengers shall be allowed a head start down the field. Game equals match. This one is for the girl, the feather barge, and everything!"

"Yes!" Volo, Curtis, and Passepout whispered a cheer in unison. Rurk had made the agreement public and would not be able to back out without losing face.

The three players, their feet shod in their customized sandals, shuffled into position down the field.

"Begin!" Rurk yelled, and the ball was put in play.

Curtis took off like a shot first, bouncing down the field in leaps and bounds that were magnified by the extra thick rubber soles of his sandals. Passepout meanwhile took his place under the midcourt ring, and began to hop up and down. With each hop, his bounce increased, aided and accentuated by the cushions of air that Volo had made sure were added to the sandals' newly padded rubber soles. With all of the agility of the tumbler training that he had learned at his father's knee, the chubby thespian began to turn somersaults in midair, mystifying the opposing team, who had never seen a fat man fly without the aid of magic feathers.

In the meantime, Volo had joined Curtis at the place where the ball was still bouncing. The master traveler and the young beachcomber intertwined their arms, and caught the ball between their two bodies, and then proceeded to hop toward their bouncing buddy.

Rurk could not believe his eyes.

"They can't do that!" he shouted.

"Why not?" Shurleen replied.

"She's right," Herve responded. "There's nothing against it in the rules."

In the time it took for that conversational exchange to take place, Volo and Curtis had maneuvered the ball to Passepout's position. On the count of three, the two ball-bearers released control of the rubber spheroid, allowing it to bounce once, at which point it was recovered between the elbows of the tumbling Passepout who, with all the force of his flabby girth, propelled himself down and up in a bounce that put him on chest level with the goal ring, at which point he released the ball with a push from his stomach, sending it sailing through the ring, and on to victory.

"Goal, game, match! The challengers win!" Herve announced in his native tongue.

"No!" Rurk screamed, overcome with rage. "Seize them!"

No one could hear Rurk's order however, and Herve failed to translate it, further accentuating the warlord's apoplectic fury.

"The raft!" Volo yelled, heading toward Herve and their featherbed deliverer.

Herve steered the raft into a hover near Shurleen.

"Hey, lady, need a lift?" he called.

"Charmed," she replied, hoisting the disguised packs on board with her.

When she was in place, she pointed to Curtis, Volo, and Passepout, who were hemmed in by the crowd who wished to congratulate them.

Herve nodded, as if to say no problem, and steered the raft directly over them.

"Gentlemen, hop!" Volo ordered, and the three travelers bounced up to their feather-lined aerial getaway raft, climbed on board, and were eastward bound in no time.

Herve, seated at the front of the plume raft, called back to the others, who were having a victory reunion. "I figured Rurk was about at the end of his reign. I took this baby out for a spin earlier today, and saw a contingent of Tethyrian mercenaries heading this way. If you don't mind, I'll get off when we hit the coast."

"What will you do?" Volo asked. Curtis was busy with Shurleen, and Passepout was still catching his breath, unaccustomed as he was to this much exertion in a single day.

"I don't know," the halfling replied. "Maybe go north, go back home, see what opportunities are waiting for me there."

"Do you want to join us?" Volo offered. "We're heading back to Faerûn."

"No, thanks," Herve replied. "The offer is appreciated, but I'd rather stay here. This is my home, and besides, from what I understand, it's not healthy to drink the water in Faerûn."

Herve and Volo laughed, and in no time at all they had reached the coast, and Herve departed, bidding them a fond farewell.

# ACROSS THE
# TRACKLESS SEA

### OR

### Until We Evermeet Again

Before he left, Herve explained to the four travelers the whys and wherefores of operating the raft of magic plumes. Steering was accomplished by gently lifting the raft's corner in the direction in which you wanted to proceed. Altitude was controlled by the mutual movements of the riders on board while clutching the feathered surface at their sides. Leaning forward would instigate a gradual dive, leaning back a gradual ascent.

"One more thing," Herve had warned. "Try not to fly too close to the surf. The feathers become weighed down with moisture, and it becomes hard to keep aloft. Also try to avoid puncturing the raft in any way. It upsets the balance of the floating spell."

"Why?" Volo had asked, hoping for a possible new notation for a revised edition of *Volo's Guide to All Things Magical*.

"Don't ask me," the halfling had replied. "I don't build them, I just fly 'em."

As before, Volo and Passepout used a combination of existing charts in the master traveler's pack, and the enchanted map that accompanied the necromancer's jewels to chart their course, as the chubby thespian cast an enchanted gem overboard at each of its appointed sites, thus marking their location on the map with the completion of each divestiture.

"Bombs away," Passepout announced, no longer surreptitious when dropping the enchanted formerly green, now red, gems. Only Volo would have heard him anyway, as Curtis and Shurleen were much too involved in silently getting reacquainted. Passepout looked back at the two young lovers, a feeling of slight heartache still present.

Once they had left the coast, Shurleen had apologized to all for her behavior, asking for forgiveness from those who had saved her from a fate she deemed worse than death. She had then apologized to Passepout personally, asking for his forgiveness for the way she treated him. He, of course, accepted her apology, and had smiled when she stated that she hoped that they could still be friends, the smile masking the internal tears that only a disappointed friend who really wanted much more would really understand. He continued to smile until she rejoined Curtis at the back of their feather airship, when he allowed himself a single tear, which he quickly wiped away before any one could see it.

*Oh, well,* he said to himself with a faint sniffle, *maybe I wasn't cut out to marry an heiress, anyway. There's always still the possibility of a reward from her father.*

"Passepout," Volo called, "when was the last time you dropped a gem?"

"Minutes ago," the thespian replied. "That's what I did when I said, 'Bombs away.'"

"Great," the master traveler replied with great enthusiasm. "By my calculations, we should be approaching the island of Evermeet very soon now."

"So?" the thespian replied, not seeing the appeal of this locale.

"Well, I've never been there," Volo replied. "It's off limits to all except the elves. Surely you must have heard that," he added with a trace of condescension in his voice.

"Well, I would have thought that no place was off limits to the master traveler of Faerûn," the thespian replied, laying the sarcasm on good and thick.

Volo realized that his tone of condescension had been uncalled for. The chubby thespian had proven himself to be an excellent traveling companion, a brave warrior, and a good friend, and deserved better for it.

"You're right," Volo conceded with a chuckle. "Unfortunately, I blew it. I was in line for a special non-elf dispensation, and well, I, uh, got on the wrong side of the head lady of those parts."

"You mean Queen Amlaruil?" the thespian replied, glad to show off what little knowledge he did have of the elves of Evermeet."

"You guessed it," Volo replied. "Give that man a cookie. She managed to get a hold of a copy of my suppressed book on magic.

*Volo's Guide to All Things Magical?*"

"That's right," he confirmed, "except she got her hands on the unexpurgated text, and sort of took offense at some of the things I said. So now I'm not just barred from Evermeet for being a non-elf, I'm also barred for just being Volothamp Geddarm."

"Too bad," Passepout offered in consolation.

"Thanks," the master traveler replied, a trace of the effervescence of enthusiasm in his voice, "but now an opportunity presents itself to us."

"How so?" the thespian asked.

"We can fly in real low, and get a good look at the place as we fly over."

"I don't know," Passepout replied unsurely. "Herve said we shouldn't fly too low, moisture weighing us down and all."

"We won't go in too low," Volo responded, "just low enough to get a good look."

"I guess so," Passepout agreed warily, wishing that they were closer to the Faerûn mainland.

At the appointed time, everyone leaned forward, and the raft of magic plumes sailed down into the mist that enshrouded and obscured the magical island of Evermeet. As they plowed through the mist, the air became clearer, and the fantastic locale no longer hidden.

The travelers traded Volo's spyglass back and forth, taking in the magical sites of the elven homeland. Elven communities grew out of forest clearings; magic and enchantment permeated the actual building structures and architecture. Sylvan creatures cavorted in the forests. Unicorns frolicked with pegasi. Sprites and fairies rode tamed dragons at play.

"It's beautiful!" Shurleen exclaimed.

"And how!" Curtis agreed.

"Not bad," said Passepout, purposely trying to appear underwhelmed. "Are you satisfied, O master traveler?"

"Why certainly!" Volo replied. "Just one last pass, and we'll be on our way."

That one last pass was one pass too many.

"What's that?" Passepout asked, pointing toward a mountain.

"Where?" Volo asked, straining to see without the spyglass.

"There," Passepout replied, pointing as he passed the spyglass to the helm-bound Volo.

Volo looked through the glass just in time to see the launch of magical spears from one of numerous elven sentries, camouflaged by cloaks of stars and sworn to protect Evermeet from all outsiders.

"Quickly! Lean back and up!" the master traveler ordered, sending the plumed raft soaring back through the damp, mist-filled cloud that shrouded the island, and forward eastward.

No sooner had they regained the other side of the cloud than they noticed that a spear had indeed hit its mark. A gaping hole now existed in the middle of the raft, and it was interfering with their steering.

"Everybody hold on!" Volo ordered, cursing his wanton curiosity that had resulted in this most recent of problems, and the pride that was the underlying cause of all of his problems so far. "It's going to be a bumpy ride!"

The feathers beneath them felt damp, having retained some of the moisture from the mists; as a result of the increased weight, the raft was unable to ascend in the manner that it had before.

The clear skies that had existed prior to the Evermeet side trip had now been replaced by storm clouds. Thunder and lightning struck on all sides, and the feathers, dampened from the two trips through the moistened clouds of mist and the present proximity to the raging surf below, began to lose their magic. The raft began to descend farther.

The storm followed them as if magically drawn to the flying raft of feathers by some elven enchantment in retribution for their invading the privacy of the Evermeet community.

Fog set in somewhere over Alaron, and the raft began to disintegrate.

"Hold tight!" Volo shouted over the roar of the wind. "She's coming apart! I'm going to try to bring her in for a landing."

With the fog obscuring his view, the maps safely ensconced in his pack (his not having the light to read them or free hand to hold them, rendering them useless for navigation at the present time), the master traveler tried to engineer a controlled descent.

They overshot landing in the sea of midnight blue just beyond the Moonshae Isles, and offshore from the Faerûn continent the raft quickly dissolved into a slick of loose feathers as the icy waters welcomed their latest prey.

# IN THE SWORD COAST

### OR

### Saved By a Dark Elf

"I can't swim!" Shurleen yelled as the raft came apart, dropping her into the icy cold waters of the Sea of Swords.

Curtis, having quickly recovered from his own shock at being dropped into the icy deep, frantically looked in the direction he had last heard Shurleen's scream.

Out of the corner of his eyes, resting among the water-sodden feathers of the raft, he spied a few petals of the Maztican orchid she had been wearing in her hair, and dove directly under it. In the darkness of the storm-enshrouded waters, though he could not make out the form of his lady love, he barely made out the glimmer of silver below him, and swam toward it, hoping that it wasn't just the iridescent glow of some fish. As he got closer he clearly made out the silvery earrings and necklace of the heiress, and their wearer as well, sinking farther into the watery depths to certain death. Kicking with all his might, he reached her and grabbed her, and holding her body in a cross-chest grip close to his own bosom, he quickly scissor-kicked, propelling both of them back to the surface.

Meanwhile, Passepout thought he was having similar difficulties.

"I'm going down!" he screamed, panicking in the swells.

"No, you're not!" Volo yelled over the roar of the storm, while trying to keep himself and his pack afloat. "Just float!"

The chubby thespian ceased his frantic motions for a moment, and indeed discovered that his bodily girth did provide him with enough buoyancy to remain afloat without any paddling exertion whatever.

"It works! It works! It *glubbbs* . . . " he cheered until a passing swell pulled him under and gave him a mouthful of water.

Volo was relieved when he saw his friend once again bob to the surface, but he knew that even under optimum conditions they would not be able to survive long in the chill of the ocean. Hypothermia would set in almost immediately.

The master traveler felt the brush of an oar handle against his outstretched arm, and immediately grabbed for it. Beyond the oar was a dinghy, and in the dinghy a pair of dark arms to help him aboard, and beyond them a pair of bright lavender eyes, glowing orbs in a body that seemed to melt into the darkness that surrounded it.

"Now to get your companions," the figure said. "There are four of you altogether?"

"That's right," the master traveler replied, just beginning to realize how cold he was, and how he couldn't stop shivering.

"There's a pile of blankets on your left," the figure said as if reading his mind. "It doesn't make sense to save anyone from drowning only to have them freeze to death from the chill."

The figure had rowed the boat within reach of Curtis and Shurleen, who were quickly brought aboard, and then turned around to pick up Passepout.

Volo was amazed at how seemingly easy the pilot was able to locate his friends in the storm-ridden darkness.

When all were on board, the pilot announced, "Wrap yourselves in the blankets. We'll be on shipboard and dry in no time."

"How did you . . . ?" Volo chattered.

"I saw you go down," the dinghy's pilot replied.

"You're a drow, aren't you?" the master traveler said, putting two and two together: the night vision, the dark skin. Though dark elves were uncommon in the surface world, occasionally drow had been known to travel the Sword Coast. Volo only hoped that this fellow wasn't a slaver rounding up cheap and expendable labor for some underworld toil. Volo was finally beginning to warm up within the thick layers of the blankets.

"That's right," the drow replied, "but you may

call me Drizzt . . . and don't worry. I'm not here to capture you, just to help. I'm alone."

With a sigh of relief Volo turned his attentions back to getting warm.

In less than an hour the travelers were dressed in dry clothes and seated around a roaring fire in the main cabin of the good ship *Leominster*, sipping hot broth.

The captain of the vessel was a taciturn dwarf named Wolflarson, who soon joined them.

"I and my companions would like to thank you for your hospitality," Volo said. "You certainly came along at the right time."

"Think nothing of it," the captain replied brusquely. "I sure don't. We're docking in Waterdeep tomorrow. You can get off there."

Volo was slightly taken aback by the offhand manner in which he treated their rescue. "Still, if you hadn't stopped the ship, and turned around to get us, sending your man Drizzt out to get us, I . . . "

In a carefully measured tone brimming with hostility, Wolflarson interrupted, "He's not my man, he's drow, and he's just another passenger. As for stopping the ship, I didn't, and woe to the person I find out that did."

"But . . . "

"And as to that drow fool Drizzt, he actcd on his own, even paid for the rental of the dinghy. Now if you will excuse me, I have to return to the wheel. I expect your clothes will be dry by the time we dock, so please leave the blankets here when you go. I won't be expecting to see you again."

With that, the dwarf captain left the cabin.

"Well," Shurleen commented, "remind me never to book passage on any ship he's the captain of. A regular charmer, he is."

Passepout detected a certain trace of Suzail slang in her voice, which was uncommon to members of the upper class. He dismissed it as probably just an affectation she threw in for effect.

Curtis looked around the cabin and stuck his head outside for a moment. When he returned he said, "I wonder where that guy Drizzt is. I mean, he fishes us out of the sea, saves us from a watery grave while risking his own life in storm-swept seas, and then doesn't even stick around so that we can say thanks."

The cabin boy, who was carefully tending the fire so that it never got out of hand, answered. "He's probably in his cabin. The captain gave firm orders that Mister Do'Urden was not to wander the ship unescorted."

"The captain doesn't like drow much, does he, lad?" Volo asked.

"Who does?" the lad replied.

"Is he getting off at Waterdeep, too?" Volo pressed.

"No," the lad replied. "He's booked all the way to Luskan. His cabin is down below, right next to the stores. Just don't tell the captain I told you."

"We should probably go thank him," Shurleen suggested without a trace of enthusiasm in her voice.

"I'll go," Volo replied, getting to his feet. "With my change of clothes from my waterproof pack, I'm pretty much the only one of us suitable for visiting. The rest of you stay here and try to dry off."

Volo left the cabin and looked for the passageway to the hold. The storms had ceased, and the fog had cleared. After a quick bit of reconnaissance, Volo discovered a rope ladder that led to the ship's hold and the stores. Balancing a lantern in one hand, he climbed down the ladder in search of the passenger's cabin.

The master traveler quickly discovered that there was a good three inches of seawater in the hold. *Surely*, he thought, *his accommodations aren't down here.* With the available light from the lantern, he quickly surveyed the hold and was about to leave when he spied a door at the far end of the stores.

The water was only about an inch deep there, so Volo trudged on over and up the incline of the curvature of the hull, and knocked on the door.

"Mister Do'Urden," he called.

*Groowwwllll!*

Volo distinctly heard the sound of a jungle cat on the other side of the door.

"Mister Do'Urden," Volo called louder. "Are you all right? It's me, Mister Volo, whom you fished out of the drink. My friends and I would like to thank you."

"One moment," Drizzt said from the other side of the door.

A moment passed, and then the sound of a bolt and a lock being undone was audible, and the dark elf opened the door and bade Volo to enter.

"Come in," Drizzt offered. "Please sit down."

Volo was astonished at the cramped quarters. Thanks to a ridge in the doorway, most of the water stayed back in the hold, although a puddle was beginning to form by the door. The bare essentials of the efficiency closet were a single rope bunk, a chest upon which a statuette of some sort was situated, and a tiny porthole that was almost eye level with the sea.

When Drizzt closed the door behind him, the

master traveler also noticed a pair of twin scimitars hanging from a hook on the door.

"Handy," Volo commented.

"But not always necessary," Drizzt replied, "particularly when making a rescue at sea."

Having grown tired of bending forward to avoid hitting his head on the low ceiling, Volo took a seat on the chest, next to the statuette, which seemed to be of some sort of panther.

"Pretty," Volo commented.

"But deadly," the drow returned.

Volo realized that his presence was making the drow uneasy, and possibly claustrophobic, given the cramped quarters.

"It looks like you are a man of few words, so I just wanted to stop by and say thank you for rescuing my friends," the master traveler said, beginning to feel oppressed by the dampness and the closeness of the space.

Drizzt pointed out through the porthole.

"I saw you crash through there. I like to look out into the night," the drow related. "I knew that the captain wouldn't have seen you . . . "

". . . or cared, for that matter. . . ," Volo interrupted.

"Oh," the drow acknowledged. "So you've met Wolflarson."

"Charming fellow."

"Would probably feel right at home in Menzoberranzan, if he were a drow, that is. That's probably one of the reasons I left," the drow said, "but I digress. I launched one of the lifeboats after being sure to attach a safety line back to the ship, and set off after you. Even in the fog you were pretty easy to find."

"You have good eyes," Volo complimented.

"Thanks," said Drizzt. "It comes with the territory."

"Well, I just wanted to say thanks," the master traveler said, reclaiming his stooped stance and heading for the door.

"You are welcome," the drow replied.

"The captain will let us ashore in Waterdeep."

"Safe home."

"The same to you."

"I can never truly go home again," the drow said, a measure of melancholy in his voice.

Volo slipped past the drow and out the door, when he stopped, and said, "I thought I heard the growl of a jungle cat when I knocked on your door."

"It was only Guenhwyvar," Drizzt replied, shutting the door after his visitor.

"Oh," said the master traveler, hearing the bolt being thrown back into place, and not bothering to ask for a further explanation.

"Well, did you thank him?" Shurleen asked as Volo re-entered the main deck's cabin.

"Yes," Volo replied absently, his mind still on their mysterious savior. "I didn't stay long. He seems to be a solitary sort."

"I thought the drow were a cruel and evil race," Curtis remarked.

"Once again, I guess there are exceptions to every rule," the master traveler replied.

"I'm just glad he came along when he did," Passepout added, starting on his tenth cup of broth.

*As am I,* thought Volo. *As am I.*

# WATERDEEP

### OR

## Back in the City of Splendors Again

After Volo had returned to them, the four weary travelers lay wrapped in their dry blankets on the deck and went to sleep in a huddle, like kittens on their keeper's bed.

Morning arrived quickly, and they awoke to the great relief that their clothes were now dry and neatly folded (by the cabin boy, presumably), and waiting to be donned.

The dwarf captain did not make another appearance, nor was any breakfast offered so the travelers had to make due with the remains of the broth from the night before.

The ship docked at noon, and the foursome quickly disembarked and availed themselves of a hasty snack from a nearby fruit cart that seemed to cater to the harbor workers. Before Passepout had dropped a red gem in place and finished his fourth pear, the *Leominster* was once again setting out to sea, its captain Wolflarson at the helm, clearly visible from the dock.

"Good-bye, you old sourpuss!" Passepout called, confident that the dwarf couldn't hear him.

Volo looked to the porthole just above the waterline; a black drape seemed to have been drawn across it as if to block out the noonday sun. For a second the master traveler thought that he had seen a dark face, but a blink of his eyes to refocus only revealed the black curtain back in place.

"Good-bye, Mister Do'Urden," Volo whispered. "I hope you find a new home to return to."

Shurleen was the first to bring up the obvious question.

"Okay, we're in Waterdeep," she said. "So now what?"

"Yeah," Passepout concurred. "This fruit is just a snack, and not really likely to tide me over for more than a few minutes. Anyone know any good places to eat?"

Volo adopted a look of mock offense. "Does anyone know any good places to eat, he asks," the master proclaimed. "Am I not Volothamp Geddarm, author of the best-selling travel guide of all times, *Volo's Guide to Waterdeep*, and is this not that selfsame Waterdeep, the City of Splendors, the metropolis of the north? Of course I know a few good places to eat!"

"So show us, then," Curtis responded with a hearty laugh.

"Fine," Volo agreed. "Follow me!"

The master traveler charged toward the city gates, and his three companions followed, confident that they were in pursuit of only the best accommodations that the City of Splendors had to offer.

Passepout huffed and puffed to keep up with the master traveler. His condition was obviously lighter and healthier than it was when they left Suzail, due to a combination of the ongoing daily exercise of traveling and the travelers' irregular supply of rations (which the still-plump thespian often referred to as slow starvation). But he was still in no condition to run the marathon around Mount Waterdeep, and he urged Volo to slow down.

"Have . . . a . . . heart . . . Mister . . . Volo . . . " he huffed, and puffed.

"Sorry," Volo replied, shortening his stride and slowing his pace just a bit. "I guess I just got a little carried away, a little overexuberant."

"Thanks," the chubby thespian replied. "Don't you think we should be careful around here?"

"Why?" the master traveler queried. "This is the City of Splendors. What do I have to fear here?"

"Well," the thespian replied. "Doesn't Khelben come from here?"

"Quite," Volo agreed.

"And isn't he the reason you and I have had to go on this gods-forsaken trip to begin with?"

"But our journey is almost at an end," the master traveler replied, "isn't it?"

"Well, we still have to get to Suzail."

"Child's play," Volo answered, dismissing the

thespian's concerns. "I'm sure that old Khelben was just suffering from some fit of pique. He's probably not even home, off on another meeting of the War Wizards or something. Heck, he's probably even forgotten the trial he's been putting us through. I'm sure that we have nothing to worry about."

"Sure?" inquired the skeptical thespian.

"Positive," the master traveler insisted. "Besides, this is Waterdeep. I have no enemies here."

"Not even the recipients of a few bad reviews?" the thespian countered, still concerned that the master traveler was taking too much for granted.

"Pish tosh," Volo replied. "Everyone loves Volo. We're almost home free. Nothing can go wrong now!"

The master traveler and the other members of his party failed to notice the chain of whispered messages that took place on the streets as they passed.

Soon, someone very well-informed and well-connected would know that the master traveler had returned to Waterdeep, and would be ready and waiting for him.

Volo managed to get accommodations for himself and his friends at the Shipmaster's Hall, a private inn and supper club not too far from the docks. It was usually reserved for captains, first mates, and ship owners and their escorts, though in Volo's case they of course made an exception.

"We would be honored to serve you and your friends, Mister Volo," the maitre d' fawned, "provided you don't mind private accommodations."

"Not at all," the master traveler replied.

"Wonderful!" the maitre d' answered, obviously

relieved, then adding, "and perhaps if you should revise that little guide book of yours, you might be able to give us a little better play. Believe it or not, there are some gentlemen sailing the Sword Coast who haven't heard of us."

"Gentlemen on the Sword Coast?" Volo replied. "Why, I can't imagine such a thing."

Both men laughed. A deal had obviously been struck.

Volo returned to his group and led them to the private area upstairs where enough food even for Passepout had been quickly laid out for them.

"Enjoy, my friends," Volo invited. "The meal and the beds are on the house." The group began to dig in, only to hear the master traveler add one more thing. "Enjoy!" he repeated, but this time adding, "Tomorrow we are Suzail bound!"

Shurleen put down her food and pouted.

"But we just got here," she whined. "I heard that tomorrow night there was going to be a battle of the bards over at the bard college, and it has been rumored that both Danilo Thann and Olive Ruskettle are going to show up."

Passepout bit his tongue. He of course would normally have jumped at the opportunity to reacquaint himself with the famed halfling bard, but thought better of it, realizing the need to bring their traveling obligations to an end.

The battle of the bards always attracted a great crowd. Musicians, singers, and the like traveled from all over Faerûn to attend. Only the best of the best (and those too well connected to safely turn away) were allowed to compete for the annual title of Best Bard. Volo had attended last year's competition and could well understand Shurleen's desire to attend.

"Tell you what I'm gonna do," Volo propositioned. "After lunch, Curtis and Passepout can restock our supplies for the journey farther east, and
I will take you to this little tavern I know where all
of the best bards hang out—in broad daylight, no
less."

"Well . . ." she answered, wavering.

"C'mon," Passepout urged. "You want to get
home, don't you?"

"Well, yeah," she replied.

"I know I do," Curtis agreed.

*Yeah, to her home,* Passepout thought. *Well, just
remember if you get the girl, then I get the reward.*

"Okay?" the master traveler asked.

"Okay," she replied, adding, "Wow! Famous
bards just hanging out."

"That's right," the master traveler said, adding,
"I promise."

The party of hungry travelers ate for a good two
hours straight.

By the time they were finished, even Passepout
relished the opportunity to walk off some of the
meal, though Volo suspected that both he and Curtis would have preferred the company that he,
Volo, was keeping rather than each other.

Volo took out a street map of the city, and showed
Passepout a route whereby they would never be too
far separated from each other, nor would they jeop-
ardize closing themselves off from their necessary
exit route out of town.

Both concurred that they would be glad when
such measures were no longer necessary.

With an agreement to be back by nightfall, the
groups split up to go about their appointed assignments.

"Eo, they were wonderful!" Shurleen exclaimed. "And imagine Danilo Thann kissing my hand!"

"I'm glad you enjoyed it," Volo replied, switching his pack bag from one shoulder to the other, and happy to see that even a spoiled, pampered child such as Shurleen could enjoy some of the simpler things in life. He noticed that when she wasn't being strident, demanding or pompous, she was actually quite cute.

"And he was just a regular guy, with regular concerns. He even mentioned that he was a little concerned about a decrease in his popularity during his last tour of Tantras. The crowds were more interested in some dwarf flying through the air on a winged lizard than sitting around a tavern and listening to good music."

*Grumby*, Volo remembered. *Oh, well, no reason to hold a grudge. I'm glad he got what he wanted.*

Shurleen went to go back the way they came, but Volo redirected her down a different alley.

"No, this way," he instructed, thinking to himself, *Lucky for us there are four entrances to the Shipmaster's Hall. I'd hate to bollix things up this late in the game.*

They ducked in and out of alleys a few more times until the master traveler said, "Now just down the next alley, and voila, we're there."

He didn't even see the rogue with the sap who came up behind them, nor feel its blow when it struck. The last thing he remembered was Shurleen starting to scream, and everything going black.

# IN THE CELLAR OF THE
# HANGING LANTERN TAVERN

### OR

### Gee, Don't I Know You
### From Somewhere?

Volo woke up with a splitting headache that he recognized as the type of borderline concussion you sometimes get from being bludgeoned upon entering someplace where you really aren't welcome.

He could feel that he was tied up but not blindfolded or gagged. He decided to act unconscious for a while until he got his bearings.

"Hey, boss!" a gruff voice called. "I think he's coming around!"

"Hasten the process," another voice answered. "Now!"

*Ooooooofffffff!*

Volo felt a kick to his ribs from an exceptionally pointy shoe and opened his eyes with a grimace.

"Boss, he's awake."

The speaker of the gruff and tough tones was a lovely young lady attired in an elegant festhall lounging frock. She was carefully made up to accentuate her beauty, a creature of loveliness, a beauty to behold . . .

"Boss!"

. . . with the voice of a longshoreman.

"I'm coming," a remotely familiar voice responded, approaching Volo from behind.

"Nice outfit," the vision of loveliness commented to the one she called boss. "Kind of kinky, though, if you know what I mean."

"Leave," the voice ordered. "I can deal with him myself."

The lovely young lady of easy virtue stood up and headed for a set of stairs that apparently led up from the cellarlike chamber the master traveler was being held in.

"Party pooper," she barbed at her boss, and with a flirtatious toss of her finely coiffed locks, headed upstairs. As Volo followed her journey, he noticed that Shurleen was bound and gagged over in the other corner of the cellar.

The owner of the voice known as Boss stepped over Volo, who was still resting on the floor like a discarded piece of cordwood, and slowly came into view.

"At last we meet again," the voice boomed. "I

trust you enjoyed your travels."

Volo's head jerked up in surprise to try to get a better look. He blinked twice and tried to focus. Boss was tall, about six foot or more, well muscled, and the light from the torch that he held seemed to reflect off the distinctive streak of gray that bisected his jet black goatee.

"Khelben!" Volo shouted in recognition.

The mage grimaced as if his ears were hurt from the loud noise.

"Don't shout," he ordered, "you might disturb the guests that are being entertained upstairs."

Volo blinked and shook his head, trying to clear away the fuzziness that still permeated his cranium.

"And you brought the map with you, how thoughtful," the mage commented, removing it from the pack that had been serving as a pillow for the master traveler's head. "I also like the cookie you traded your fat friend in for, though I am sure he is still in the area, given that the magical bond from the jewels is still in effect. I'm sure we'll find him shortly; after all, we just have to follow the trail of red gems. It is only a matter of time. Your traveling days, on the other hand, have just about come to an end."

With a bit of a struggle, the master traveler managed to attain an upright sitting position.

Out of breath from the exertion, pain still cracking through his head, Volo only managed to get out one word. "Why?"

Khelben laughed. "I know," the mage replied jovially, walking back and forth. "I'll keep giving you clues until you tell me to stop. Then you get to guess." Khelben crouched down to eye level with the master traveler. "First," the mage said, "the building upstairs is a festhall."

"Go on," Volo instructed.

"Second, because of you it had to be shut down."

*A festhall I gave a bad review to*, Volo thought. *Maybe I should have taken Passepout's concerns more seriously, . . . but what does this have to do with Khelben?*

"You're thinking," the mage commented. "I like that. Here's two clues that should give it away. The festhall upstairs used to be called the Hanging Lantern . . . "

*Doppelgangers!* Volo thought.

". . . and I usually look like this," the mage replied, throwing off his black cloak with a flourish.

The familiar, muscular form of the famous mage began to melt and shift, taking on a grayish aura that soon became the predominant color. Gone was the thick black hair, trademark beard, and manly figure, now all replaced by an almost featureless humanoid with a thick, hairless hide of gray.

". . . and my real name is Hlaavin," the figure who formerly answered to the moniker of Khelben Arunsun concluded.

*Hlaavin!* the master traveler thought. *I know that name from somewhere.*

"You can talk out loud, you know," the doppelganger said. "I can read your thoughts easily enough, but I would much rather hear them from your own lips."

The doppelganger known as Hlaavin once again began to pace back and forth, as he provided Volo with the background he desired.

"Now, you were thinking that you've heard my name before," Hlaavin said. "Probably so. You might have heard that I was the head of a certain consortium of shapechangers, rogues, and assassins known as the Unseen. The Lords of Waterdeep would quake in my wake if they knew the actual extent of my influence. The Hanging Lantern was all a part of it, a really nice setup, actually. High society patrons of influence and wealth would come to our classy festhall to meet the girl of their dreams. If they couldn't be co-opted to our cause, or corrupted in some other way, we just had them replaced by a doppelganger who was waiting in the wings. Easy as pie. That was, until you and your stupid little book came along!"

Hlaavin kicked out his knobby, taloned foot, assaulting the upright seated Volo in the stomach.

The doppelganger continued, his composure restored. "Where was I? Oh, right. We reestablished the festhall under new management and began to rework our power base back into position ever so slowly. I was experimenting with the viability of having a false Khelben working Suzail when I recognized you in the Dragon's Jaws Inn, and immediately formulated a plan for discrediting you, getting even with you, and getting rid of you all at the same time while also having you carry out the preparations for another plan I had in the offing."

"The necromancer's gems," Volo interjected.

"Exactly," Hlaavin confirmed. "Not only did they succeed in dampening your magical abilities and imposing wonderful restrictions on your travel, they also aided my first expansion of the Unseen's influence all over the world. With the wonderful map that you so generously brought with you I will be able to teleport my minions all over the Realms. Nothing will stop me now!"

The doppelganger kicked Volo in the chest again, this time toppling him over onto his side.

"You, on the other hand," Hlaavin resumed, his composure once again restored, "will disappear. Rumor will pervade Faerûn and abroad that Volo was a fraud, that he lost a challenge or perhaps shied away from one after he had already given his word. Maybe he didn't deserve to be known as *the* master traveler of the Realms. Perhaps Marcus Wands was the 'real' Volo, the one who really deserves the title. You know how people gossip and speculate."

"Not wishing to sound trite," Volo said with a grimace, "but you'll never get away with this."

"I think I will," the doppelganger replied, reassuming the Khelben form right before Volo's eyes. "Tomorrow you and your friend will be taken to a waiting boat at Skullport, taken out to sea, and dumped. You'll drown, your bodies swept out to sea, and all that sort of stuff. Your fat friend will meet a similar fate. If we don't catch him first, the gems will exert their influence. He will find himself drawn to the sea with the new day, and then his life will be snuffed out at the exact same moment as you breathe your last breath. Bound in life, bound in death."

Hlaavin grabbed his cloak and, with a flourish, threw it over his shoulder. "But tonight," Hlaavin said, "I feel like doing the town, and as what better person than old Blackstaff himself?"

"Aren't you afraid of running into the real thing?" Volo queried. "This is his home stomping ground, after all."

"As the fates would have it," the doppelganger replied, "he's out of town. Do you know what the beauty of it is? He is in Suzail for a meeting with Vangerdahast. Isn't that wonderful? But don't worry. I'll be back in plenty of time to give you and your little friend a proper sendoff."

As he went up the cellar stairs, he called back down. "And don't even think of trying anything. I'm sending a guard down to baby-sit. Ta-ta."

In less time than it took for Volo to re-upright himself to a sitting position, he was rejoined by the 'young lady' who had been there when he first came around.

"Sorry to take you away from your fun," Volo commented.

"No problem," the tart/doppelganger replied. "I was about due for a break, anyway."

Within a few moments, Shurleen regained consciousness and made eye contact with Volo. He tried to reassure her nonverbally but feared that he was doing a poor job of it since he himself thought that they were very probably doomed.

The music and frivolity of upstairs was interrupted by a pair of raucous voices.

"This is that festhall I told you about! Ain't it great!"

"Wow! Look at all the good-looking girls!"

*Passepout and Curtis!* Volo thought, then quickly tried to clear his mind in case their guard was listening in on his thoughts.

She/it wasn't.

"I guess the fleet's in," she/it commented. "I hate it when they get rowdy."

A great commotion quickly commenced above, the sound of running feet and doors slamming.

"Fire! Fire!"

"What in the . . . " the guard asked out loud, climbing up the stairs to take a peek, whereupon she/it was immediately hit over the head and fell down the stairs, coming to an unconscious rest on the cellar floor between Volo and Shurleen, legs and frock all akimbo.

Her body was quickly followed by the heroic figures of Passepout and Curtis.

"We saw you being taken down the alley and decided to follow. We waited until Khelben left to make our move," the rescuers explained.

"That wasn't Khelben," Volo corrected. "It was a doppelganger, and this is all part of an insidious plot by the Unseen."

The thespian and beachcomber quickly undid the bonds of their friends and surveyed the cellar scene.

"We can't get out upstairs," Curtis announced. "The girls, uh, things were barring the door."

"How about there?" Passepout asked, pointing to a loose sewer grate in the corner.

Volo quickly surveyed the room and decided that no other options presented themselves.

"Sounds good to me," the master traveler replied.

Shurleen, her bonds undone and her gag removed, commented, "Well, I guess it isn't everyone who gets taken to a bards' club and given a tour of the Waterdeep sewer system by the master traveler of all Faerûn."

The rapid approach of footsteps to the cellar entrance hastened their resolve, and the four travelers dropped themselves down the sewer pipe, Volo last, replacing the grate to cover their tracks.

# SEWER & UNDERMOUNTAIN

## OR

### A Ghost Gives A Chance

The drop down the sewer pipe was longer than any of them imagined it would be. The pipe was slick and situated at a slight tilt so that their fall was soon replaced by a slide, complete with a network of turns, hooks, and drops that threatened to make them dizzy.

After what seemed like hours but was really only minutes, the pipe disappeared beneath them and the four escapees from the festhall formerly known as the Hanging Lantern were deposited into an underground canal about ten feet around, and filled with about three feet of water. The distinctive odors of garbage and excrement wafted around them.

"Someone should package that ride for a fair," Passepout pointed out. "They would make a fortune, provided they supplied each customer with a nose clip to compensate for the smell."

"I can just hear my little braddah saying, 'Oh, let's do it again!' " Curtis replied.

"You have a brother?" Shurleen asked.

"Several," Curtis replied. "I'm sure you'll meet them soon."

"Wonderful," Passepout interjected, rolling his eyes.

Volo concurred with the thespian's sentiments, if not his comments.

"We can't stop now!" Volo said. "We have to get out of this sewer, then out of Waterdeep, and back to Suzail to tell Khelben and the War Wizards about Hlaavin's insidious plot."

"Quickly, this way!" Passepout said, for no other reason than to get them moving again, and it was the way the water was flowing.

The other three looked at each other and, seeing no better alternatives, shrugged in agreement and followed the path prescribed by Passepout.

As they walked, the water level continued to go down and the water itself became clearer and cleaner. The travelers were soon able to cleanse themselves of the sewerage residue. Eventually the water was no more than a trickle that escaped through various cracks and grates, clouds of mist wafting upward. The air cleared, and the four companion's clothes dried on their backs, as the underground sewer canal took on more of the appearance of a tunnel, complete with forks, stairs upward and downward, and a requisite amount of dead ends.

Their footsteps on the paved floors echoed through the tunnels, and they also began to hear various frightening noises in the distance, the owners of which none of them hoped to run into.

After two rest stops, the group stopped for a third time, this time at a juncture point that went off in five directions in addition to the one from whence they came.

"Undermountain," Volo murmured, louder than he had intended.

"Say what?" Passepout asked.

"Undermountain," the master traveler repeated. "Elminster called it the largest mass grave in all Faerûn today."

"Wonderful," Passepout replied in his familiar sarcastic manner.

Volo walked around the brick-and-mortar-walled chamber, examining the passageways out as he filled in the rest of the group on a few more details. He wished that he had his magics at his disposal to help him find a way out. He concentrated for a moment to see if they had returned, accepted that they hadn't, and once again began his tour guide spiel.

"It was constructed and designed by Halaster Blackcloak. Only one of his apprentices ever made it out alive. That was Jhesiyra Kestellharp, who later went on to Myth Drannor and adopted the moniker of the Magister."

"Wonderful," Passepout repeated.

"Meaning no offense, Mister Volo," Curtis interrupted, "the history lesson is nice and all, but do you have any idea of a way of finding the way out?"

"Many have tried," Volo continued, taking a torch down from the wall. "No one knows how far down it goes, or how far the network of tunnels stretches. Rumor has it that Halaster, a master of illusion, weaved an enchantment so that travelers could lose their way, thinking that they were going up when instead they were traveling farther down into the bowels of Mt. Waterdeep, down to the deepest levels of Undermountain."

"Is this Halaster guy still around?" Shurleen asked.

"No one knows," Volo replied. "He disappeared down here ages ago. Some say he still wanders around down here, leaving an occasional torch or message in a passage vestibule to lend some assistance to the wayward treasure-seeker."

"That guy must have been crazy," Curtis said.

"They called him the Mad Wizard," Volo said, a touch of finality to his voice signaling that the story was over.

"Maybe he wasn't really mad," Passepout said. "Maybe he was just misunderstood."

"I think I see a light down this way," Volo said, indicating the tunnel of his choice with his torch in hand. "Let's try this way."

The group agreed and continued down the tunnel.

Eventually they came to another juncture just like the other.

A new torch was waiting in the exact same position as at the previous juncture.

"Here we go again," Curtis replied, trying not to sound too pessimistic for Shurleen's sake, as she was obviously becoming frightened.

"I want to get out of here," she whimpered.

"We all do," Passepout answered gently, "and we will."

An old gentlemen dressed in the robes of a wizard from years gone by stepped out of one of the walls as if it were no more than a cloud of fog.

"You want to get out of here," the apparition said with a cackle. "Why didn't you say so? Just take the tunnel over there, you'll be on the surface and out of here in no time. And by the way, the chubby guy is right. I was just misunderstood."

The apparition walked through the opposite wall and disappeared, though his continued cackling could still be heard off in the distance.

Volo looked at the group, and then looked down the tunnel that had been indicated by Halaster.

"Why not?" the master traveler replied. "It's not like he's ever lied to us or anything."

An echoing voice was heard in the distance, repeating the statement, "I'm just misunderstood."

"That settles it for me," Passepout replied with a sense of finality to his voice. "Always obey the directions of a ghost, particularly when he is the only one who knows the way out. Feet, do your stuff."

Taking a torch down from its holder, Passepout started down the tunnel that had been indicated by the apparition.

After an hour, the tunnel's incline steadily increased.

In another hour, they were out, and the sun was high in the sky.

Volo stopped a passing milkmaid for their location.

"Why, you're in Baldur's Gate, of course," the maid replied, and continued on her way.

"Baldur's Gate," Curtis replied in disbelief, "but that's miles down the coast from Waterdeep. We couldn't have been walking for that long."

"I guess Mad Monkey isn't the only immortal with a passion for portals," Volo replied.

"Well," Shurleen commented, taking on the unlikely role of the optimist of the group, "at least we're closer to Suzail."

"We'll go into town, hire some horses and head due east," Volo suggested.

The group agreed, and they headed toward the outskirts of the city, though Volo noticed a certain sense of apprehension and reluctance on Passepout's part.

The master traveler thought he heard the thespian mutter under his breath, "Baldur's Gate, where all the chickens come home to roost." Volo couldn't be sure if those were his exact words, but thought that it would be better not to ask him for clarification at the present time.

# JAILBREAK!

## OR

## Imagine Their Gaol!

As per usual, Volo took upon the role of tour guide as they approached the city, giving his fellow travelers a little background.

"Known as 'the place that is halfway to everywhere,'" the master traveler began, "Baldur's Gate is actually two cities, one walled and the other, more recent, addition to its borders outside the wall. It seems that the city thrived like a sprouting child and had to burst its seams. It is ruled by the

Four Grand Dukes who are also called the Council of Four. The city is renowned as one of the most tolerant but also quietly well policed places in the western Realms."

Volo saw that he was beginning to lose his audience to wandering thoughts and decided to bring his spiel to an end. "From what I understand it also has a thriving thieves' guild, which has been known to work with the local authorities to crush illicit and illegal activities that they might consider unfair competition."

"You can say that again," Passepout whispered under his breath.

Volo paused for a moment, thinking that he had heard something. Curtis and Shurleen were quietly enjoying each other's company as if this were no more than a walk on a summer's day. Turning to the chubby thespian, he asked, "Did you say something, Passepout?"

"No, Mister Volo," the thespian replied, resuming his distant silence.

Volo's offhand comment about Baldur's Gate being well policed turned out to be true.

Passepout was arrested within moments of his entering the city. The guards were well mannered but firm, and the chubby thespian did not put up a fight.

"Passepout!" Volo demanded. "What's going on?"

As the guards slipped a pair of shackles on him, he asked, "Can I just say good-bye to my friends?"

"All right," the captain of the guard, whose name was Gehrard, replied, "but be quick about it."

"I'm sorry, Mister Volo," the chubby thespian replied dolefully.

"What is going on?" the master traveler demanded.

"As I'm sure you know, acting is not always the

most lucrative of professions. My dear parents Idle and Catinflas often had to occasionally pick pockets to help make ends meet, a trade they were all too willing to pass on to their son. We were performing to meager audiences on the outskirts of town and found that we once again had to supplement our earnings with a little unvolunteered gratuity from some of our audience. How were we to know that the thieves' Guildmaster Ravenscar was in the audience? He called out the city guard, and we were arrested. I managed to escape, but Mom and Dad are still in prison."

Volo turned to Gehrard, and said, "Surely, we can work something out?"

"Afraid not," the captain replied. "When this here fellow escaped, I was held to blame and demoted. On that day I swore out a magical warrant on the city gates that would let me know when, if ever, he returned to the city, because if he did I swore that I would once again bring this fugitive to justice."

"It doesn't sound like justice to me," Shurleen interjected.

"Doesn't matter," the captain stoically replied, beginning to escort the thespian to the jail. "A nice long prison stay is waiting for him, but cheer up; the last fellow I brought in was sentenced to have his arm hacked off before being sent to gallows, but then again he *did* murder the wife of one of the city's most famous clerics."

Passepout looked back at his friends, and said, "Sorry."

Hanging his head in shame, he was led off by the guards.

"What can we do?," Shurleen asked. "We can't just leave him here."

Volo was very aware of this. He had grown attached to his rotund companion and had no desire to see him left rotting in some dark prison cell. The fact that he and Passepout were still magically bound together was entirely secondary.

"Well, if we're going to do something, we'd better do it fast," Curtis replied. "We have to get back to Suzail to inform Khelben and the War Wizards of Hlaavin's plans."

Volo was torn.

"You two go to Suzail," he decided. "I'll stay here and think of something."

"We won't go without you and Passepout," Shurleen demanded. "Right, Curtis?"

"Right," the beachcomber responded in agreement without thinking, which Volo always accepted as a necessary talent for any good husband.

"I guess that leaves us no choice," the master traveler replied. "We have to arrange a jailbreak."

Volo knew that the jail was one of the oldest buildings in the city, and that the holding cell for new prisoners was near an exterior wall on the surface level of the structure, the dungeon being reserved for serious criminals and killers. He was sure that Passepout would be classified as neither.

"If I'm not mistaken, the salt air has been playing havoc with the external walls of many of the local structures that have been around a while, and since usually the first two buildings that are put up when one builds a city are the temple of the patron's choice and the prison, I'm sure that the prison's wall are the worse for the wear. I understand that the Council of Four has funded an extensive city renovation program to shore up the old structures, but I sincerely doubt that the prison is high on their list of priorities. All we have to do is break through the exterior wall into the cell Passepout is being held in, and get out of town before anyone is the wiser."

"Not an easy trick, if you ask me," Curtis replied. "Don't you think we're going to need a little help?"

"Sure," the master traveler replied. "I know this tavern not too far from here, where sell-swords of good standing and reputation have been known to frequent. I'm sure we'll find some willing assistance there."

The Inn of the Bovine Lad catered to mercenaries and wranglers for hire of all types, and as usual it was packed to the seams with brawling and boisterous sell-swords looking for employment and/or trouble.

Volo scanned the crowd as if looking for someone in particular.

"Who are you looking for?" Shurleen asked.

"A mercenary who is obviously not a local," the master traveler replied. "We can't afford to have our plan given away due to someone's personal loyalties. A newcomer to Baldur's Gate would be best, and I have to find one without appearing too obvious."

"What should we do?" Curtis asked.

"Stand around and try to look tough," Volo replied. Then, looking at Shurleen still clad in the water-stained remnants of her Maztican finery, he changed his mind. "On second thought, wait outside and, I know it's hard, but try to look inconspicuous."

Curtis and Shurleen left, and Volo resumed surveying the crowd. He settled on a likely candidate, a reddish-haired warrior woman dressed in battle-worn chain mail with a singularly opportunistic opening in the pectoral region that showed off her ample cleavage. A pair of azure tattoos adorned her arms, seeming almost to glow and move in the smoky tavern's interior. She appeared to be keeping company with a lizard man of some sort who sat across from her at a table for two. As lizard men were not indigenous to the Western Heartlands, Volo figured that they were a good bet.

Volo approached the couple cautiously, hoping to eavesdrop on their conversation, but unfortunately could only make out an occasional growl or snort from the nonhuman member of the pair. Upon closer examination, the master traveler discerned that it was not a lizard man at all but a saurial with a blunted muzzle, green scales, and yellow eyes, with a single fin running down the back of its head.

"Don't just eavesdrop," the warrior woman announced. "Drop in." With that she reached up and grabbed the master traveler by the collar, pulling him down to a place at the table.

"Sorry," the master traveler said.

"What do you want?"

"I'm looking for a pair of mercenaries . . . " Volo began.

"We're not mercenaries," she replied churlishly. "We're adventurers. What do you want?"

"I need help to rescue a friend," Volo replied.

The saurial snorted again, and Volo detected the distinct aroma of honeysuckle.

"Dragonbait here seems to trust you," she said. "My name is Alias. What can we do for you?"

Quickly and quietly, Volo told her the whole story, from the challenge in Suzail, through the trip to Kara-Tur and Maztica, and right up to

Passepout's incarceration. For some reason he trusted this strange woman and her saurial companion, and he realized that they were his and Passepout's only hope.

Dragonbait growled, and then snorted again.

"Okay," Alias said. "We'll help you. What's the plan?"

Volo and the two newly recruited adventurers left the tavern and rejoined Curtis and Shurleen, who were trying to look inconspicuous.

"We're going to need at least eight horses," Alias said. "Two of the strongest draft horses we can find, and six of the swiftest steeds available. After the break, Dragonbait and I will draw the pursuers after us. My saurial friend here sticks out in a crowd, and we didn't plan on staying around here long, anyway. I know a place we can lose the guards in the mountains, and we'll be home free in no time. You, on the other hand, have to get to Suzail, as soon as possible. This doppelganger conspiracy can endanger the stability of all of the nations of Faerûn, and beyond."

The conspirators went off in different directions and rendezvoused at the rear of the prison where Passepout was being held. Alias and Dragonbait brought the horses with them, evidently obtained through a Harper contact.

"I'm pretty sure he would be in this cell," Volo said, pointing to a barred window.

"No problem," Alias replied. "Shurleen, stand around the corner and be the lookout. Give a holler if anyone comes."

Shurleen kissed Curtis on the cheek and left, taking her position just out of sight.

"If Volo is right, we should be able to pull out

these bars from the window with a minimal amount of help, which is why I brought these fine specimens," she said, indicating the draft horses, "Bush and Heiser, to help us out."

Volo and Curtis wrapped a rope around the window bars, and handed it back to Alias, who attached it to Bush and Heiser.

"Pull!" she ordered.

They did. Nothing happened.

"Pull!" she repeated.

Once again the horses strained with all their might. At last, something began to give . . . but instead of just pulling the bars out, the entire wall section collapsed, showering the jailbreakers with ancient mortar dust and pebbles. Instead of a single inconspicuous hole into a lone cell, the entire back cellblock was exposed. This turned out to be quite fortunate as Passepout, as it turned out, was being held in the cell next door to the one that was being seiged. A chunk from the wall to his cell, however, was loosened by the horses' efforts, and with a little extra help from Dragonbait and Curtis, a hole was made that was large enough for the rotund thespian to get through.

The prisoner in the neighboring cell, who had obviously spent a long time in the prison by the length of his hair and beard, also took the opportunity to make his escape.

"Free at last," he cried. "Now I must seek revenge on those who have wrought pain and suffering on myself and my family."

Dragonbait snorted his disapproval.

"It's all right," Passepout explained. "He's an innocent man framed by jealous rivals."

"Yeah, sure," Alias replied sarcastically.

"It's true," the thespian insisted, and then, turning back to his fellow prisoner, added, "Good luck, Edmund."

"Thanks, Passepout," the long-haired prisoner replied, "and to you, too. If you get the chance, look me up. The world hasn't seen the last of me, Count Dantes, by a long shot."

With that the prisoner took off in the direction in which Shurleen was stationed, and disappeared down an alley.

Alias called to the others. "Quickly, you go west, and we'll go north."

Dragonbait snorted, and Alias joined him at Passepout's side.

"My friend here is a paladin," she explained. "Once this crisis has passed, he wants you to turn yourself in and make restitution for the wrongs you have done in the past."

"I will," the rotund thespian replied.

"Swear," she commanded.

"I swear," he replied, "and thank you."

Alias and her saurial friend mounted their steeds and made ready for a gallop.

"Give us a few seconds to draw the pursuers, then make haste for Suzail," she instructed.

Without waiting for further thanks, she and her companion rode off at a gallop.

In a matter of seconds, Shurleen ran back to the group.

"The guards were about to come back here when Alias and Dragonbait rode past," she replied, out of breath from running. "They all took off after them."

"Time's a-wasting," Volo announced.

"I know," Passepout replied, thankful to be out of the cramped confines of the holding cell, " 'We're burning daylight,' right?"

"Right," the master traveler agreed. "Eastward

ho! On to Suzail!"

Quickly mounting their steeds, they headed eastward.

Keeping his horse apace with Volo's, the chubby thespian called to the master traveler, "Well, at least Captain Gehrard won't be held accountable for my escape this time."

"How so?" Volo queried.

"Certain people were so happy that I was to be made an example of that they gave him the day off for bringing me, the dangerous fugitive, in after being at large for so long a time. Gehrard's not such a bad guy, really," Passepout commented, "just a bit obsessed."

They were out of the city and on their way in no time, and not a single member of the city guard pursued them.

# SOUTHEAST

### OR

## Back to Cormyr, and Step On It!

When they had ridden beyond sight of the city, Volo brought the group to a stop.

"In the interests of time, I'm afraid that we are going to have to take the fastest route, which unfortunately also happens to be the most dangerous," the master traveler announced.

"We are with you, my captain," Curtis intoned.

"This is no time for theatrics," Volo instructed.

"First, we will have to pass the legendary Fields of the Dead, and then the site of the infamous Battle of the Bones."

"Yeah, yeah, the possibility of encounters with undead, orcs, and worse," Passepout replied, anxious to bring their quest to an end. "Go on."

"We will then have to pass through Zhent-infested mountains."

"Fine," the thespian answered for the group. "Let's just get moving."

"Don't you even want to stop for lunch?" Shurleen asked.

"There will be plenty of time for eating at the Dragon's Jaws Inn," he replied. "Now, are we going or staying?"

Volo was heartened by the change in the thespian; it was as if he had discovered a secret bravery and courage from within that heretofore he was unaware of.

"Let's go!" Volo replied, leading the group at a full gallop toward the Fields of the Dead.

The Fields of the Dead made up a barren wasteland that had withered away all that had tried to grow in it. This, however, was a veritable garden compared to the next leg of their journey.

They entered the site of the legendary Battle of the Bones.

The soil had a dusty white pallor that mirrored the bones of long-dead warriors that jutted out from the landscape surface.

"Watch where your horse is stepping," Volo called back to the others. "Many a horse has broken a leg by getting its hoof caught in some long-abandoned rib cage."

The steeds kicked up clouds of white and gray as

they passed through the bleached battleground of carnage, where humans and orcs had engaged in mortal combat for almost a full week of nonstop fighting. Skulls were trampled under their fiery hooves, and shards and splinters that had been once part of human limbs were blown to the side by galloping cascades.

Shurleen had narrowly missed being thrown from her horse, when it stumbled before leaping over an ossified orc carcass, but she quickly recovered, reining her horse to the side for a moment before rejoining the others in midgallop.

Several members of the undead watched from their graves, never deigning to give their presence away. There are some sights that hold even zombies and specters in awe.

The travelers passed out of the fields of former carnage without a single incident.

Sometimes leading their steeds on foot so as not to be seen, the four travelers carefully navigated the Zhent-infested mountains.

A single robber brigand who had mistakenly assumed that Shurleen was traveling alone was the only obstacle encountered, and before Curtis had a chance to double back and subdue the pugnacious thief, Shurleen had already disarmed him with a quick kick to the tender parts and was back on her way.

After many miles of short rations, and hours of riding that were happily shorter than expected due to an unexpected enchantment of speed that the steeds had been blessed with, the foursome soon entered Cormyr.

Even sooner, the city of Suzail loomed in front of them.

# SUZAIL

### OR

## There and Back Again

Kirk had retired a matter of days ago and Duke was already missing his old friend. Stewart, Kirk's replacement, was a nice enough fellow, but a bit too much of a talker, which was a real problem since he also had a tendency to stutter. Duke had seen it take him close to a half hour to tell a passing traveler that it was necessary for him to register at the gate before entering the city due to another one of Vangerdahast's meetings of the War Wizards. Kirk might have been a bit pugnacious at times, but at least he got the job done quickly and efficiently.

"St-t-t-t-t-t-t-top! St-t-t-t-t-t-top!"

*What is he up to now?* Duke thought, getting up from his seniority-has-its-privileges chair in the watch station in just enough time to see four riders race through the gate.

"Whoa!" the leader stopped the steeds.

Duke recognized him as the legendary Volo, whom he had first met back when Kirk was assigned to the gate.

"Khelben," Volo puffed. "Where is he?"

"Probably at the Dragon's Jaws Inn," Duke replied, "raising a tankard or two with Vangerdahast. The Council of Mages doesn't meet again until tomorrow, and old Vangerdahast likes to take the occasional visiting dignitary out to the local hot spots."

"Thanks," Volo replied. "We'll register later."

"No problem," Duke answered, thinking, *Fame has its privileges*.

Stewart had just caught up to the horsemen, as Duke signaled for them to go.

"B-b-b-b-b-u-u-u-t, Duke," the junior geriatric Purple Dragon stuttered. "They didn't sign in."

"Don't worry about it," Duke replied, and resumed his place of seniority in the watch station while Stewart turned his attentions to an new group of arrivals.

Khelben was feeling very uncomfortable as he and Vangerdahast arrived at the doorstep of the Dragon's Jaws Inn.

"Honestly," the ramrod-straight mage with the distinctive streak of gray in his beard said to the older mage, "do we really have to make an appearance here?"

"Yes," Vangerdahast replied. "The citizens of Suzail enjoy it. It is but a small sacrifice of our time in the larger scheme of things."

"Speaking of time," Khelben remarked, "I really feel that we are spending too much time in meetings. I've lost count of the amount of times in the past year that you've called a gathering of the War Wizards. Sometimes I feel like I'm spending more time in Suzail than I am in Waterdeep."

"Well," Vangerdahast replied, "having spent so much time in our fair city, it is only proper that you take advantage of this opportunity to dine at the Dragon's Jaws Inn, the one tavern that any visitor to Cormyr shouldn't miss."

The two mages opened the door and stepped inside and were immediately greeted by the always-on-the-spot Milo Dudley.

"Mister Vangerdahast, you honor our establishment, and Mister Arunsun, I'm glad you decided to pay us another visit. As I said to you before, though, had you given me a little notice I could have arranged something special for you, but I guess we will have to make due with our typically exceptional service."

"I beg your pardon," Khelben interrupted, somewhat confused. "What did you just say?"

"Our typically exceptional service?" Milo repeated with a touch of uncertainty in his voice.

"No, before that."

"Oh, about the last time you were here," the majordomo replied.

"But I've never been here before," Khelben corrected.

Milo was puzzled. He never forgot a face, particularly one as famous as the Lord Mage of Waterdeep himself. *I know,* the dwarf concluded, *he doesn't want Vangerdahast to know that he's been here before. That must be it. I wonder why? Oh, but wizards are a strange sort anyway.*

"I'm sorry Mister Arunsun," Milo replied with a sly wink. "I must have been mistaken."

. Khelben was now even more confused by the majordomo's subtle wink, but decided to let it pass.

"Gentlemen," Milo announced, "your table awaits." He proceeded to hustle through the crowd to one of the prime tables that were always reserved for VIPs.

"First time, eh?" Vangerdahast whispered to his companion, having also caught Milo's subtle wink.

Khelben just harumphed a response.

The two mages were quietly enjoying the dwarf-tossing festivities over two tankards of ale; an elven ranger who did not seem to know his own strength had just sent a particularly rotund dwarf sailing out of the playing area, through the kitchen door, and out of the kitchen window into the backyard compost heap. Suddenly a great commotion ensued at the door.

"Khelben! Vangerdahast! Are they here?"

Milo was once again on the spot, greeting his rather boisterous and demanding, but also very important guests at the door.

"Mister Volo," the dwarf attended, "it is wonderful to see you again, but please calm down and observe the simple rules of common courtesy. This is a respectable establishment, after all."

"Khelben and Vangerdahast," the master traveler repeated, this time as a demand. "Are they here?"

"They are at one of our special tables in the back," Milo replied, studiously controlling his temper, as a good host is expected to. "Would you like me to see if they will permit you to join them?"

Having received the answer to his question, Volo and his companions barged across the tavern floor toward the table where the two mages were sitting, despite the audible protestations from Milo whom they had left standing in their wake.

"What is the meaning of this intrusion?" Vangerdahast demanded, both he and Khelben standing up as the four travelers approached.

"Sorry for the intrusion, your eminence," Volo apologized, "but there is a grave matter we must discuss with you immediately."

"You're Volo," Khelben interrupted, "that guide book author."

"At your service, Lord Arunsun," the master traveler replied with a bow, "but there is a great deal of urgency to the matters at hand. A dark conspiracy is underfoot. It is based in your own Waterdeep, and it threatens the stability of all Toril."

Khelben began to finger his beard, which Volo immediately realized meant that he was giving the matter serious consideration.

"Well, then," the Lord Mage of Waterdeep replied, "why don't you and your friends pull up a few chairs, and tell us just what seems to be going on?"

Volo immediately sat down and began to relate their story.

"My friend Passepout and I were having a good time here at the Dragon's Jaws Inn when a fellow who looked exactly like yourself accosted us . . . "

Volo told the tale as swiftly and efficiently as possible, with Curtis and Shurleen chiming in at various points in the story to allow the master traveler to catch his breath. No one noticed when Passepout withdrew from the table for a moment to pass a piece of paper to a messenger who was waiting by the bar.

"Get this to Lord Bleth immediately," the thespian instructed.

The messenger left, and Passepout rejoined the group just in time to wrap up the tale of their adventure. ". . . so they busted me out of the jail at Baldur's Gate, which was for minor previous offenses for which I am truly sorry," the master thespian rambled, "and we hightailed our way here."

"We have been aware of the insidious group known as the Unseen for quite a while," Khelben said, "but we were unaware that their influence was spreading and that their powers were on the rise."

"If they succeed with their plans to establish teleporting gates throughout Toril, there will be no way to control their insidious infection of our social structure. You won't know whom to trust. Anyone, even yourself, Lord Mage, could be a doppelganger," Volo concluded.

"Quite," Khelben replied.

Vangerdahast put out his hand toward Passepout.

"I need one of these necromancer's gems so that I can neutralize the whole lot of them," the mage said. "Please hand one to me."

Passepout reached into his pouch and felt nothing but air.

"Oh, no," the thespian said. "I must have dropped the last one on the way in here. What will we do?"

"I must have one of the gems in order to counteract the influence of the others," the mage insisted. "Without it, we are powerless."

Shurleen reached into a hidden pocket in her belt.

"Here," she said, passing a red gem to Vangerdahast, and then turning to the others in the group, added, "I just thought I would keep a souvenir. I didn't mean anything by it. I guess we're lucky I did."

Vangerdahast examined the red gem carefully, holding it up to the light.

"This isn't just any necromancer gem," the mage announced. "This is one of the legendary jewels of Verne. With just this one stone, I should be able to scry the locations of all the others."

The mage stared into the facets of the red stone.

"I see a desert, a roadway, an ocean, Storm Silverhand's farm, some place very hot . . . "

"That's probably the volcano on Chult," Passepout explained.

"That will do," the mage announced, and taking Khelben's hand for added strength and magical support, he concentrated with great intensity, and squeezed the gem with all his might.

When he reopened his hand, the gem had disappeared.

"Now all of the gems will act as gates to that volcanic location on Chult," he replied. "It won't affect their locations on Hlaavin's map, though. He won't discover what we have done until he tries it out himself."

A faint trace of a smile appeared on Khelben's lips. "It will serve him right," the Lord Mage of Waterdeep replied.

"Oh, and by the way," Vangerdahast added, "the magic that had bound the two of you together and restricted your movements has been removed, as has the buffer that has restricted your magical abilities, Volo."

"*Wonderful!*" Passepout replied.

"Agreed," said Volo, adding, "not that I didn't enjoy your company and all."

"I'm afraid that I won't be good company for much longer," the thespian replied. "Now that the crisis is over, I have sworn to turn myself in."

"I don't think there will be any need for that," Khelben volunteered. "I have a few friends in the Baldur's Gate hierarchy. I think an amnesty is in order in lieu of the service you have provided for the security of all Faerûn."

"*Wonderful!*" the chubby thespian replied, for once without a trace of sarcasm.

"I'm sure that I can also arrange the release of your parents as well. It sounds like they've served their time."

Turning to Volo, the thespian whispered, "You know, I'm beginning to like some of these wizards."

Volo just smiled.

*Slam!*

A messenger barged into the inn and made an announcement.

"I have here a message from Lord Gruen Bleth," he proclaimed.

"Read it," Passepout said thinking, *Reward money, here I come!*

The messenger read: "Lord Bleth is pleased to hear of the rescue of Miss Shurleen Laduce, but feels that there is no need for a reward since a replacement for her services has already been secured."

"A replacement for his daughter?" Passepout sputtered in disbelief.

"No," confessed Shurleen, "for his daughter's dresser. His daughter had already been ransomed home before I was traded to the other tribe."

The messenger continued reading: "Lord Bleth

also wishes to assure Miss Laduce that he will be providing her with a most favorable recommendation when she seeks employment elsewhere."

"So you're not an heiress?" Curtis asked.

"No," Shurleen replied, with a quiver in her voice, "just an heiress's dresser."

Shurleen looked at the young beachcomber with tears in her eyes. Before this trip, her sole desire was to marry money; she only hoped that he did not share the same ambitions.

"Well, it doesn't matter to me that you're not an heiress," Curtis replied. "I still want you to be my wife."

"Oh, Curtis," she replied, giving him a big kiss, "for richer, for poorer, till death do us part."

A cheer went up through the tavern and much merrymaking commenced, which didn't finish till the dawn's early light.

"Three cheers for Curtis and Shurleen," Volo shouted.

*Hip, hip, hooray!*

"Three cheers for Volo, the true master traveler of all Toril!" Passepout added.

*Hip, hip, hooray!*

"And three cheers for Passepout, son of Catinflas and Idle, famed thespian and part-time hero," Volo shouted.

*Hip, hip, hooray!*

# YONDA

### OR

## The Story Concludes

Rosy-fingered dawn was just creeping its way over the horizon when the four world-weary travelers decided to leave the Dragon's Jaws Inn, despite invitations from Gnorm, Milo, and even Vangerdahast himself to take advantage of the best accommodations in all Suzail.

"No, thanks," Volo replied to all, adding, "Maybe later."

"Where do you think you'll go?" Passepout asked.

"I thought I might drop by Yonda," Volo replied.

"Your old friends, eh?" Passepout responded wistfully.

"Why not?" the master traveler replied. "That is, if it's all right with you."

"What do you mean?" the thespian queried.

"Well, I remember saying that I thought your time would come," Volo answered. "Well, that time is now."

"I'm going to stay at the Bernd estate?" Passepout asked incredulously.

"Why, certainly," Volo replied. "Bernd has an eye for theatrical talent. I'm sure he would consider giving you an audition—that is, if you are indeed looking for a patron."

"Wonderful!" Passepout replied. "I'm going to the Bernd estate!" he shouted.

Curtis and Shurleen, who were still holding hands, came up from behind, and Curtis patted Passepout on the back.

"Why, that's really great," Curtis said. "Congratulations!"

"I hope you remember us little people when you are a rich and famous actor," Shurleen added, a twinkle of a smile on her lips.

"I could never forget you," Passepout replied, looking into her eyes and then, quickly turning to Curtis, adding, "neither of you, particularly after all we've been through together."

"You can say that again," Volo affirmed.

"Do you mind if we walk with you?" Shurleen asked.

"Not at all," Volo replied. "Do you need a place to stay?"

"No," Curtis replied. "I have a few connections in this neck of the woods."

Volo just smiled, and continued walking.

Duke was asleep at the watch station, and Stewart was busy interrogating a druid who wished to bring in unidentified fruits and plants to Suzail without the proper papers and authorizations, so the travelers passed through without stopping.

The sun was rising, and it looked as if it were going to be a beautiful day.

The Bernd estate was not too far from the city gate, and the group ambled along in no particular hurry, just enjoying their walk and being together.

Two gray-striped cats were curled up at the entrance to the Bernd estate, the manorly castle just visible in the midmorning mists. Upon their approach, the two cats immediately came to attention, rushed over to Curtis, and began rubbing themselves against his legs and feet.

"Sparky, Minx," he said affectionately, "it's good to see you, too. It has been a while. I didn't think you'd remember me."

The two felines meowed welcomingly in their catlike way.

Shurleen stopped in her tracks. "You know these cats?" she asked quizzically.

"Sure," Curtis replied.

Volo also stopped.

"These are Lord Bernd's cats," Volo pointed out.

"That's right," the young beachcomber agreed.

"You've been here before?" Passepout asked incredulously.

"Sure," Curtis replied, "whenever I come to visit my faddah."

"What?" the dumbstruck threesome said in unison.

"That's right," Curtis clarified. "Yonda is the castle of my faddah."

"Faddah?" Passepout queried.

Volo chuckled, regaining his composure.

"His father . . . so you're old man Bernd's son," the master traveler replied, "the one who kept putting off entering the family business."

"That's right," Curtis answered. "I wanted to see the world first, and now that I have, I guess it is time to get serious . . . "

Curtis gave a quick look to Shurleen, and smiled, adding, ". . . about a lot of things."

The two young lovers kissed. Volo and Passepout looked on, stole a glance at each other, and said in unison, *"Wonderful."*

# APPENDIX

## Dramatis Personae
### in order of appearance or mention

*Once Around the Realms* includes many familiar faces of Realmslore. Following, I have listed book authors who have previously used these characters, and have provided titles in which the characters made major appearances. Any discrepancies with Realmslore or canon is solely my responsibility, and not the fault of the characters' marvelous creators.

— *B. M. T.*

**Kirk and Duke:** over-the-hill veterans of the Horde campaign, now assigned to watch duty at the gate of Suzail.

**Purple Dragons:** King Azoun's large standing army, whose name comes from the emblem featured on the banner of Cormyr.

**Vangerdahast:** royal magician of Cormyr, chief advisor to King Azoun IV, chairman emperius of the College of War Wizards.

**King Azoun IV:** just king of Cormyr, protector of Tilverton, and victor of the Horde incursions, who has proven himself an able leader both in peace and at war.

**Passepout:** son of thought-to-be legendary thespians (and thieves), self-proclaimed famed actor and ladies' man, now serving as a traveling companion to Volo.

**Catinflas and Idle:** parents of Passepout.

**Elminster:** 'nuff said, even though he doesn't actually appear in this book.

**Volothamp Geddarm:** roguish magician who has written a number of best-selling travel guides and *Volo's Guide to All Things Magical,* a suppressed work on magic for the common people. He is truly the master traveler of the Realms.

**Bernd Family:** wealthy family of Suzail, whose family estate is just outside the city limits.

**Milo Dudley:** dwarven mayordomo of the Dragon's Jaws Inn.

**Gnorm the Gnome:** secret owner of the Dragon's Jaws Inn.

**Mindy, Sara, Wolfgang, and Molly:** "the hired help" at the Dragon's Jaws Inn. Molly is a personal favorite of Volo's.

**Marcus Wands:** imposter, rogue, and ne'er-do-well black sheep of the Wands family, who passed himself off as the real Volo (using the alias "Marco Volo") on a trip from Waterdeep to the Dalelands.

**Khelben "Blackstaff" Arunsun:** the most powerful and influential archmage of the Sword Coast (and probably a secret Lord of Waterdeep).

**Kalen Verne:** doppleganger necromancer and alchemist.

**Stew Bone:** cook for a herding caravan bound north from Cormyr.

**Elam Jack:** disreputable rogue temporarily employed by the herding caravan.

**Malpasso:** strong silent ramrod of the caravan, an honest man from humble origins.

**Catlindra Serpentar:** born in Impiltur to merchant parents, she used her inheritance to found an adventuring company after a doppleganger slew her mother (from *Campaign Guide to Myth Drannor*).

**The Company of the Catlash:** female adventuring band founded by Catlindra Serpentar. Originally from the Vilhon Reach, they have chosen a wandering life and are not likely to throw it away in exchange for any of the many handsome princes that cross their paths (from *Campaign Guide to Myth Drannor*).

**Hlaavin:** doppleganger crime lord whose origins have been traced to both the Rat Hills and Skullport. Set up the Hanging Lantern Festhall in Waterdeep as a front for his criminal activities until its doppleganger affiliation was inadvertently exposed in *Volo's Guide to Waterdeep*.

**The Unseen:** consortium of shapechangers, thieves, illusionists, and assassins headed by Hlaavin. Their purpose is to supplant various powerful people of the Realms with their own minions.

**Lord Gruen Bleth:** head of the Seven Suns trading company and one of the most powerful merchant families in the Realms.

**Jhaele Silvermane:** proprietor of the Old Skull Inn and shrewd observer of new faces passing through Shadowdale.

**Storm Silverhand:** one of the legendary Seven Sisters, also known as the Harper of Shadowdale, now thought to be retired.

**Mystia and Mandy:** Storm's horse and donkey.

**Marks the Harper:** mute Harper agent in the Moonsea region.

**The Red Plumes of Hillsfar:** mercenary-based militia and standing army of Hillsfar whose red-plumed helms were provided by Maalthiir, first lord of Hillsfar, in order to forge the diverse companies into a unified and identifiable fighting force.

**Captain Bligh Queeg:** legendary ship captain and disciplinarian in command of the merchant vessel the *Amistad's Bounty*.

**The Cormyrean Freesails:** King Azoun's legendary seagoing privateer corp.

**First Mate Nordhoff:** first mate of the *Amistad's Bounty*, Captain of the *Balding Quaestor*, and secret Harper agent. He was an orphan.

**Marlon:** cabin boy serving on the *Amistad's Bounty*.

**Starbuck:** flogged crewman on the *Amistad's Bounty*, who became first mate of the *Balding Quaestor*.

**Captain Ahib Fletcher:** villainous pirate captain with a whip fastened to one wrist stump and a hook forged to the other. He is missing a leg as well.

**The Brotherhood of the Red Tide:** villainous pirate brotherhood whose patron deity is Cyric.

**Cyric:** God of Strife and Intrigue, Patron of Murder, and Prince of Lies. He is also sometimes called the Mad God, but only behind his back (featured in the Avatar Trilogy by Richard Awlinson and *Prince of Lies* by James Lowder).

**Hannibal:** former captain in the Purple Dragons, now leader of a ragtag mercenary band.

**Eli of the Wallachs:** balding and flea-bitten halfling bandit leader known to terrorize travelers along the Golden Road.

**Jonas Grumby:** foul-smelling dwarven captain of the airship *Minnow*.

**Curtis:** a young man in search of adventure.

**Ffogg:** archmage proprietor of the *D. Niven* (later rechristened *Minnow*).

**Artus Cimber:** legendary Harper explorer and adventurer known for his famous Chult expedition (featured in *Ring of Winter* by James Lowder).

**Olive Ruskettle:** famous halfling bard of dubious reputation (featured in the Finder's Stone Trilogy by Kate Novak and Jeff Grubb).

**Olav Ruskettle:** true and famous bard who lost his name and reputation to Olive in a dice game.

**Gherri, Aahnnie, and Modesti:** Tabaxi warriors who invented the parachute.

**Aleekhan:** minor Horde warlord.

**Sammhie:** lesser cousin of Aleekhan known for his passion for art.

**Shurleen Laduce:** young woman of humble birth mistaken for the daughter of Lord Gruen Bleth. She is actually his daughter's dresser.

**Danilo Thann:** legendary Harper bard, known for his good looks and musical talent (featured in *Elfshadow* and *Elfsong* by Elaine Cunningham).

**Chiun de Lao:** unflappable old coot avatar of the demigod Mad Monkey.

**Mad Monkey:** martial arts master and chaotic good demigod of Kara-Tur (featured in *Mad Monkey vs. the Dragon Claw* by Jeff Grubb).

**Blackthumb:** sailor from the Moonshae Isles who settled in Kara-Tur and opened a western-style inn called the No Bull House on the coast of the continent.

**Tai Pan:** friend of Blackthumb and proprietor of boatyard called Pan's Sampans (thought to be the most honest shipbuilder on the Celestial Sea).

**Dragon Claw:** petty fiend martial artist (featured in *Mad Monkey vs. the Dragon Claw* by Jeff Grubb).

**Rurk:** Tethyrian expatriate mercenary who has set himself up as a Maztican warlord (known by his native subjects as Mis Ta Rurk).

**Herve:** opportunistic halfling who serves as Rurk's mayordomo.

**Queen Amlaruil:** elven ruler of the Isle of Evermeet.

**Drizzt Do'Urden:** renegade drow ranger who has escaped the oppressive regime of his underground homeland (featured in the Icewind Dale Trilogy, the Dark Elf Trilogy, *The Legacy, Starless Night,* and *Siege of Darkness* by R. A. Salvatore).

**Wolflarson:** bigoted dwarf captain of the good ship *Leominster.*

**Guenhwyvar:** otherworldly panther companion of Drizzt.

**Halaster Blackcloak:** known as the Mad Wizard, he is the long-thought-dead master of Undermountain.

**Jhesiyra Kestellharp:** Halaster's sole surviving apprentice who eventually moved to Myth Drannor and became known as the Magister.

**Captain Gehrard:** captain of the city guard of Baldur's Gate, known for his dogged pursuit of escaped criminals.

**Dragonbait:** saurial paladin companion of Alias (featured in *Azure Bonds* and *Song of the Saurials* by Kate Novak and Jeff Grubb).

**Alias:** a magical construct, though to all appearances a normal woman warrior. Her right arm is marked by a set of azure tattoos (a vestige from her creation), and she currently makes her living as a free sword (featured in *Azure Bonds* and *Song of the Saurials* by Kate Novak and Jeff Grubb).

**Stewart:** Kirk's equally over-the-hill replacement at watch duty at the gates of Suzail.

**Sparky and Minx:** two striped cats who are the Bernd family pets.

# Elminster:
# The Making of a Mage

## Ed Greenwood

**From the creator of the FORGOTTEN REALMS® world comes the epic story of the Realms' greatest wizard!**

Elminster. No other wizard wields such power. No other wizard has lived as long. No other book tells you the story of his origins. Born into humble circumstances, Elminster begins his life of magic in an odd way – by fleeing from it. When his village and his family are destroyed by a being of sorcerous might, young Elminster eschews the arcane arts. Instead, he becomes a journeyman warrior and embarks on a mission of revenge . . . until his destiny turns in on itself and he embraces the magic he once despised.

*Elminster: The Making of a Mage*, in hardcover, is coming to book, game, and hobby stores everywhere in December 1994!

TSR #8548

ISBN 1-56076-936-X

Sug. Retail $16.95; CAN $21.95; £10.50 U. K.

# COMING FALL/WINTER '94

## The Ogre's Pact

**Book One in the new Twilight Giants Trilogy by Troy Denning, *New York Times* best-selling author**

When ogres kidnap Brianna of Hartwick, her father forbids his knights to rescue her. Only a brash peasant, who covets Brianna's hand, has the courage to ignore the duke's orders. To Tavis's surprise, slaying the ogres is the easiest part . . . the challenge has only begun!
**Available September 1994**

ISBN 1-56076-891-6

## Realms of Infamy

**The incredible companion volume to the *Realms of Valor* anthology**

From the secret annals of Realms history come never-before-published tales of villains – Artemis Entreri, Manshoon of Zhentil Keep, Elaith Craulnober, and many others – told by your favorite authors: R. A. Salvatore, Ed Greenwood, Troy Denning, Elaine Cunningham, and others.
**Available December 1994**

ISBN 1-56076-911-4

Sug. Retail Each $4.95; CAN $5.95; £4.99 U.K.